"JUST GO AWAY AND LEAVE ME ALONE! LEAVE US ALONE!"

"I can't do that." Kyle stared down at her. Her parted lips invited his invasion. But he was coming to realize that he wanted more than just a moment's coerced pleasure from Charmayne.

"Why?"

"Because . . ." He stopped. What could he say? He really didn't know.

"Can't you see you're not welcome?" Charmayne was trembling with anger. "You might come back to Kearney with your money and your company . . . and people might let you. They might even accept you, to a degree! But you can't buy your way into people's hearts, Kyle."

As her hurtful words ended, the pressure of his grip on her arms increased until she thought her bones were going to snap.

A wall of pain seemed to close in on Kyle. Emotions from childhood churned those of adulthood. For a moment he forgot where he was. Then as some of the suffering faded, his gaze focused on Charmayne.

Hours ago he had wanted to kiss her; he had wanted to overwhelm her, storm her emotions until she gave him everything that he could ever possibly ask. But he had quelled the desire. "Well, to hell with waiting," he said to himself.

CANDLELIGHT ECSTASY SUPREMES

A
HEART
DIVIDED

Ginger Chambers

A CANDLELIGHT ECSTASY SUPREME

Published by
Dell Publishing Co., Inc.
1 Dag Hammarskjold Plaza
New York, New York 10017

Copyright © 1984 by Ginger Chambers

All rights reserved. No part of this book may be
reproduced or transmitted in any form or by any
means, electronic or mechanical, including photocopying,
recording, or by any information storage
and retrieval system, without the written permission
of the Publisher, except where permitted by law.

Dell ® TM 681510, Dell Publishing Co., Inc.

Candlelight Ecstasy Supreme is a trademark of
Dell Publishing Co., Inc.

Candlelight Ecstasy Romance®, 1,203,540, is a registered
trademark of
Dell Publishing Co., Inc.

ISBN: 0-440-13509-5

Printed in the United States of America
First printing—March 1984

For Carolyn, Nancy, and Susan.
For being there when I needed them.

To Our Readers:

Candlelight Ecstasy is delighted to announce the start of a brand-new series—Ecstasy Supremes! Now you can enjoy a romance series unlike all the others—longer and more exciting, filled with more passion, adventure, and intrigue—the stories you've been waiting for.

In months to come we look forward to presenting books by many of your favorite authors and the very finest work from new authors of romantic fiction as well. As always, we are striving to present the unique, absorbing love stories that you enjoy most—the very best love has to offer.

Breathtaking and unforgettable, Ecstasy Supremes will follow in the great romantic tradition you've come to expect *only* from Candlelight Ecstasy.

Your suggestions and comments are always welcome. Please let us hear from you.

Sincerely,

The Editors
Candlelight Romances
1 Dag Hammarskjold Plaza
New York, New York 10017

CHAPTER ONE

The main floor of the department store was filled with shoppers, yet few seemed to notice that the others were there. Most were intent on their own affairs, considering the occasional jostle they received more of an annoyance than anything else. What mattered to the majority was deciding on their purchases and claiming the attention of a sales clerk. To them, shopping was something to be done and over with, a reflection of their hurried city pace.

But to Charmayne Brennan, fresh from the less complex life of the country, a store of this size was a wonderland of undiscovered treasures, something to be savored, like precious wine. She fingered the softness of a silk scarf, gazed appreciatively at the golden chains and earrings resting behind the protection of a glass case, sampled the exotic fragrance of a tester bottle of perfume that caught her rapt fancy; her eyes widened at the countless displays that vied for a user's attention.

It was not often that she came to Dallas, but when she did, she was always amazed at the array of glittering choices. In Kearney there was a definite limit to the number of stores available, and each of them was concerned more with the functional than the frivolous. A reflection of their customers' nearness to their Puritan origins.

Charmayne moved closer to a counter that contained a well-known cosmetic company's wares, the rainbow of color drawing her. Lipsticks and eye shadows in impossible shades met her view and she reached out to touch a jet-black plastic case. If only she could use something of this sort! A wistful smile came to rest on her sensitively drawn mouth. No, it was not for her, and for more than one reason. With her bright, carrot-red hair and cursed freckled complexion she would look more like a clown at a circus than a vixen bent on seduction. She could just imagine how the townspeople would react on seeing their mayor's conservative administrative assistant suddenly transformed into a glamour queen. Her smile increased as her imagination played out the fantasy scene: the shock, the dismay, the disapproval.

Involved with her thoughts, Charmayne had no knowledge of the saleswoman's approach until a practiced voice prompted her pleasantly, "Yes? May I help you?"

The question caused Charmayne to give a starled jump. A wave of embarrassed heat rose up to cover her cheeks as her fingers immediately withdrew from the case.

"Ah—no. No. I was just . . ."

The woman's eyes narrowed and made a lightning quick assessment of her person. Charmayne was tall, almost five feet eight, but she was built like a graceful willow. Extremely slender, she looked as if a strong puff of wind could possibly uproot her and carry her away. Her breasts were small, her waist tiny, her hips slim, her legs long and lean, the shirtwaist dress she was wearing only emphasizing her fragility.

The suspicious gaze swept over her face, noting the leafy greenness of her eyes and the noticeable freckles that covered a small slender nose and spread outward over what could be seen of her body.

"Yes, well . . ." she said at last. "If you decide you want something, just let me know."

Charmayne nodded and moved jerkily away, sensing the woman's attention still upon her and feeling more than a little like a fool. Because of the suddenness of her recall from reverie, she had been disconcerted enough to lose all sense of time and place and had been instantly catapulted back into childhood, reacting as if she were a little girl caught with her hand in the forbidden cookie jar. Charmayne hadn't liked the experience at all. She was the type who didn't like being caught off guard. She needed to feel in control of each and every situation.

Intent on putting the experience behind her, Charmayne lifted her chin and straightened her shoulders. It had been six months since her last visit to the city and she wasn't about to let such a trivial matter ruin it for her. She forced herself to relax, and as she strolled down the aisle she fixed her attention on the colorful displays: huge urns filled with peacock feathers resting on Oriental rugs to complement the various mannequins' clothing. And soon she was back to her normal self. There were so many things she needed to buy! But she didn't want to rush. She wanted to take her time, to indulge herself. She looked at dresses, sorted through blouses, toyed with the idea of purchasing a special pair of designer jeans. . . .

Finally she reemerged into the area where her journey through the store had begun: the cosmetic/ jewelry/accessory counters. She paused as she neared an umbrella display, knowing that she was now going to have to get serious. She had to start her shopping somewhere. The proprietors of the store would probably take a dim view of her camping inside for the night. Even if it was barely midday she knew that if she didn't exert some form of control, she might have to do just that in order to finish. She had to be back in Kearney Monday morning and since this was Saturday and the stores were closed on Sunday . . .

Charmayne pulled first one umbrella then another from its slot, looking at color and at style. Eventually she decided on a suitable candidate, a compact collapsible model which she took over to the nearest cash register. The umbrella tucked under her arm, she had just approached the counter and was reaching into her shoulder bag for her checkbook, when a huge woman pushing a child in an old-fashioned stroller whipped around the corner and rolled the conveyance directly over Charmayne's foot. That one indignity was soon followed by another: the woman herself jostled against Charmayne, causing her to make a desperate grab for the counter in order to keep her balance. Charmayne's oversized shoulder bag slipped off her arm, spewing its contents in all directions. To add insult to injury, the stroller's reckless driver hardly seemed to notice and only grunted at her victim—possibly an apology?—before barreling on.

Other shoppers, however, were more sympathetic to Charmayne's plight and several stooped down to help her collect her scattered belongings. Murmuring her thanks, Charmayne hurriedly scooped her wallet, hairbrush, keys, lipstick, and the rest of her lost treasures back into her bag as they were handed over to her.

Charmayne righted herself and glared at the woman's disappearing back. Of all the rude, inconsiderate . . . She started again when another unfamiliar voice questioned solicitously, "Are you all right? Are you hurt?"

Charmayne tentatively wiggled her injured toes and decided that everything seemed to be in reasonable, if painful, working condition.

"Yes . . . I'm fine. Thank you." She hugged her purse close against her side as she readjusted the shoulder strap, relieved that the mishap hadn't been worse. She could have been sprawled out on the floor, a victim of one of the best off-field offensive blocks known to history.

"I saw her coming," the clerk explained. "And then I saw you, but there wasn't anything I could do! There wasn't time to warn either of you."

Charmayne's tight mouth relaxed and pulled into a wry smile. She could understand that feeling. She had been there more than once herself.

"It's all right. Really," she reassured the woman. "I just hope I don't meet up with her in the parking lot."

The saleswoman laughed, some of her tension leaving as she saw that Charmayne was able to see the humor of the situation. "No, I imagine not. I don't think I would want to, either. I wonder what she drives—a tank?"

Charmayne joined in with her laughter. "Probably."

"Well, I'm glad everything is okay." She hesitated, then asked. "Is there anything I can help you with? I suppose I should ask that now."

Charmayne's mind went momentarily blank. There was something she had been intent on doing

. . . something that needed to be done. . . . But for the life of her she couldn't remember what it was. Slowly she began to shake her head. "No, I don't think so. I—"

Again she was interrupted. "I'll be right around the corner if you change your mind. I was about to ring up a sale when all of this happened."

Charmayne dipped her head in acknowledgment, a small frown making a furrow on her forehead. She was sure that there had been something. Yet when a more intense search of memory yielded nothing, she gave a mental shrug and moved slowly into the flow of pedestrian traffic in a center aisle. If it was important she would remember it later. In the meantime there were those jeans she wanted to try on . . . and a blouse.

She had walked only a few steps on the plush carpeted area of the sportswear department when a hand came out to take firm possession of her upper arm.

"Hold up, miss." The rough masculine directive came at the exact moment she was pulled around. "I think we'd better have a little talk."

Charmayne gazed across at the man in surprise. He was only a degree taller than herself and was dressed in an ordinary suit, his silver-gray hair the most striking feature about his otherwise plain appearance.

"What? I don't understand." She tried to control the sudden rapid beating of her heart. Was she about to be assaulted? Right here? In the middle of the store? Hadn't enough already happened to her today?

The man's grip firmed. "About the umbrella," he

stated levelly. Then, at her still perplexed look, he explained further. "The one you have hidden in your purse—the one you neglected to pay for."

At that, Charmayne suddenly remembered what it was she had forgotten earlier. The umbrella! That was what it was! She had been on her way to pay for it when she had been stopped by the reckless mother. She looked down at her purse and saw the baby blue material of the umbrella peeping out. She reached with her free hand and pulled it out before her. In the confusion of gathering her belongings up from the floor someone must have handed her the umbrella and she had just put it into her purse with all the rest.

"Oh, thank you," she breathed in relief, flashing a grateful smile. "I almost forgot about it. I'll just go back and pay for it now. I wouldn't want anyone to think I was trying to steal it."

The man's face didn't give even the remotest glimmer of a returning smile. Instead, he reached into his jacket pocket with his free hand and pulled out an identification badge that showed he was attached to the store's security department. "I'm afraid that someone already does, miss. You're going to have to come with me."

Charmayne stiffened. "Oh! But no! I didn't . . ."

The man started to move away, pulling her with him. Charmayne tried to resist, but her efforts did no good. Finally she planted her feet and halted him, causing him to release his grip.

"Look," she insisted. "I didn't try to steal anything! Something happened and I put the umbrella into my purse by mistake. I would have seen it eventually and come back to pay for it. I'm an honest

15

person. I wouldn't take something that doesn't belong to me!"

"That's what they all say," the man murmured dryly and reattached his fingers to her arm, this time with more determination.

"But it's true!" she protested.

"They all say that, too."

Charmayne's heart continued to beat quickly. Surely she could make him believe her.

"But I haven't left the store yet! Doesn't that tell you I'm not a shoplifter? That I just forgot?"

"Look, lady. All I know is what I saw. And just because you didn't leave the store doesn't mean a thing anymore. You left the area where the merchandise you have in your possession is controlled, that's all that counts."

"But—"

"You can tell your story to my supervisor, if you like."

A cold spark of fear shot through Charmayne's body. He really was convinced that she was a thief!

"Yes," she decided quickly. "Yes, I will. Maybe I'll be able to convince him."

"Don't count on it," he advised, and then motioned for her to accompany him.

A healthy anger had now come to be a companion to Charmayne's fright. She was innocent. She knew she was innocent. She would *make* them believe her!

But during the next fifteen minutes the nightmarish quality of her situation only increased. She was shown into the office of the security supervisor and seated in a chair across from his desk. Then she was forced to listen as the guard who had apprehended her made her sound as if she were one of the worst hoodlums since the notorious Bonnie Parker and her accomplice, Clyde Barrow, were free to roam the streets of Texas. He had been keeping his eye on her for some time, it had seemed, his suspicious nature piqued by her unusual activities. He had secretly watched as she wandered from department to department—acting, to his mind, strangely. He had seen her surprise at the cosmetics counter, where she had jumped in an unnerved fashion when the sales-clerk caught her handling a case of eye shadow. The guard felt she was about to steal it but had been interrupted before she could spirit it away. Then he had seen her tuck the umbrella under her arm and the next thing he knew she was leaving the accessory department, bold as brass, with the umbrella slipped into her purse, just like one of the best pros.

The security supervisor watched Charmayne impassively as the guard completed his story, his brown eyes half closed as he leaned back in his chair. He was younger than his fellow worker, in his mid-thirties, his sandy hair still thick without any signs of gray.

"Do you have anything to add to that, Miss . . . ah . . ." He looked down at the name on her driver's license, which was exposed along with the rest of the contents of her purse on the desk surface before him. ". . . Miss Brennan?"

Charmayne lifted her chin, the light of battle in her green eyes. "Just one thing," she snapped. "There's been a mistake. I didn't intentionally take the umbrella." She turned to the silver-haired guard. "Didn't you see that woman run me over?"

"What woman?" he asked, his arms folded across his chest as he stood beside her, as if he was afraid she might decide to make a break for it and he wanted to be prepared.

Charmayne lifted her hands and let them fall in exasperation, again turning to face the younger man. "There! You see? That's the problem. He wasn't really watching me all the time! There was a woman who ran into me with her child's stroller. Everything got knocked out of my purse and in the confusion, I put the umbrella in my bag with everything else and forgot to pay. You can ask the sales clerk. She'll tell you."

"Did she know you had the umbrella in your purse?" the supervisor asked quietly.

"Well, no, but—"

"Then all she can do is tell us about the alleged accident."

Charmayne's eyes sparked. "It wasn't alleged!"

The man shrugged.

Charmayne took a deep breath. She had to make them see. "And I wasn't about to take the case of eye shadow. I was just looking at it!"

"Then why did you jump?"

"Because the saleswoman startled me! Is that a crime?"

"No, but shoplifting is."

"I didn't shoplift!"

The man sat forward, his expression still impassive, and began to look through her possessions. "You don't exactly have a lot of money here."

Charmayne's nerves were strained. "No. I don't usually carry a lot of cash."

"And you have no credit card with this store."

"No . . ."

He examined her checkbook. "I suppose you were planning on writing a check."

"Yes." Her answer was tight.

He fingered her driver's license and an eyebrow rose at her address.

"You're from out of town?"

"Yes."

"Kearney, Texas?"

"Yes."

"You're a long way from home."

Charmayne said nothing, a sinking feeling taking hold in the pit of her stomach.

Following his last statement, the man said nothing more and a silence stretched among the three people in the room.

Charmayne's heart was pounding, the adrenaline that had at first come to her rescue by promoting anger now signaling a return of fear. She wanted to rush away. Maybe the guard was right. Maybe he knew what he was doing in positioning himself so that she couldn't escape.

She broke the silence. "Please . . . I didn't mean to take it. It was an accident."

The supervisor's eyes rose to her face. "The best shoplifters I know can talk themselves out of almost any situation. I pride myself on not letting them do it to me."

"But I'm not a shoplifter! I've told you that! It's all a horrible mistake!" A wash of tears came to life in her eyes and she immediately tried to blink them away. She had to maintain control in order to be convincing. She couldn't break down; let herself be arrested for stealing! What would the people back home say if they came to know? How could she hold up her head? And even worse, what would happen to her job? Up for reelection, the mayor was having to be so very careful because his opponent would take advantage of any opportunity to blacken his name. What would the man do with ammunition of this kind? No! She couldn't let it happen! She couldn't! "Please!" she cried.

Her pleading had no visible effect. The supervisor's calm attention was still directed solely on her, not a flicker of compassion in his gaze.

Then into the echoing silence the door to the outside hall swept open and a man strode into the room. Charmayne's hazy gaze saw his entrance, but at first the only thing she noticed was the fact that he wasn't wearing a policeman's uniform. Her first thought was that the security man had somehow magically placed a call to the police station and she was about to be taken to jail!

Yet a second later she was blinking her eyes even harder, trying to clear them, because the voice, now apologizing for his precipitous entry, was achingly familiar.

"I'm sorry, Mark, I didn't realize—" Then his words were cut off in midsentence and the familiar voice questioned incredulously, "Charmayne? Charmayne Brennan? Is that you?"

The supervisor pushed to his feet and extended his hand to the newly arrived man.

"I was hoping you'd be early for our meeting, Kyle. So you do know her."

The man seemed thunderstruck, and coming further into the room, he completed the handshake automatically. His pale gray eyes were fastened intently on Charmayne's bright head, taking in the fact that she was so pallid her freckles were standing out in stark relief.

"Yes," he replied slowly. "What's going on here?"

Of all people in the world to show up at this moment, Charmayne would have picked anyone but Kyle Richardson to be the one! Yet she was in such a position that she would have welcomed the devil himself if he had been willing to say that he knew her and would vouch for her honesty. If such a thought had come to her at any other time, Charmayne knew, she would have added the postscript that Kyle *was* the devil! But at this moment she didn't care. He was here! He knew her! At least he knew her to a degree! He knew of her position within the Kearney city government; they had dealt enough together over the past few weeks. And even if the dealings hadn't been exactly amicable, surely he wouldn't leave her to the tender mercies of the supervisor and the Dallas police.

"Miss Brennan was caught shoplifting, Kyle. She says it was an accident. My guard here says differently."

Kyle's attention was momentarily diverted to the guard, who nodded his silver head. "She did it, all right," he pronounced.

Charmayne could no longer remain silent. She sent the guard a distasteful look and contradicted, "That's not true! I just forgot to pay, that's all!"

She felt Kyle's gaze shift back to her and saw his eyes narrow. He was much taller than the guard, several inches over six feet, and heavier because of his height. But there was not a spare ounce of flesh on him; his body was in excellent condition. His hair was a deep burnished brown, almost showing red in

21

some lights, crisp with untamed curls that clustered on his head in a wholly masculine way. His mouth was strong and firm, his nose straight, his eyebrows marked the same dark shade as his hair. The rugged angles and planes of his face could be described as handsome by some people, but Charmayne had resisted being one of them. Kyle already thought too much of himself. She wasn't about to join the throng of worshipers. Not after what had happened all those years ago; the hurt his family had inflicted, the pain. And he seemed not to be aware of the sorrow that had resulted from his uncle's scheme in the least, or if he was, he didn't seem to care. But now was not the time to dwell on differences. She needed help and he could provide it. She met his gaze straight on.

Kyle held her look and a spark of amusement soon appeared deep in his eyes. Charmayne saw his dawning humor and stiffened her back. So he thought this was funny! Well, she would like to tell him a thing or two! But she forced herself to remain quiet. Now wasn't the time or the place. And knowing what she did of him, if she in any way slipped into her usual manner of polite combativeness, he just might find it even more amusing to leave her to her fate.

Kyle's smile grew until it crinkled the lines at the sides of his eyes and pulled his lips into a sloping quirk. He seemed to have completely regained any loss of equanimity he might have suffered.

"I think you can believe the lady, Mark. She's usually the epitome of honesty."

"Usually?" Characteristically his friend pounced on the qualifying word.

"Well, right now I think she'd like to tell me exactly where I can go and what I can do when I get there. But discretion is forcing her to keep her tongue."

"Hence the 'usually.' "

"Correct."

"Do I detect a bit of strained relations?"

"Correct again."

"I never thought I'd live to see the day!" The supervisor shook his dark head. "Kyle Richardson finally meeting a woman who didn't fall all over him."

Charmayne had with great difficulty remained silent throughout this masculine exchange; the tongue Kyle had spoken of so accurately stood in danger of being shredded if she had to keep a curb on it much longer. Finally she could stand it no more and said, "I think we've settled the question of my guilt satisfactorily. Whenever it's convenient, I'd like to leave."

All three men turned to look at her, the taller two in amusement, the third in remaining suspicion.

The security supervisor lost his smile, his expression once again impassive.

"Yes, I suppose we have. Technically, you were shoplifting. But considering how well I know Kyle—and know that he wouldn't lie—I guess I'll have to believe you. It's the first time I've ever run across an excuse like yours and swallowed it. Just don't ever let anything like that happen again, especially in this store. Next time I won't be so lenient."

A wave of embarrassed heat emanated from Charmayne's face. He was lecturing her! As if she was still under suspicion! And in front of Kyle Richardson! Taking her word only because of his friend's! Didn't the man know a swindler when he saw one? Or at

23

least a swindler's nephew? Hurriedly she swept her belongings back into her purse and got to her feet, a mixture of emotions—outrage, indignation, and a sick kind of relief—causing her to tremble.

The guard moved out of her way as she started for the door. Charmayne refused to meet his condemning eyes. In his mind she could be wearing a halo and he would still swear that she was guilty.

She was almost outside when the security supervisor's voice made her pause. "Miss Brennan?"

"Yes?" She didn't turn.

"Do you still want to purchase the umbrella?"

It took all of Charmayne's considerable strength of will not to give him the answer he so richly deserved. Instead she answered as calmly as she was able, "No, thank you."

She started to leave but was again stopped by his "Miss Brennan?"

"Yes?"

"I'm sorry if you've been inconvenienced."

Charmayne did turn at that, her eyes bright with all the emotions that were seething within her. She said nothing, just looked at the supervisor. Then her gaze transferred itself to Kyle, who was standing where he had been throughout this ordeal. Again she said nothing; her ability to put across her feelings without words was more than adequate. Possibly she should thank him, but she couldn't make herself do it. His gray eyes were even more deeply amused than they had been before and her recognition of that fact only irritated her more. She turned her back pointedly and gained the comparative safety of the hall.

If she had had the option, she would have collapsed back against one concrete wall and let her limbs shake until they were all shaken out. But as it was, she couldn't take the risk of one of the men coming out, especially Kyle Richardson. All in all this had to be one of the most humiliating days of her life! And she wasn't going to compound the effect by being seen again in a weakened condition. She was free. She could leave. And that was exactly what she was going to do. She wasn't going to stop to buy one thing; all she wanted to do was get back to the haven of her hotel room so that she could try to forget.

Forget . . .

Charmayne was pushing open the swing door that led into the main area of the store when the sudden thought hit her. Would she be able to forget? She had been so relieved to see Kyle Richardson; he had been the key to her release. But after gaining for her one objective, would he be the ruination of another?

She hadn't thought of it before this moment, but could she depend upon him not to spread the story about her apprehension for theft all over the small town where they both lived and worked? All it would take would be a whispered word in one avid ear. . . . It wouldn't matter whether she had been at fault or not. Gossip would soon have her sentenced to ten years at Sing Sing!

Charmayne gave a small defensive groan. Oh, God! What was she going to do? Would he keep quiet? And if he did, what price would he extract?

She walked blindly along the aisle, sure that she had not as yet heard the end to this particular fiasco.

CHAPTER TWO

The morning air was cool and damp and smelled of the earth as Kyle Richardson let himself out of the house he had been calling home for the past three weeks. It was an essence that he remembered well . . . an echo of the past that had never been forgotten. Waking up to each new day in Kearney was like being a witness to rebirth. There was a freshness that could never be duplicated anywhere but in these dry, rocky hills of the Texas heartland.

As he moved down the flagstone walkway that lead to a well-traveled path along the edge of the highway, his fingers tightened about the slender parcel he was carrying. The package was wrapped in jaunty floral print paper with a frilly pink bow attached. It had all the appearance of being an eagerly anticipated gift.

Yet as he mentally projected the impact this present would have, Kyle allowed a small smile to tilt the fine lines of his lips. Somehow he didn't expect the recipient to be very appreciative. In fact, he would be lucky if he escaped the incident with no major injuries. Redheads weren't known for keeping their tempers and where this particular redhead was concerned, a short fuse seemed to have been issued in the same package with those beautiful pale green eyes—or at least that seemed to be the case whenever the catalyst of his presence was added.

Yes, he knew what he was asking for and that Charmayne would probably deliver, but something was driving him on—a devil within himself. The two of them were like powder and flint and he had a need to once again experience the resulting explosion.

Not that it had always been that way, he reminded himself wryly. When he had lived in Kearney for one summer all those long years before, Charmayne had been a tomboyish eight to his thirteen and he had been her idol. She had wanted to tag along with him wherever he went, and since her family's farm and the one on which his uncle was employed neighbored each other, there had been ample opportunities.

But then that had been before the *great misunderstanding,* his uncle's term for the occurrence that had preceded their quick departure from the area, in the dead of night after short whispered words of direction and a hurried gathering of their possessions.

Kyle gave an infinitesimal shake of his head, as if trying to shake off a bad memory. He didn't like to remember that time. Really, he didn't like to be reminded of very much of his boyhood, at least not the years after his parents died and he had been sent to live with his father's younger brother. Not that Martin had ever been mean to him or raised his hand in anger; it was just the general atmosphere of neglect, of deceit, of traveling from one town to the next with the uneasy feeling of having barely escaped an unnamed shame.

Kyle's long gait finally turned onto the path that led to the entrance of a newly constructed two-story building of brick and steel. But since this was not his destination, he spared it only a single satisfied glance. The name emblazoned on the front gave no hint that a Richardson had anything to do with it, which was exactly what he had planned. He hadn't wanted people to know. He had wanted to come in, set up his business, make it a success, and then and only then reveal himself. And his plan had worked, thanks mainly to his partners and their dedication.

As he continued walking, the beginnings of a formal sidewalk soon replaced the hard earth of the previous path. This signaled that the central nervous system of Kearney was being approached. Trees were planted along the widening street, curbs were in evidence, and grander homes which had been preserved from an earlier era were resting on their spacious lawns. Then finally the center of town itself appeared as the street he was following intersected with others and a parallel companion to form a square. A white gazebo sat in parklike atmosphere beneath the branches of a huge spreading oak.

Kyle paused a moment to enjoy the pastoral sight, then his gaze was drawn to a building directly across the way which housed the tiny town's lifeblood: the municipal offices. Once again tightening his hold on the package, he gave a slow grin and completed the remaining distance.

The main entryway gave access to a hall and three separate doors. From past experience he knew that the first door led to the police station, the second to the tiny town library, and the third to the mayor's office. Kyle didn't pause until he reached the last. Then, after taking a deep bracing breath, he twisted the knob and entered the room, causing the secretary stationed at the gray metal desk to look up.

Her expression of polite inquiry quickly changed to one of appreciative interest as soon as her gaze took in Kyle's lean, muscular build. A hand came up to pat her frizzy blond hair into place as she fixed a welcoming smile on her lips.

"Why, Mr. Richardson . . . hello."

The lines on either side of Kyle's cheeks deepened. He was accustomed to the ripple of sensation his appearance normally caused among persons of the opposite sex. Frankly he didn't comprehend the reason, but he had learned to live with it and wasn't above using it during certain strategic moments. He wouldn't have been human if he had not.

"Hello yourself, Tina." He silently acknowledged the other women who were occupying the remaining two desks in the room. He had been here so often recently he was beginning to know the small staff almost as well as his own.

"Ah . . . did you have a meeting scheduled with the mayor?" The secretary tore her gaze away from him long enough to check her appointment book, then leveled her attention back on his face, her big blue eyes wide. "I don't seem to have anything down. . . ."

"No, I don't." Kyle replied. "Not this time."

The secretary was visibly relieved. "Oh, good! Because I was wondering how I was going to break the news to you that he isn't here. He went out to inspect some roadwork near Tom McNeil's place and he won't be back for a couple of hours." She paused and confided, "He's always making appointments that I don't know about, then he cancels others and forgets to tell me. Honestly, sometimes I don't believe the man trusts me to keep everything straight. To him I'm not grown up yet."

Kyle let his eyes travel over the woman's undeniably impressive shape and murmured, "Then he must be blind."

The secretary preened and gave an affected laugh.

"Well, I suppose that's one of the curses of working for a relative. They just can't seem to forget the time when you were in diapers and screaming your head off for something to eat!"

Kyle laughed and the secretary joined in as well, enjoying the moment of shared intimacy.

It was that moment Charmayne chose to enter the room. A scowl was settled on her face because so far her day had been wholly miserable and it was barely ten o'clock. For administrative assistant to the mayor, her job description should actually read "general flunky." If a recent downpour clogged a street drain . . . if a car was parked in a no parking zone along the main street and the police department hadn't seen it yet . . . if a raccoon decided to make someone's attic its nighttime playhouse . . . if anyone had any sort of problem whatsoever, did the mayor's schedule get interrupted? No-o-o-o! The administrative assistant's did. And that was she.

Up until the present she had loved her work, loved the challenge. But today her duties seemed to be only added weight to the invisible load she was already carrying. Maybe it was that she was tired, or maybe it was a leftover feeling of unease from the weekend . . . a waiting for the other shoe to drop. She didn't know.

But walking into the laughter-filled room and immediately focusing on one of the participants resulted in the increase of her bad temper to such a degree that she almost left the office without saying a word.

The only thing that stopped her was the quick realization that she would be playing directly into Kyle Richardson's hands. He would enjoy seeing her turn tail and run, enjoy the hold he undoubtedly thought he had on her. Hadn't she spent most of the previous night worrying about just that? So she stood her ground, her normally softened features frozen, and waited for the laughter to subside.

Her unsocial demeanor soon had the desired result. Tina Cliburn changed her laugh into a series of short coughs and, keeping an eye on Charmayne, quickly recovered herself.

For as many years as Charmayne had worked for Mayor Cliburn, his decision to have his niece serve as his secretary was the one bone of contention between them. Not that Charmayne had ever tried to persuade him to fire her—she just considered the woman an airhead, uninterested and unconcerned with her office responsibilities and only occupying the job until something better came along. Preferably, something better in the shape of a man who wanted to marry her. That so far no one had was regrettable from all points of view.

Charmayne decided that the best approach to the situation was to go on with the premise of business as usual. She advanced farther into the room and placed the folder she had been carrying on the secretary's desk. She pretended to ignore the large man standing next to her.

"I found the error in the account, Tina. Next time it would help if you'd post the numbers directly to the ledger as they come in instead of waiting so long."

"I will, Charmayne. I promise I will. I'm sorry things got into such a mess."

Charmayne nodded coolly to the apology and turned as if to leave. If she could just play her role convincingly for a little bit longer. Just a little bit longer.

She was almost to the safety of her office when the sound of masculine footsteps came up close behind her.

"Miss Brennan. If you have a minute . . ." The hateful voice sliced into the sensitivity of her ears.

She paused with her hand on the doorknob. "I'm busy, Mr. Richardson."

"So am I. But I'd still like to talk. I don't plan on taking long."

Charmayne could feel the interested gazes of the other women in the office. Over the past three weeks she had tried to stay out of Kyle Richardson's way as much as possible. To her mind he was just as guilty of trick-playing as his uncle. He must have stayed up a succession of nights burning the midnight oil planning his return to Kearney. Insidious! That was the word she had been looking for ever since the news broke that he was the person responsible for the new business in town. As far as she could remember, *insidious* was defined in the dictionary as "sneaky, treacherous, evil." And that was exactly what he was! The townspeople had been so happy to have the hope of the small manufacturing firm. It meant jobs when jobs were scarce. To most it meant that they would not lose their farms . . . or that their sons and daughters would not have to go to the city to find work. Everyone had been so grateful, herself included because her father had been one of the farmers saved by the extra money. Then, after it had been fully established in the consciousness of the community, the business's founder appeared: Kyle Richardson, unrepentant about his uncle's deception and as arrogant and self-important as if he enjoyed the role of humanity's savior.

"I can give you five minutes," she stated, giving him the benefit of a glance over her shoulder, only to whip her head back around when she saw the amused light deep in his gray eyes. She hated the way he always seemed to be laughing at her!

"That's all I imagine it will take," he drawled.

His reply irritated Charmayne even more. Where did it read that he could make such enigmatic statements? He seemed to have a positive talent for finding the right things to say that made her react as if he had just run a fingernail down a blackboard!

She walked stiffly into her office, knowing that he was following.

When he closed the door and encased them in privacy, Charmayne took her position behind her desk, hoping that the official act would bolster her confidence. She made the first parry.

"What can I do to help you, Mr. Richardson?" The formal question satisfied her. She folded her hands on the scribbled-on blotter.

Kyle's pale eyes ran over her. Why did this woman fascinate him so? He had seen prettier. And her figure certainly wasn't anything to write home about; in fact, for all intents and purposes she was flat on top and as thin as a reed everywhere else. But there was a certain appeal there that he couldn't deny. And considering all the sparks that flew whenever he came near, that was enough to interest any man. But did her hostility go back to the time of his uncle? Or was there something else—something he just didn't have a handle on yet?

Instead of immediately answering her question he

took the chair positioned across from her desk as if he was planning to be comfortable for the amount of time they were to spend together.

"Did you enjoy your trip to Dallas?" he asked at last.

A flush rose into Charmayne's cheeks. She knew it! She had known it from the beginning! The other shoe was dropping loudly!

She answered crisply, "I believe you already know the answer to that question."

Kyle allowed a small smile to pull at his lips. "Well, I just thought I'd ask. Were you afraid you were on your way to jail?"

Charmayne's fingers tightened against themselves. "If you don't mind, I'd rather not talk about this, Mr. Richardson. Now, I've told you I'm very busy. If that's all you have to say, I'd appreciate it if you would leave."

Kyle sat unmoving and Charmayne experienced a helpless sense of frustration. Mentally she began to speculate about filling out a work order to have him physically removed—one forklift truck, one driver. And just where would the destination be? The town dump? Yes! That would be perfect!

Kyle saw the quick flicker of self-directed amusement that entered her eyes and wondered at its cause. He hadn't expected humor in any form, at least not from her.

"I've brought you something," he said slowly.

Charmayne gazed at him with polite dismissal. "I want nothing you have to give."

The barb struck Kyle squarely, but he shrugged it off. The battle was beginning to warm. "It's something you need," he continued.

34

"I don't care—" she began but was stopped when he placed the gaily wrapped package in front of her on the desk.

Seconds passed as Charmayne gazed at it. The shape was familiar.

"What is it?" she demanded.

"Open it up and find out."

Curiosity warred with pride and curiosity won. She didn't have to keep whatever-it-was. What would it hurt to look?

By the time the ribbon and the paper were removed Charmayne wished that she had listened more intently to her first inclination. The umbrella was the same one which had caused her such embarrassment in Dallas.

She stared down at it in momentary disbelief. Then, visibly having to restrain herself from thrusting the offending object away, she flashed her eyes upward and demanded, "Is this your idea of a joke?"

Kyle was unmoved by her anger. "Isn't that the one you wanted?"

His pretense of innocent concern was too much for Charmayne.

"You know it is!" she retorted. "But I don't want it now. I changed my mind when I was in the store. If I had wanted it, I would have bought it. I certainly don't need you to buy it for me!"

"I thought you might have been a little too unnerved at the time to be thinking clearly."

"I was not unnerved!"

Though her teeth were clenched when she uttered the denial, Kyle didn't know if it was from increasing animosity or from having to make up such a lie. He smiled.

35

"Oh?"

Charmayne jumped to her feet and leaned forward over her desk.

"Get out!"

Kyle took his time about shifting forward in his chair, prolonging the seconds it took to unwind his long frame. Then, standing to his full height, he, too, leaned on the desk, his hands splayed out scant millimeters from her own.

"I'll get out when I'm damn good and ready and not a second sooner. I saved your butt, lady. And you didn't even thank me for it. I don't think you realize just how close a call you had."

"I said, get out!" The words were a hiss.

"You've changed, Charmayne. In some people growing up looks good. But on you it doesn't. I think I prefer the little girl I used to know who was so anxious to learn how to bait a fishing hook, how to skip rocks, how to build a fort out of brush. . . ."

Charmayne clipped back the reply that was on the edge of her tongue. She clearly remembered the days when she had so foolishly thought him her special hero. But those days were gone. They had disappeared the minute a member of his family had caused her family so much grief.

Well, he might be able to worm his way back into the good graces of some of the people in this town, with his money, with his good looks. But he wasn't going to sweet talk her.

"I have an idea," she began calmly, sweetly. "Why don't you take your umbrella and ram it up—"

"Charmayne!"

"—up the nearest tree!"

Even in her furious state Charmayne was aware of his closeness. She could see the fine lines of charcoal that radiated outward from the pupils of his gray eyes, making the irises a darker shade than she remembered. She also had a closer view than she wanted of the texture of his skin, his thick lashes and dark brows. She thought about pulling back a degree, but she forced herself to hold her ground.

Kyle met her furious gaze and was satisfied, in a perverse way, that he had gotten the reaction he had hoped for. In country terms she was spitting mad and he was inordinately proud that he had been the cause. A reaction of this sort was much better than the frigid display of disdain she had at first showed him upon his return. Little by little he had been successful in eating away at her control, until now it simply required a word or two from him to strike sparks off her volatile temperament. Curiosity about the reason for her interesting behavior carried him on to further prodding.

"Do I need to remind you just whom you're talking to?"

Charmayne drew a quick breath. There were so many replies she could make to that question! But the fact he wanted her to remember—that he was regarded as the salvation of the town with his printed-circuit-board assembly operation—she was going to stubbornly reject. Instead, she dredged an answer from the past that reeked with dislike.

"Oh, no! Certainly not! If you could have been found eighteen years ago, you and that uncle of yours would have been hung on the spot, and I would have been ostracized from the community for what I'm doing now: talking to you!"

Kyle's hands had curled into fists, although he was still resting them, knuckles down, close to hers.

"Then I guess it's a good thing that eighteen years have passed."

"Oh, have they?" She strove for blitheness.

"Do you still fight the Civil War every day as well?"

"Only when I consider it helpful."

Kyle laughed, a short disdainful sound. "Well, what if I bring in some ammunition of my own?"

Charmayne's daring instantly evaporated because she had an idea of just what his "ammunition" might be. But she didn't let her expression falter. Her eyes remained steadily on his.

When she didn't reply, Kyle continued, "Like, won't it be interesting to find out how the good people of Kearney react when they find out that their mayor's administrative assistant got herself arrested for shoplifting the last time she went to the big city?"

"You wouldn't dare." Her voice was low with menace.

"Want to try me?"

"What would you have to gain?"

Kyle shrugged.

"Anyway, I wasn't arrested." Charmayne tried to regain her equilibrium. "It was all a mistake."

"The guard didn't think so. He caught you red handed. And my friend—you remember my friend? —he believed you took it." He motioned to the umbrella resting close beside them.

Charmayne's gaze dropped to the baby-blue material and she almost hated it. Her eyes flashed back upward. Her arms were getting tired from their aggressive position on the blotter, but she maintained it nonetheless.

"I go back to my earlier claim: *I wasn't arrested!*"

Kyle's lips drew into a smug smile. "On my say-so."

The soft answer galvanized Charmayne into action. She jerked upright, her hands clenched at her sides, wanting for all the world to lash out at him. But some semblance of sanity prevailed. She was in her office and her office was in the mayor's office. And if he so desired, Kyle Richardson could add battery charges to go with his contention that she was a shoplifter! All she would have to do was touch him. . . .

With her back ramrod straight and her soul bursting with impotent fury, Charmayne marched to the door and pointedly opened it.

"You've had your five minutes."

She waited for him to leave.

Kyle straightened, a smile still lingering on his mouth.

"All right. I suppose you're right. But I don't think we've reached a satisfactory conclusion to our conversation yet. So"—he paused—"we'll just have to continue it. How about tonight? I'll pick you up at six."

"Absolutely not!"

"Six thirty?"

"Six *nothing!* If you think I'd be willing to go out with you after the things you've said, you're totally and completely out of your mind!"

Kyle moved to the door, but before completely executing his exit he paused and asked, "I don't suppose you happen to have John Marshall's telephone number handy? I know I could look it up, but if you have it, it will save me some time . . . make everything much more simple."

Mayor Cliburn's political opponent's name rolled so easily off his tongue. The name John Marshall was never mentioned in the office, as if the mayor were subconsciously afraid of the challenger's strength and the staff understood his fear. To hear the name sounded aloud seemed a sacrilege.

Kyle's strategy had the planned-for effect. He could see Charmayne's mind working rapidly behind her wide eyes before, tight lipped, she snapped, "Make it seven!" Then she slammed the door closed in front of him, causing the wind to whoosh on his face and almost catching his sleeve in the crack. She seemingly wouldn't have cared if she'd trapped his entire arm!

As Kyle turned toward the staring women in the outer office, he tipped his head, nodding courteously, and gave them the benefit of one of his most charming smiles. Then he began a confident, congratulatory walk out of the building and back down the sidewalk which led to his office, located in the building held responsible for changing so many lives.

Within her own office Charmayne gathered the umbrella from the top of her desk and threw it into the trash basket, grimly deciding that the town dump wasn't a good enough place for one Kyle R. Richardson. He deserved something much more foul, like permanent resident status on land set aside for the disposal of dangerous nuclear waste! Add to that a few hazardous chemicals and the mixture might be just about right.

CHAPTER THREE

Charmayne fumed to herself for the remainder of the workday. She didn't like being blackmailed. And there was no getting around it, that was exactly what he was doing. He was blackmailing her! And to make matters worse, he seemed to be enjoying it. *And* there wasn't a darned thing she could do about that, either.

She couldn't let him tell the world about what had happened in Dallas. Not for herself so much—she could weather the storm and hope that eventually public sensibility would win out. But there were others she had to think about, people who would be adversely affected by the revelation of her purported action.

Mayor Cliburn was one. With a conservative constituency that made William F. Buckley, Jr., look as if he were writing for *Rolling Stone* magazine, there would be an outcry that someone in her sensitive position should have allowed herself to become involved, innocent or otherwise, in such a dastardly deed. Of course a number of townspeople wouldn't want to believe the tale about a person they had known since childhood; but, small towns being what they are, the damage would be done. As any slick trial lawyer fighting for his client knows, a hint sometimes taints. And she did often do a lot of the bookkeeping involved in running the town. What if a penny here or a penny there somehow managed to disappear occasionally? Would anyone ever learn of it? That suspicion would be a burden the mayor would have to carry into the election and it would hurt. She would be honor bound, for his success, to resign her job. Yet if she did, it could be looked upon by some as an admission of guilt. Catch 22.

Then there was her sister, who had just become the blushing bride of the local Baptist minister. How could she explain to Lynn and how could Lynn explain to Bob that his new sister-in-law was suspected of being a shoplifter?

And last of all, her parents, who still somehow thought the sun rose and set on their elder daughter.

No, as Kyle Richardson had said. It would be easier this way. No muss, no fuss. Just a great deal of irritation. She would be the only one to pay the price.

At that Charmayne's thoughts came to a sudden halt before moving on in another direction. Why should she be the only one to pay the price? Why shouldn't there be another? A wicked smile came to play along the edges of her soft mouth. She didn't know exactly what Kyle had in mind for tonight, but if she had anything to say about it—which she did—their time spent together was not going to be something he would enjoy. And he certainly wouldn't be tempted to coerce her into granting him more.

Charmayne left her office that evening feeling much more positive than she had when she first entered it.

The next problem presented to Charmayne was her parents. Although she was twenty-six, she still lived in the same frame house where she had grown up. She did this because the extra income she contributed helped keep the family farm financially afloat. When she was eight, they had been forced to sell a great deal of their land to meet a certain debt. Then again, when she was twenty, another large amount of acreage had had to be sold. Now the farm was half of what it had once been and they were still having trouble meeting their annual debts.

Her other reason had to do again with living in a small town. She had a perfectly good home, people would say—why leave it? Especially when her job was only a twenty-minute drive away. What was she planning to do if she set up a place of her own? Something of which her parents would disapprove?

Yet Charmayne didn't feel trapped. She lived at home willingly. Her parents respected her as an adult, as a productive member of the family, and she didn't resent the necessity that kept her there. One day she would leave, but she didn't worry about when that would be. She would deal with it when it came.

Charmayne's fingers tightened on the steering wheel of her car as she approached the familiar fork in the road near her home. To the right was the Stratton place, the farm where Kyle and his uncle had once lived. To the left was her parents' farm. A quick vision of Kyle and herself as they had once been flitted through her mind: she gangly with her carrot-red hair drawn into rubber bands on each side of her head and plaited into long pigtails, her freckles, her youthful hero worship . . . Kyle, tall for his age, slim, his skin burned brown by hours of play in the sun, his curling chestnut hair alive with living tongues of flame as that same sunlight glinted off of his head, his pale gray eyes which always seemed to be laughing . . .

Charmayne gave her head a dismissing shake and purposefully directed her car to the left. She had to put the past—or at least that part of it—out of her mind. There was something much more important to remember. The very same something that made it distinctly impossible for her to tell her parents whom she was going out with tonight. Disapproval would be the understatement of the century!

As the car drew into the long drive leading to the quaint one-story farmhouse, Charmayne was still grappling with the problem of how she was going to leave the house this evening. She wished she had told Kyle she would meet him somewhere else, but since she hadn't, she was just going to have to come up with an idea. She didn't know what, but—

Charmayne's worried thoughts came to a halt when she saw her mother. She was busy gathering clothing from a series of outside drying lines. When she heard the car, she glanced over to the sound and waved. Charmayne waved in return. After depositing a collection of wooden clothespins into a fabric bag hanging close by, her mother folded a newly released sheet over her arm and came to greet her daughter.

The two women looked nothing alike. Where Charmayne was tall, her mother was small. Where Charmayne was thin, her mother showed the effects of her too-long affair with the sampling of goods produced in her own kitchen. But it was from Margaret that Charmayne took the color of her eyes.

Eyes the exact shade of the tree leaves above them met Charmayne's own with a warm smile.

"Hello, sweetheart. Did you have a nice day?" Her voice was low and pleasant.

For as long as Charmayne could think back in time, those same words had greeted her. When she was a child, it was the signal for her to tell everything that had happened in her day. Now, as an adult, she kept some things to herself, but she still appreciated the caring the question embraced.

"I sure did. How about you?"

Her mother's smile deepened. "Well, it didn't rain on my wash, so I suppose I should count myself as lucky. With all the showers we've been having lately I felt like I was taking a gamble choosing today."

Charmayne shifted her purse strap to a more secure position on her shoulder and took the sheet from her mother's arm. "You could have used the dryer, you know," she teased.

"I know." Her mother turned to walk beside her.

"But you'd rather not," Charmayne stated drolly.

They covered the short distance to the clotheslines before her mother agreed, "No, I'd rather not."

Charmayne drew the sheet close to her face and breathed in the scent. It smelled of warm grasses, sunshine, and that special something that only fresh air can impart. "Hummm. I don't blame you. This smells wonderful!"

Margaret Brennan started to gather more clothes, expertly pulling the fastenings free and stacking the partially folded garments in a basket until only several pairs of her husband's blue jeans remained on the line. These she felt and rejected.

"I hope the rain will hold off a little while longer." She scanned the horizon. "Your father's pants are going to take more time."

Charmayne examined the sky as well. Gray clouds were gathering, but they were still a distance away.

"I'll help you keep an eye out," she promised.

Her mother smiled her approval and bent to pick up the loaded basket.

Charmayne quickly stopped her. "Here, let me," she offered.

The interior of the Brennan home was at once spotless and somewhat cluttered. Margaret believed in cleanliness, but she also believed in comfort. She felt that a home was meant to be lived in. So as a result there were times when what could only be termed "organized chaos" was the most noticeable feature of the decor. In the living room an easel and all the accompanying paraphernalia associated with a work-in-progress oil painting of a tall sailing ship was positioned in one area (Margaret's own hand-iwork) and a leather tooling kit with a partially finished belt spilling off the side of a worktable (her husband's hobby) was stationed in another.

The only person who didn't seem to contribute to the disturbance of the room was Charmayne, and that was because she spent her spare time writing poetry, which was supposed to be a deep, dark secret, something that she did only in the privacy of her room and under the impression that no one knew. But some months before, Margaret had happened upon one of her poems, quite by accident, and she knew. Yet she kept her daughter's secret, feeling that when Charmayne wanted to share what was, in her prejudiced view, some superior verses, she would do so.

The rest of the house was equally unorganized, yet in a wonderfully relaxed way. A shopping list with accompanying cents-off coupons were spread out on

46

a kitchen counter. A collage of bills was scattered on the table. One letter in the process of becoming an answer to another was resting on a desk inundated with both recent and old issues of subscription magazines.

Charmayne set the clothes basket down beside the kitchen table and gathered the bills into a neater stack, sighing at the height. On a farm there always seemed to be places for money to go. But at least now there was optimism that a number of their debts would be paid, whereas before . . . well, before there had been serious doubts and a number of extensions.

Charmayne turned toward her mother, who was testing the tenderness of the chicken she had left baking in the oven.

"Dad's not home yet?" she asked, glancing at the clock above the stove that showed he was late . . . again.

Her mother shook her head.

"Is he having to work late tonight?" If he was, a part of her problem would be lessened. Of everyone in the family, it was her father who disliked the Richardson name the most, even if he was now working for one, a fact that Charmayne suspected added to his dislike. Her father was a proud man. It had been hard for him to learn that the job he had thought of as a salvation was instead a blessing of mixed origin. He had toyed with the idea of quitting when he first discovered his mistake, but in the end he had decided not to, for purely financial reasons.

"I'm not sure. He didn't say anything about it this morning, but—" Her words were halted by the sound of another car turning into the drive. "That must be him now. He probably just got to talking and lost track of time."

Charmayne frowned at the excuse. It wasn't like her father to tarry. There were too many chores to be done in the evening for him to waste time talking with his coworkers. And for that matter, few of them had extra minutes to spare, either. Holding down full-time day jobs and keeping up with the outside work on their farms didn't leave much time for idle conversation.

Narrowing her eyes, she peered through the leaves and twisting branches of the bush that had grown to enormous proportions outside the kitchen window. She could see a smattering of dark blue paint: her father's pickup truck.

"Yes, it's him."

"Good."

An unmistakable tension had crept into her mother's voice and Charmayne's frown increased. It remained in place until the tall man, whose once red hair was now almost totally silver, let himself into the kitchen through the back door.

At fifty-eight Raymond Brennan was still a handsome man, his roughly hewn features seeming to be carved of stone. And even though he was normally a quiet, introspective person, he had the kind of no-nonsense look about him that made people pay attention whenever he decided to talk. Logical and straightforward in all matters there were only two things that he knew could make him lose his head. He could take anything else with calm deliberation, but he couldn't tolerate any threat of injury to either his family or his farm. Anything that threatened them, threatened him. And he reacted accordingly.

Charmayne's mother closed the oven door with a snap and turned to greet her husband. As her eyes ran over him, they reflected a deep concern. But when she moved forward, her hands coming out to grasp his arms while she tiptoed to plant a kiss on his cheek, the worry was successfully hidden.

"You look tired," she said soothingly, yet with a slight edge that possibly only Charmayne could discern.

The light of love grew warm in Raymond's heart as he accepted his wife's nearness. But not being a demonstrative man, he kept himself in check, content with the feel of her soft back beneath his hand.

"I am . . . a little." He stepped away, continuing forward until he was able to take a seat at the table. There he almost fell into a chair, his long body collapsing against the wood. He ran a weary hand over the back of his neck. Then his attention was switched to Charmayne.

"Hi, honey," he said, his pale blue gaze softening.

"Hi, Dad." Charmayne bent to hug him, then drew back. Examining her father closely, she could see no reason for her mother's tension. She agreed that he looked tired, but the earlier emotion she had sensed had been rich with something more, something she didn't understand.

Margaret's voice interrupted her thoughts. "You had to stay late again, Raymond?"

Charmayne's gaze still locked with her father's, she saw the instant shuttering that closed the world out. He would resist any attempt anyone might make to pry into an area he did not wish to discuss.

For an answer Raymond merely grunted. It was neither an affirmation nor a denial.

Margaret immediately turned away, her shoulders stiff.

Charmayne could feel the increasing strain in atmosphere and she was helpless in its presence—an uncomfortable witness. For as long as she had been alive, her parents had never experienced any kind of marital misunderstanding more serious than an occasional tiff. But over the past week or so she had gradually begun to perceive a new evasiveness, a new hurt. She could have excused herself from the room, but that would merely have drawn unwanted attention. So she remained silent and started a calm refolding of the clothing from the basket onto the table, smoothing the fabric of wrinkles, making sure the edges were straight, all the while hoping that the emotional squall would soon pass. She could have been a young child again, so deeply did it affect her.

The room existed in silence for elongated minutes before Raymond broke the quiet with the scrape of chair legs against the linoleum floor. He seemed not to notice the tension.

"Well, I'm going to change and then see about the stock."

Charmayne waited for her mother to answer, but when she didn't, she gave a soft "All right" to her father's departing form.

Again there was a stillness in the room, but as if to cover what had passed, her mother soon put on a forced bright expression and stated, "I believe I'll make a peach cobbler for dessert tonight. It's one of your father's favorites."

Charmayne continued to pull clothing from the basket to add to the growing stacks on the table, each representing the portion of the house to which it eventually would be taken. "That sounds good," she concurred, her mind still grappling with speculation as to what was happening between her parents. But at mention of the evening meal, she was immediately reminded of the further ordeal she was going to have to face tonight. Kyle hadn't mentioned eating out as a part of their bargain and since the thought of sitting civilly across a table from him was repellent to her, she discounted the possibility. But she was going to have to get away from the house soon after dinner. She couldn't possibly let her family know that she was in any way, even against her will, fraternizing with the enemy.

She decided it would be best if she fabricated a little story. Not a lie, she reassured herself. She didn't lie. But a gentle coloring of the truth, a bending of reality, a considered protection of loved ones . . .

"Ah, Mom—" she began, then jumped nearly out of her skin when a loud clap of thunder that seemed to come from nowhere shattered the air space around them. Her words were lost in the reverberation.

Margaret Brennan started as well, but not for the same reason as Charmayne. Charmayne's thoughts centered mainly on the idea of divine retribution and Margaret's only concern was for the blue jeans hanging nearly dry on the line. With a little squeal she hurried from the house and raced across the yard to gather them before the first hard drops of rain should start to pound the rocky soil. When she rushed back into the kitchen, her cheeks were flushed, her lips were slightly parted, and her dark brown hair with its streaks of silver-gray was tumbling over her forehead. With a new perception Charmayne could see

51

the beauty of the young girl her mother used to be. Her eyes were shining with triumph, her troubles momentarily forgotten in the victory she had just wrested from nature. Large splashes of rain were now drumming against the roof, making a lively roar in their ears.

Her mother laughed. It was a nice sound.

"There! I did it! That rain came up so fast! I didn't think I was going to make it, but I did!"

Charmayne took the jeans from her mother's hands and allowed the woman to rest from her exertion. Margaret dropped into the seat her husband had recently occupied and began to fan her face with her hand.

"Whew!" She laughed again. Then her head tilted as she watched Charmayne feel the jeans. "I know. They have to go in the dryer!" She stated the conclusion before Charmayne had the opportunity to do so.

"Want me to do it?" Charmayne offered.

"Yes, please. You know I try to pretend the darned thing isn't there." She sighed. "But I will admit that there are times when it comes in handy."

When Charmayne returned from setting the machine, her mother was still seated in the chair, her hands resting on the folded clothing, her vision attached to nothing in particular.

Once again she decided to broach the subject she had tried to voice a few minutes before. If lightning was going to strike her, it would just have to go ahead and do it.

"Mom. I've got something to do after supper tonight. I'm meeting someone."

Instead of tickling her mother's curiosity, the statement seemed not to interest her at all.

"That's nice," was Margaret's abstracted reply.

Charmayne's forehead creased. This was definitely not like her mother. She respected her daughter's freedom. After all, she was old enough to run her own life, but normally, motherlike, Margaret still could not contain her desire to know who she was going out with, and where she was going.

Charmayne tried again. "I'm leaving a little before seven."

"All right."

"I'm not sure when I'll be back."

"Have a nice time."

Charmayne sighed. If only her father would be as easy to deal with.

Much to Charmayne's amazement, he was. He, too, seemed distracted over dinner, eating his chicken and vegetables with little appreciation. Then, when he merely picked at his peach cobbler and received her news with a preoccupied grunt, it only underlined in Charmayne's mind that something was definitely wrong.

But at least, if it had to be, it came at a good time for her. She could just imagine her father's reaction if Kyle Richardson drove his Cadillac up their drive and then knocked on the front door, asking to see her. Mount St. Helens would have better odds of keeping its top in place.

So, at fifteen minutes before the hour of seven, after having given a silent prayer of thanks that the rainfall had stopped a short time before, Charmayne let herself out of the house and walked the short distance to the fork in the road. At exactly the appointed time the stylish black car appeared and Charmayne stepped forward.

Kyle immediately drew to a stop, her presence surprising him. He rolled down his window as she came near and said dryly, "I certainly never expected to find you waiting for me. I thought I'd have to come to your house and drag you kicking and screaming from the door."

Charmayne's lips tightened and she reacted childishly, resenting him for being so sure of himself. "Oh, why don't you just shut up? I'm here. That's all that matters."

Kyle's eyes moved over her assessingly. She looked so much like a schoolgirl in her pale yellow sundress. Her disposition at the moment only reinforced it.

"How old are you now, Charmayne?" he asked slowly, knowing the question would nettle her but asking it anyway.

"Old enough to resent being asked!" she responded shortly.

"Sixteen going on fifteen?" he prodded.

Given free rein to do as she wished, Charmayne would have turned around and walked straight back to her house. She didn't want to have to talk with this man. She didn't want to have to suffer his superiority.

"Why don't you take another guess?" she answered sweetly.

Kyle smiled, his teeth showing white in the evening sunlight. He liked the way she crinkled her nose when she got angry. He wondered if she was aware of the gesture.

"No, that wouldn't be fair." He continued to play his role. "Because I already know."

"Then why did you ask?" she demanded, hating him all the more as the seconds passed.

Kyle's only answer was a shrug and Charmayne wanted to hit him.

He had changed out of the suit he had worn earlier and from her close position, she could see that he was now wearing a pair of dark corded jeans topped with a lighter blue shirt. The color of his shirt only heightened the darkness of his tan and made his eyes look strikingly pale. A smile started on his lips.

"I'm sure we could carry on this brilliant conversation all night, but I made arrangements for us to eat at Gibson's. If we don't get started soon, we won't have time for a drink." Gibson's was a specialty restaurant in a nearby town. It was *the* place to go for entertainment if a person lived in Kearney.

"I don't drink," Charmayne answered flatly. "And I've already eaten."

As part of the plan to make him uncomfortable, he had given her the perfect opening.

Kyle's smile wilted a moment, but it didn't stay away for long.

"All right," he pronounced. "We don't do either."

"What are we going to do, then?"

A second passed. "There's not a whole lot."

"Then why do anything?"

"Would you be shocked if I said it was because I wanted us to get to know each other again?"

Charmayne was temporarily disconcerted. She hadn't expected that for an answer. But she didn't allow her hesitancy to carry on for long. She folded her arms across her midriff and stated, "I already know enough about you. I don't want to know more."

The lines beside Kyle's pale eyes deepened as his lips curved winningly into a smile that caused Charmayne to feel the strong pull of his masculinity.

"Is that supposed to crush me?" he asked softly, effectively blunting her challenge.

His response gave Charmayne the excuse she needed to break the hold of his unexpected attraction. She released her arms and leaned forward aggressively.

"Look," she stated, giving her emotions back to indignation with some relief. "I only came here because I can't let you come to my house. Don't read anything more into it than that. And I didn't agree to go anywhere with you tonight. You said we needed to talk more and we have. Now I consider the matter settled."

Kyle leaned across the front seat of his car and opened the opposite door. Charmayne watched his action warily.

"Come around and get in," he directed.

"No."

"Charmayne . . ." he warned, then suddenly he switched approaches. "Charmayne, would you *please* get in?"

"The answer is still no."

Kyle draped his hands over the steering wheel and stared forward for a moment. Then his head swiveled back around and he looked directly at her through narrowed eyes.

"I'll follow you to your house if I have to," he stated evenly. "You agreed to give me some of your time this evening and now you're reneging. That's not a very honorable act."

Her voice rang with incredulity as she countered, "*You* dare to talk to me about honor?"

Kyle's eyelids flickered at her words. It was a small action, but she saw it and knew that she had struck blood. She started to turn away but was brought to a halt by his "I meant what I said, Charmayne. I'll come to your house."

Slowly Charmayne returned her gaze to his and saw the steady resolve in his expression. He meant what he said. She thought of the already strained conditions in her home and the fact that the man before her was, in reality, her father's employer—albeit a resented one, one whom it wouldn't take a lot of pushing for her father to punch in the nose. A quick flashing daydream of Raymond doing just that took occupation of her mind for a moment before she shook it away. No. She couldn't allow that. She was just as helplessly caught in his power now as she had been earlier. Her father needed to keep his job, she needed to keep hers—the farm needed the money from both sources. And she couldn't let herself be their downfall.

Without another word she moved around the car to the released passenger door and climbed inside. But as she took her position on the soft leather seat, she angrily adjusted her skirt and muttered, "I should have known I couldn't trust you to be anything but nasty." It wasn't in her to let him get away with his despicableness so easily.

Instead of coming back with an equally stinging reply, Kyle let his eyes rove over her profile, appreciating the way her nose tilted upward, the way her curving bottom lip showed full, almost in a pout, and the manner in which the soft skin of her cheek was kissed by hundreds of tiny freckles with just the hint of a delicate pink color applied by nature's hand and not practiced artifice. Without warning a chord deep inside of him was struck and the vibration caused him to give a defensive, mocking little laugh. For the space of a second he was unsure of just what was happening to him.

Then, when he had shaken his confusion, once again regaining some degree of stability on his mental legs, he shifted the car into gear and moved forward a distance, only to make a short quick reversal that was soon followed by a forward burst of speed. Dust and gravel spewed from beneath the tires of the rapidly moving car as it retraced the route that led to the main highway.

Charmayne sat as far away from Kyle as was possible, her side and arm touching the paneling of the passenger door, the forward thrust of acceleration causing her back to be pressed against the rear seat, the echo of his disregard for her opinion bouncing along the sensitive corridors of her mind. But what bothered her most was the memory of her earlier momentary abdication to his attraction. She hadn't expected that. She had thought she was immune. And now that she realized there was a tiny crack in her invulnerability, she could see that this had all the possibilities of being a long hard night—a much worse one than she had expected.

If only he weren't such a handsome devil! Why couldn't he be cross-eyed and have buck teeth? The very least he could do was to be balding. Weren't some men totally void of hair by the time they turned thirty-one? But no, oh, no. Not Kyle Richardson. He had to be a combination of Richard Gere, Tom Selleck, and Mel Gibson all rolled into one living, breathing human being who happened to be sitting across from her.

It wasn't fair, Charmayne fumed to herself. It just wasn't fair!

CHAPTER FOUR

Silence reigned supreme in the car as mile after mile clocked past like an invisible marker. A number had been added together before Kyle broke into the reserve by saying, "Charmayne? How does your father like his job? Somehow I never expected to find him holding down a spot in a production line. He always seemed so much a part of the out-of-doors."

If that was supposed to be a conversational ice-breaker, he had chosen just the right vehicle. Charmayne took a sharp breath, sat forward, and flared, "Your sense of humor is really sick, Kyle! Did you know that?"

Kyle took his gaze away from the road long enough to see that she had meant every word. He mulled over what he had said. He hadn't expected such a reaction.

"Is it?" he asked provisionally, still unsure of his ground.

"Yes!"

Kyle shrugged, deciding to try to make amends. "Well, I didn't mean for it to be."

"Are you going to tell me that you just didn't think?" Her reply was scathing; his effort unappreciated.

"I guess I am."

Charmayne resettled her shoulders against the material of the leather seat and observed, "That's typical!"

The irrepressible smile on Kyle's lips surfaced as he began to enjoy her bad temper.

"Is that another loaded observation?"

"A twenty-two is loaded. An observation is made."

"I stand corrected."

Charmayne tipped her chin upward, proud of her small victory.

Another mile went by before Kyle spoke again, this time with more seriousness.

"I'd really like to know, Charmayne. Does your father like his job?"

Charmayne thought over all the answers she could make and chose the one more amenable to her father's employer.

"I suppose," she granted distantly.

"Does he have to have it?"

Charmayne's fingers closed in her lap. "Don't you think that's just a bit too personal a question to ask?"

"Let's just say that since I'm in for a penny I might as well be in for a pound."

"That's a cliché."

"But it fits. Answer me."

Charmayne wasn't about to. She looked pointedly out the window at the scenery passing by.

Kyle sighed and his grip tightened on the steering wheel. He decided to make another approach. She had to be handled so carefully.

"Do you feel that Orion Enterprises has helped Kearney?"

"In what way?" She was going to be as obstinate as she was able. It was all part of the plan.

Kyle kept his temper with difficulty. Not a shade of impatience showed in his voice as he rephrased his question.

"Do you think Orion Enterprises has made a difference to the financial condition of Kearney?"

Charmayne looked around, her eyes flickering over him before she forced them to focus on the upcoming road. "Of course."

"In what way?"

"Any new business helps."

"I'm speaking of Orion Enterprises in particular."

Charmayne gritted her teeth. "Do you want a medal or will a simple citation do?"

"Your sarcasm is misplaced. I don't want anything."

"Well, you did seem to be hinting."

Kyle shifted in his seat. What he had said could have been taken that way—and leave it to her to take it wrongly!

"I want to know if what I feel about my company is correct."

Charmayne slid him a withering glance. "Why? So you can get more jollies when you shut it down?"

Barely two seconds passed after the words left her mouth before Kyle was directing the car to leave the road. A cloud of dust and gravel washed over them as they came to an abrupt stop under the shade of a gnarled oak.

With one fluid motion he switched off the ignition and leaned an arm over the wheel, shifting his body toward her.

"Would you like to explain that little dig?" he asked softly, with deceptive mildness.

Instantly Charmayne knew she had gone too far. She was playing with fire and was about to be singed. Yet she didn't give any indication of the thoughts that were catapulting through her brain when she answered coolly, "I don't understand."

"That little dig . . . What have you heard about my operation being shut down?"

"Why, nothing," Charmayne denied. Truly she hadn't heard a word, but she wasn't going to give him the satisfaction of saying it in such a way that he would believe her. She felt that her denial was a masterpiece of charged evasion.

Kyle watched her through narrowed eyes. This wasn't the first time he had become aware of such a rumor. He had first overheard it in muted conversation between two of his employees. The second time had been when one of his partners had come to him with the information that he had been asked if what was being said was true. It was a niggling little problem; one Kyle wanted quickly put to rest.

"It's not true," he stated firmly.

"I didn't say that it was."

"Then what did you mean about my getting my jollies?"

Charmayne examined a fingernail. Anything to keep from looking into his detested face. "I learned a long time ago not to trust a Richardson. And you are a Richardson."

Kyle thrust the door open and got out. He came around to Charmayne's side of the car and pulled her door open as well.

"Come on," he said. "Let's walk."

"I'd rather not," she returned obstinately.

"You don't have a 'rather' in this case." He took possession of her arm and made it physically impossible for her to remain sitting down.

Charmayne sputtered when she was brought to

her feet and forcibly led across low-lying grass to a barbed-wire fence. Kyle stopped at the taut wires and then, much to her surprise, bent to lift her into his arms and swiftly deposited her on the other side. He followed in a more conventional method, one learned as a boy. Coming away unscathed, he grinned at Charmayne and then took her arm, urging her again to move forward.

Charmayne registered her resistance to his high-handedness with one freeing, imperative jerking movement. But when this attempt failed to gain her release, she kept pace with him as he started up a gently rising hill. What would be the use of remaining alone? It would be hard to recross the fence in a dress, and even if she did, what waited on the other side? His car? She could just see herself sitting inside, passing time until his return. That vision did not please her. No, it would be far better if she went along with him, listened to what he had to say, and then continued to bait him.

"I've missed Kearney," Kyle confided, switching subjects. "—the people and the land."

Charmayne made no reply.

"It was my favorite place to live when I was a boy."

Again Charmayne remained silent.

Kyle sighed and when they came to the crest of the hill, his eyes ran over the surrounding pasture. The panorama was striking. Springtime wildflowers were almost entirely covering the fields: huge patches of bluebonnets, scarlet thrusts of paintbrush, a number of pale pink primroses. There had been some flowers growing among the grasses they had walked over, but nothing had prepared him for this. It was spectacular! Because of repeated rains, everything was so green and fertile looking . . . so very different from the last time he had lived here. A drought had taken hold of the land then and worry about livestock and crops was the main topic of conversation when any two people came together. Maybe if it had rained then—just a little—the sequence of events that led to his and his uncle's disgrace would not have happened. But it hadn't rained. And he was still paying the price to this day.

A gleam of water in the near distance caught Kyle's attention, and dropping Charmayne's arm, he set course toward it.

The late evening sun was still warm on Charmayne's back as she automatically started to follow his lead. Then a sense of déjà vu overtook her. How many times in the past had she followed him in just such a way? Her eyes ran over his broadened, now mature back, and acknowleding the folly of her childhood, she quickened her pace, not content to follow any longer. Soon she was beside him, matching him step for step.

Kyle sensed her determination but made no comment. He wasn't sure just what she was trying to prove, but if it was important to her, then he wasn't about to stand in her way.

The shade beneath the trees lining the stream was dappled by rays from the sun and the water reflected both lightness and dark. Various sets of animal prints along the dampened edge showed that the stream was used by domesticated and undomesticated species alike to cool the heat of their thirst.

Kyle chose to take a seat on a gnarled cypress root that twisted its way to the water. Charmayne selected another root a little distance away. In order to have something to do, she plucked a stray primrose blossom and began to twirl the stalk between her fingers.

Kyle did the same, only his subject was a long finger of grass. Ultimately he slid the bottom tip into his mouth. When he saw that she was watching him, he flashed another grin, his teeth white and strong on the tiny stalk. He pulled it from his mouth and explained, "I haven't done this in ages. Not since I was a boy. I was just checking to see if it still tastes the same as I remember."

"Does it?" Charmayne couldn't help the question.

He laughed. "I guess it's lost some of its appeal over the years."

A small smile twitched at Charmayne's lips as she thought about the saying that a person can never go home again. Then her smile disappeared. Because Kyle seemed to be trying it and succeeding, at least to some degree.

Kyle noted the sudden tightening of Charmayne's lips. If only he could get her to relax with him. But maybe that was asking too much. Maybe armed combat was the only course available to them just now. He flicked the stalk of grass into the creek and watched as it slowly made progress floating downstream.

Charmayne fixed her attention back on the flower in her hand, its delicately formed petals and pollen-loaded stamens a miracle of nature. She tried not to be aware of the man sitting across from her, but she was finding it increasingly difficult.

When he spoke again her reaction was similar to her startled surprise during the thunderstorm earlier in the day. But this time all the quaking was done internally. It seemed to go on for an inordinate amount of time.

"Did your umbrella come in handy this afternoon?" he asked, a droll humor flavoring his words as if he was perfectly aware that the question could be put in the same category as waving a red flag in front of an infuriated bull.

Charmayne took refuge in a resurgence of resentment. She wasn't at all happy about the way she seemed to be overly sensitive to each and every move of his lean muscular form, nor was she at all enthralled with her overly dramatic reaction to his softly spoken question.

"No," she answered stiltedly, still trying to right the confusion within her.

Kyle let his eyes run over her leisurely. She was the epitome of unruffled femininity just waiting to be provoked. And he was just the man to provoke her.

"You left it at the office?" he goaded.

"You could say that."

Kyle smiled. "Do I detect that something has been left unsaid?"

"If it has, then there must be a reason. I'd advise that you take the hint," she snapped.

A low soft whistle escaped his lips. "I think I detect something more. What happened to it, Charmayne?"

"I put it away," she said stiffly.

"Where?"

The flower still remaining in Charmayne's grasp came closer to being beheaded.

"In a safe place."

"How safe?"

"Safe enough."

There was a pause. "Charmayne, are you telling the truth?"

"Yes!"

It wasn't really a lie. The hateful umbrella *was* in a safe place—safe from her being bothered by it again!

"Are you sure?"

If the Maker of the heavens wanted to hold this against her on Judgment Day, she would just have to face up to it at that time. She wasn't about to admit to anything now. "Of course I'm sure!"

"Then you must have had another one with you. Either that or you left before it started to rain."

"Yes." She was on safer ground with either speculation.

"Ahh."

"Yes," she replied again to emphasize her position.

"You don't have to repeat yourself. I believe you."

Charmayne was desperate to get the spotlight off herself and onto something else. She chose him.

"What you do and don't do, Kyle Richardson, doesn't interest me in the least. And since when have you started to worry so much about minor little things like honesty? You and that uncle of yours certainly didn't let anything so mundane affect either of you." She took a quick breath and motioned in the air with one hand. "It wasn't bad enough that you had everyone's trust! Oh, no. The two of you had to go it one better! You had to steal from us as well!"

Kyle sat forward and hunched over to hug his updrawn knee, a dull red stain creeping onto the back of his neck. *The sins of the father* . . . But in this case it was the uncle.

"I stole nothing, Charmayne," he denied softly.

Charmayne didn't hear him. She had found a defensive tack and she wasn't about to relinquish it so quickly.

"You didn't care what havoc you caused . . . what heartache! You didn't care about the shambles you left of so many lives! People scraped together all the cash they had—some even turned over their entire savings—and they gave it all to you because they trusted you!

"Water! A farmer and rancher's lifeblood!" She threw the flower down a mangled mess. Unconsciously she had destroyed what nature had worked so many seasons to perfect. "Why didn't the two of you just come in here and start shooting people? That's what I'd like to know.

"A series of deep water wells . . ." she stated bitterly. "Did your uncle really have all the contacts he said he did? Or was it all just a part of the scam? A lie from the beginning . . ."

Charmayne rose to her feet, the agitation within her building until she couldn't remain still any longer. She threw a disgusted look at Kyle and turned on her heel to begin the trek back to the car. She didn't care if he came or not. It would be night soon, but she would walk back to the farm if she had to. It wasn't all that far. Just ten or so miles. She would be in around midnight; her parents wouldn't have cause for alarm, if they missed her at all, that was.

But she had got no farther than the ascending slope beside the creek bed when Kyle came up rapidly behind her. His fingers wrapped around her arm and whirled her around.

Fiery green eyes met stone-hard gray.

"You've made some serious accusations, Charmayne. Don't you think it would be a good idea to stick around long enough to listen to a few replies?"

Charmayne tried to wrest her arm from his grasp, but his fingers were like clamps attached to her skin.

"I don't believe you can possibly have anything to say to me that I want to hear!"

"Oh, no?"

"No!"

A smile that could only be described as lethal settled on Kyle's mouth. "Do you always think you're so damned right, Charmayne? Isn't anyone ever given the chance to make an explanation?"

"Not you!"

"Yes, me!"

Charmayne tried again to free herself. But once more it did no good. She stopped her struggles and instead drew herself upright, deciding that cold hauteur might have more effect in gaining her release than outright fury.

"Let go of my arm."

The frigidness of her request blew frost on Kyle's soul, but he held firm.

"Not until you agree to listen."

A gigantic struggle began to take place within Charmayne. One part of her wanted to cross over into physical battle; the other was urging her to agree, though she had no compunction about breaking her word.

The second course to freedom won out. A short

nod of her head resulted in his hand slowly falling away.

As soon as the action had been completed, an electrical spark shot through Charmayne's body and she began to run, clawing her way up the embankment when the going became especially rough because of loose stones.

She didn't take the time to look around, to see whether Kyle was coming after her. She knew that he was. She could hear his breathing directly behind and beneath her.

When she broke into the open pasture, her flying feet made short work of the low grasses.

As her breath came in short quick gasps, Charmayne spotted the fence outlining the road where the car was parked. Then, at once, she realized her foolishness. She didn't want to run toward his car! That was not a route of escape for her! It would be to *his* advantage if she kept to the road.

As soon as the thought entered her head, Charmayne broke stride and tried to execute a quick turn to the right. She would go across country, keep to the fields. There her agility would give her an advantage.

But before she could take many steps, something happened to her balance. It must have been the fast turn, because her legs no longer wanted to keep up with the rest of her torso. Her feet seemed to get tangled each time they came near the ground.

Kyle saw the trouble she was having and instantly knew that she would falter. A rush of something like primal elation surged through him as he intensified his pursuit.

The ground came up fast against Charmayne's body, and for a moment the air was pounded from her lungs, the cool darkening of the Texas sky repeated in her brain. But the pungent smell of earth and crushed wildflowers was too vivid to be ignored. It acted as a natural stimulant to keep her conscious.

The seconds seemed long as she lay there, stunned. Then a great weight was hitting the ground beside her and a viselike object was pressed across her back.

Harsh breathing sounded in her ear that soon became a masculine chuckle.

Reality hit at that same instant and Charmayne tried to struggle against the entrapment. But a sudden pain in her side, the result of her having fallen against an upthrust rock, made her quickly cease all movement.

"You shouldn't have tried to run away, Charmayne," the aggravating voice advised.

The victorious pleasure in his tone added provocation to her already injured pride as well as her physical being. Didn't he care that she might be hurt? Couldn't he at least ask?

"Oh, shut up!" she hissed, wishing that she could wound him in return.

"All I wanted you to do was listen," he persisted.

Charmayne turned her head away in pointed silent response, causing Kyle to give another little laugh.

"Well, since this might be the only chance I'll have, I'm going to have to make the best of it."

His arm loosened a degree, yet kept her under firm control. "Some of what you said is true, Charmayne. My uncle did cheat the people here. But it wasn't me. I didn't have anything to do with it. I was just a kid!"

When she remained stubbornly silent, Kyle continued, "I'm ashamed of what my uncle did. But I couldn't have influenced the situation then, and I

72

can't now. There are times when things are out of a person's control, Charmayne." He paused, waited, and then went on, "Even if I had tried, I couldn't have stopped what happened. These farmers were desperate. They *wanted* to believe that my uncle could find water for them. He told them what they wanted to hear. I would have been telling them something totally different. It's human nature not to listen to the truth when it goes against what you wish. Still, I didn't know."

Slowly Charmayne turned her head until she was facing him.

"You didn't know what was going on?"

"No."

"I don't believe you."

"All I have is my word."

"Which isn't worth much!"

Kyle's eyes remained steadily on her, and she could see the tiny lines of darker color that radiated outward from the pupils. She was aware of the mussed state of his hair—a condition that somehow only managed to add to his physical appeal—and she could sense the warmth of his body, the strength of his arms and chest, and the hard muscles of his thighs as they pressed against her.

All at once a sexual tension flooded through Charmayne. It was as if super-hot lava had replaced the usual liquid in her veins. Under this assault the harshness of her anger melted. Forgotten was the momentary pain in her side, the fact that Kyle was holding her down against her will, that she came as close to hating him as she did any individual on the face of the earth. . . . Her green eyes widened as her emotion deepened.

Kyle was instantly aware of her body's stiffening, then of its quick rush of heat. And looking deeply into her eyes, he saw the dawn of desire as it was born. Without thinking, satisfying only the building demand in his own body he lowered his head until his lips were in contact with hers.

At first Charmayne was still, as quicksilver fires burst through her system like explosive charges. His lips were warm and soft, urging her to even greater sensation. Then, as the tension within her mounted and her arousal became complete, her eyes closed, her body shifted to face him, and she actively sought whatever sensual pleasure would come next. She began to kiss him back, her arms coming out to enfold his neck.

Her willingness came as no surprise to Kyle. In fact he gave it little notice; he simply accepted it. His mind wasn't working well now, looking for causes, searching for reasons. He didn't question. He was alive only to the feel of her soft pliant body next to his and her growing need that merely echoed his.

Caught in the sensual spell of their own making, they quested forward, unaware of the lengthening shadows of evening, unaware that the next day would come.

Kyle's lips moved from her mouth to her ear, his tongue tracing the fragile outline.

Charmayne drew in a sharp breath as his course lowered and his breath came warm on her throat, blazing a trail across her sensitive skin. Her fingers threaded through his hair, feeling the crispness of his curls, the shape of his head. Her senses were alive to his masculine scent, the lingering spicy aroma of his cologne, the heat emanating from his long form.

With a reflexive tightening of her own womanhood, she was overwhelmingly aware of his body's response as he strained against her, a knee separating her legs, a thigh heavy and moving on hers.

Then one of his hands released its fevered hold on her back and came between them to smooth over the fabric covering her breasts. The small bounty responded accordingly, swelling as she arched forward. Using his thumb, Kyle played with the hardening nipple.

For a moment Charmayne felt as if she were on fire. Then, when he untied the delicate bow at the shoulder of her sundress and smoothed it free, replacing the lower covering with his lips, she realized she'd had no previous idea of what fire was!

Her fingers dug into his hair, her body arching again as passion took wing and the incessant demand that had been growing from the first moment obliterated all but the need for total possession.

A rapturous moan escaped her lips as she moved against him.

Kyle's breath was coming short and fast, and he recaptured her lips as he covered her body completely with his own, keeping most of his weight from crushing her by placing his hands on the ground above her shoulders.

The kiss they exchanged then was soul destroying in its intensity. It was a prelude, a promise, a tantalizing taste of what was to come. Finally Kyle broke away and raised her hand to his chest.

"Touch me, Charmayne," he directed huskily. "Touch me here . . . and here." He moved her hand over his shirt then lower, past his belt.

Charmayne's heart jumped at the intimate contact and Kyle gave a low ragged groan.

"God!" he rasped, then said, "Charmayne . . . I—"

No further words were allowed to pass his lips as Charmayne sat up and covered his mouth with her own.

Quickly the buttons of his shirt were disposed of, followed by the shirt itself.

The warmth of his skin was like a blessing to her. She smoothed her hands over his chest, then around to his back, where the strength of his well-developed muscles rippled and moved as he drew her closer.

The weight of his body molded her into the soft earth, but Charmayne didn't care! She didn't care about anything except what was happening this very moment. There was no right or wrong. No good or bad. No past, no future.

If she had never wanted a man so strongly before, it now seemed as natural as drawing breath that she wanted Kyle. Somehow it seemed right to be Kyle.

Then slowly a feeling filtered through to first one and then the other that they were no longer alone, that someone was watching them. It was a prickly kind of sensation that went back in time to the early days when human beings had to be alert for any kind of threat to their safety.

Kyle's body's stiffening was soon followed by Charmayne's as her breath seemed to catch in her throat. His eyes met hers and several silent seconds passed before each turned.

What they saw gave them both a shock.

Several cows, who had been ambling by in the pasture, were now standing only inches away, their jaws working as they stared at the couple with dulled bovine brown eyes.

Charmayne blinked and blinked again. Then she started to laugh. She couldn't help it. She could just imagine what the scene must look like through the animals' eyes. She and Kyle had invaded their territory; they had no grounds for complaint!

Kyle's attention came back to her immediately, his eyes holding a mixture of emotions in their depths. Then, as he watched her amused reaction to the interruption, the crinkles at the corners of his eyes deepened until he was laughing as well.

"Shoo! Go away!" He waved an arm in the cows' faces. It did no good. They just considered his action a part of the show.

Kyle pushed to his feet. "Shoo, I said! Go on! Go away!"

Three white faces were directed from one human to the other. Then, as Kyle came closer, a decision must have been made that the entertainment was over because the great beasts turned almost in unison to move slowly on their way once again.

With his hands low on his hips Kyle watched their unhurried departure. Finally he turned back to Charmayne, the light of amusement still curving his lips.

"Well, that's a first!" he murmured.

Charmayne gave no response. It had taken those short few seconds for her to realize just what she had been doing. She was so ashamed, she was so mortified. What had happened to her great plan? It had melted the instant he had gotten near her! How stupidly ridiculous!

They had come so close. . . . Thank God for the

creation of cattle! If they hadn't come . . . She promised never to eat red meat again.

Kyle narrowed his eyes as he saw her closing expression. He didn't need the full light of day to see what was going on. He could feel it.

"Charmayne. Charmayne, look at me."

Charmayne stubbornly would not. She occupied herself with straightening the top of her dress.

Kyle moved close and crouched down to reach out and tip up her chin. Her freckles barely showed in the twilight. But her green eyes were large and wet looking, as if she might burst into tears at any moment.

"Don't pull away from me like this, Charmayne," he said softly. "What happened was . . ." He paused to search for words, more than a little shaken himself. Was what? It certainly wasn't planned. He didn't know what had come over him! He wasn't an animal that he had such little control. He hadn't even known that he felt that way about her. All he knew was that he enjoyed teasing her, getting a rise out of her. In some ways when they were children he had looked upon her almost as a kid sister! Yet note the past tense, "had." After what had happened he couldn't say that any longer. The memory of her willing response still contained the power to excite him.

"Crazy!" Charmayne supplied the word. "That was what it was! Crazy!"

She pulled her chin away from his hold and shakily got to her feet. He saw her sway, but he didn't attempt to offer help.

"Take me home, Kyle."

Kyle was silent for a moment; then he reached forward to retrieve his shirt from the ground.

Charmayne turned away as he stood up and slipped it back on, her face a brilliant red as she remembered how anxious she had been to take it off. And when she remembered how she had touched him so intimately only a moment before . . . Without waiting for him to finish attaching the buttons, she started for the car.

Oh, God! What was she going to do? How would she ever be able to face him again? Could she make herself forget?

Her burning hand answered the question. It was so easy to remember. . . . A shooting need drove through her that she immediately quashed. No! She had to forget! There was no other way!

The drive back to her home was even more silent than the drive away, Kyle not seeming any more anxious to converse than she.

For his part Kyle was reliving each moment of their lovemaking over and over again, reveling in it with a kind of wonder. He had made love to women before—the first time had been when he was sixteen —but somehow with Charmayne there was a difference. And as he neared the fork in the road that led to her home, he made the resolve that he was going to see that it happened again.

As the car slowed to make the turn, Charmayne spoke for the first time since they had left the pasture.

"Stop here." The direction was stiff.

Kyle did as she directed, but protested, "I think I should take you to your house."

"Why? So I won't be attacked twice in one night?" Her sarcasm was deadly.

"I didn't attack you," he reminded her.

She snorted.

"Charmayne!"

She pulled at the door handle, but it wouldn't budge.

While she searched for the release, Kyle reminded her, "You didn't exactly fight me off, you know."

"I don't pretend to be a saint."

"You admit that you enjoyed it?"

"I admit nothing."

"But you did."

"Help me get out of here, Kyle. Before I—"

"Before you what? Hit me? Or kiss me?"

At that moment Charmayne wanted nothing less than to scalp him! Maybe it was some of the much diluted Comanche blood coming out in her at the right moment. She pictured his curly hair hanging by a cord from her fireplace.

When she remained silent, Kyle decided that he had pushed her far enough for the moment and released the lock from the controls at his side.

Without another word Charmayne exited the car, then slammed the door with unrestrained antagonism. The entire chassis rocked.

Kyle smiled tightly as his gaze followed her straightly held back for as long as he could see her in the glow shining from his car's headlights.

CHAPTER FIVE

When Charmayne awoke the next morning she was not fit company for anyone. She felt mad at the world. A perky "Good morning" would likely receive a snappy "What's good about it?" So she hurried through her shower, her dressing, and her breakfast so that she wouldn't give her parents cause for wishing that she had never been born.

When she arrived at her office it was to find the mayor standing beside her desk using her telephone.

Mayor Drew Cliburn was a hefty six footer with steel-gray hair and a face that only a mother could love. He had been a Marine during World War II and still was proud to the core of that fact. But his once trim, fighting-machine body had succumbed to late middle age and one too many helpings of his wife's special apple pie.

He noticed Charmayne's presence and winked at her while continuing his broken conversation.

"Yes, Mrs. Miller. I'll get someone on it right away. No ... Yes ... I agree. Yes, I understand. You have my promise on that. Well, yes, thank you. Thank you. I expect it will, too. Now, you take care of yourself and just let me know if you have any more problems. All right?"

When he hung up the telephone, he heaved a great sigh.

"Mrs. Miller," he explained needlessly.

"Yes, I heard."

"She's having trouble with Harry Winston's dog getting into her garden again. Lord, I don't know what she expects. That danged dog just loves carrots and will do anything he can to get them, even if he has to dig them up! Stopping him would be like the canine equivalent of a James Bond movie! I can see it now: a sophisticated radar system sweeping the area between her house and the Winstons', a deputy on duty watching the screen. Suddenly he sees a moving blip. . . . It's the dog! Using wire cutters to slip through the reinforced barbed wire fence . . ." He laughed shortly. "Do I really do all of this for a measly dollar a year, Charmayne?"

Considering the mood she was in, and since the task of dealing with Mrs. Miller and her various problems were usually pawned off on her, it was all Charmayne could do not to give the mayor the answer he so richly deserved. But she wisely held her tongue. The mayor did see to a number of obligations himself. He visited the town's elderly regularly, checking to see if they needed anything, from the most basic necessities of food to being sure that they kept their doctors' appointments. And whenever one of the town's more derelict citizens fell off the wagon and became too drunk to drive, he knew he could call Mayor Cliburn and the mayor would be sure he had a ride home, sometimes even coming to get him himself. So he had his good points and they made working for him easier.

"Maybe we could see about getting you a raise." Charmayne smiled tightly, trying to join in with his wry humor. "Maybe even double your salary to two dollars a year."

The mayor grunted and pushed himself from his half-sitting position on the edge of her desk. "Yeah, maybe. Don't know why I do it sometimes, though.

More problems that it's worth. And to want to do it again : . ." He shook his head. "I must have a screw loose in my head somewhere!"

Charmayne's smile became more genuine. She really liked Mayor Cliburn, even if she did occasionally become impatient with him. "You do it because you're a good mayor," she reassured him.

His sharp brown eyes bored into her. "You really think so?"

"Yes." She moved to a position behind her desk and put her purse into a side bottom drawer. "I do." She had to handle all the nitpicky occurrences in the running of the town, but the mayor dealt with some problems that she wouldn't accept for anything. Like wrangling with the city council, dealing with the state politicians, and the larger financial picture of Kearney itself.

"Mrs. Miller says she hopes I'm reelected," the mayor remarked, breaking into her thoughts.

"Good."

"She says she thinks it will be a hard race."

"Oh, I don't know," Charmayne said consideringly. "John Marshall's base isn't all that large."

"But he doesn't mind fighting dirty. Remember, I've come up against him before."

"And you won."

"I know. But I—"

"You'll win again. Stop worrying."

"I get paid to worry, Charmayne."

"A dollar's worth. And in today's economy that doesn't buy very much."

The mayor broke into a slow grin and gruffly patted her shoulder. "Why does talking with you always make me feel better?"

"Would you like to give me a raise, too?" she teased. She knew the likelihood was nil.

The mayor looked into the freckled face turned up to him, at the smiling eyes and vibrant red hair.

"I would if I could."

"And if a pig had wings he could fly, right?"

Mayor Cliburn thought a moment, then said, "I'll tell you what. If I am reelected, the first thing I'll put on the docket to take up with the council is a raise for you. How does that sound?"

"You've got my vote!"

The mayor's grin was even wider as he moved to the door. "Never let it be said that I don't know how to make friends and influence people."

"I won't tell a soul," Charmayne called after him.

When she was alone she collapsed against the back of her chair. Oh, God! she thought. She should have called in sick. She didn't feel up to making the day. But what would she have done with all her spare time? Mope around the house feeling sorry for herself? Hadn't she done enough of that already—like all through last night? No. The best thing to do was to bury herself in her work and try to forget.

The simultaneous ringing of two telephone lines assured her that this was going to be a busy day.

Charmayne looked up from proofreading a letter Tina had typed—she always proofed Tina's letters before sending them on to the mayor, otherwise she never knew what chaos might ensue—when a bright head the same shade of red as her own thrust itself through a crack in the door.

"Hi! Are you busy?"

On seeing her sister's happy face, Charmayne put the letter aside.

"Hi, yourself. You mean you've finally surfaced long enough from conjugal bliss to pay a call on a relative?"

A vivid pink blush stained Lynn's cheeks, the color clashing wildly with her hair. "Hush, Charmayne. Bob is a minister, after all."

"And ministers don't—"

"Hush, I said. Or I'm going to turn around and leave."

Charmayne's lips twitched.

"All right. I'll be good. Come on in. It feels like it's been a year instead of just one month. How are you? Have you gotten settled yet in the rectory?"

Charmayne reached out to hug her younger sister.

Lynn was shorter by several inches and her eyes, instead of being green, were their father's pale, pale blue. The combination of her coloring was striking. Lynn had always been the prettier of the two sisters and instead of being reed thin, she possessed at least twenty more pounds than Charmayne. Of course Charmayne never let her forget it, lovingly teasing her even though she knew her younger sister's curves were all in the right places.

"Sort of. There are still a number of boxes sitting around. Some of the church members volunteered to help, but Bob and I would really rather do it ourselves."

"Is that why it's taking you so long? Put away this, make a little love. Put away that, make a little love. . . ."

Charmayne enjoyed teasing Lynn.

"I warned you, Charmayne."

"Okay, calm down. Now, seriously, how are things going?"

Lynn began to beam as she took a seat in the chair across from Charmayne's desk. "Fine, really. As I told you on the phone, Padre Island was wonderful! Camping out on your honeymoon is so much fun!"

Privately Charmayne doubted that. She couldn't bear the thought of any creepy-crawlies coming into her tent, but she said nothing, just continued to smile.

"And then when we got back, the rectory had been repainted and all we had to do was start putting things away. Do you realize how many wedding presents we received? My fingers are going to be worn down to stubs by the time I finish writing all the thank-you notes!"

"Is that a hint? Do you need some help?"

"Thanks—but I'm enjoying it, actually."

"You always were an independent little cuss."

"And you're not?"

"We should have been twins."

"We nearly were!"

"Mom and Dad were a little off on their timing," Charmayne agreed, referring to the fact that she and Lynn had been born only ten months apart.

There was a moment of silence, then Lynn broached the subject that had brought her to the office.

"Charmayne?"

"What?" Charmayne sensed her sister's sudden seriousness.

"About Mom and Dad . . ."

Charmayne's moment of lighthearted relief came to an end. Talking with Lynn had taken her mind from her troubles; now everything came back with a rush.

"What about them?"

Lynn's brow wrinkled. "I don't know. It's just something I feel. Are they having some kind of a problem?"

Charmayne shrugged. "There's always the farm."

"No, I don't mean that. It's something else. Something personal." She paused. "Maybe it's because I've been away for a while, but something seems to have changed between them. I went out for a visit last night—you were gone, of course. The least you could have done was be there!—and I felt it. A kind of silent tension. Do you know what I mean?"

Charmayne picked up the pencil she had been using and twirled it unconsciously. So Lynn felt it, too!

"Yes."

Lynn's troubled expression increased. "I was hoping it was just my imagination."

"I know."

"What do you think it is?"

Charmayne shrugged again. "I don't have the slightest idea. I started to notice it a few days after your wedding."

"Do you think it has anything to do with my marrying Bob?" The thought startled her.

Charmayne was quick to reassure her. "No, that's something I'm positive it's not."

"Have you noticed anything in particular?"

"Just that Dad doesn't come home from work on time like he used to. And when he does, Mom kind of closes up."

Lynn stared at her. "That's exactly what I felt, too. Only with both of them. They seem to be growing a wall between them." She stopped, then asked hesitantly, "Do you think they don't love each other anymore?"

All children worry about the possibility of their parents' breaking up, even after they've grown.

Charmayne dropped the pencil decisively. "Don't be ridiculous."

"It happens, Charmayne."

"I know! But it's not happening to Mom and Dad!"

For once the younger sister felt like the older one. She looked at Charmayne and her blue eyes softened.

"You're probably right."

"I know I'm right."

"Yes . . ." Lynn stood up. "Well, I've taken up enough of your time and Bob is waiting for me to fix lunch. He had a meeting this morning."

"The real world is setting in with a thump."

"I guess so."

Charmayne accompanied her sister to the door, then hugged her and whispered, "Don't worry. Nowhere does it read that a honeymoon has to end the minute you get back."

Lynn's blue eyes began to shine and she answered in like manner, "I know. That's why you haven't seen very much of us!"

"Now who's going to embarrass who?"

Lynn gave a covert glance about the outer office. Tina was calmly applying Wite-Out to a paper in her typewriter and the other two women were industriously involved in their own work.

"Me, I suppose. I'm going to have to learn to watch my tongue!"

"Why?"

"Oh, Charmayne, you're hopeless! Call me when you get a chance, okay?"

"Sure. You do the same."

"I will."

Tina looked up as Lynn passed through her office and smiled a friendly good-bye.

Charmayne's smile was tight when Tina's gaze moved back to her.

So far this had been another horrible day!

Maybe it would get better.

She should have known! Do bad days ever get better? No, they usually get worse.

As if it weren't enough that what had passed between them yesterday was never far from her mind, Kyle had called just before midday to audaciously ask if she would like to have lunch with him.

Charmayne had stared at the phone and almost growled.

Kyle took the hint and didn't press the issue. He wished her a good day and hung up.

Purposely she waited until long after her usual time to leave the office for her lunch break. Kearney had only so many places to eat out and she didn't want to run into him in one. When she finally left, it was past two and her temperament wasn't improved by the young waitress in the café who took her own sweet time about writing up her order because she was busy flirting with her boyfriend, who followed her everywhere.

Indigestion was added to irritation and Charmayne returned to the office ready to attack anything that moved. But, of course, she didn't. She was the model of calm efficiency, dealing with all problems large and small with a high degree of professionalism.

She remained that way for the rest of the workweek, and only someone who knew her well would have sensed the toll such repression was taking.

Kyle was experiencing little better of a week. And to top his Friday morning off, he had learned that somehow the papers had been switched on two orders—the travelers that went with each printed-circuit-board order telling what process was needed—which had resulted in the finished orders being sent to the wrong customers. Representatives of both computer manufacturing firms were extremely displeased and after dealing with them, Kyle felt as though he had been put through the wringer. Quality control was the watchword at Orion Enterprises. How had they slipped up?

If this had been the first time it had happened, he might feel differently. Human error was an inescapable factor. But for it to happen twice in as many weeks!

Kyle looked up from rubbing his forehead with his fingertips, his elbow resting on the top of his desk, as Dak Stevens, one of his partners, voiced exactly what he himself had been thinking.

"Sabotage . . ." he repeated, not wanting to face the suspicion.

"I'm sorry to say it looks that way."

Dak and Tony Campo had come with Kyle from one of the larger electronics firms in Texas. Each had been enthusiastic about the idea of starting their own small assembly operation that would contract with the larger firms for jobs that could be done with more ease by a smaller plant. Both had contributed monetarily what they could and Kyle had come up with the rest, an accumulation he had been adding to for years with a special idea in mind.

"I don't want to believe that."

Dak shrugged, his thin, intelligent face sober.

"Who would do it?" Kyle asked.

"Anyone. Do you have any enemies here?"

If Dak only knew! When he had recommended Kearney for the location of their operation, he had only told his friends that he had lived there as a boy. If they had heard anything else, it had not come from him.

"A few."

Dak remained still.

"Possibly more than a few. But hell, Dak! These are good people. And they need this operation almost more than we do! We can go back to Dallas if we fail; they have to stay here. It would be financial suicide for anyone to want to harm us."

"Then how did the travelers get switched?"

"By accident?"

"A second time?"

Kyle took a deep breath and pushed away from his desk. He felt the need for physical exertion. He walked to the window that looked down onto the parking area one story below.

"Dak, I don't know."

"I think we should scale up our security."

Kyle turned. "In what way?"

"Just keep our eyes and ears open a little more—at least for right now."

"Yes," Kyle agreed at last. "I suppose you're right. But I still don't like it."

"No, neither do I. But we have to look at things realistically. First there was the rumor about us closing and now this. If someone's out to cause trouble, I think we should be prepared."

Kyle abdicated to wise counsel. "You're right. Okay. Let's do it. Does Tony know?"

"Not yet."

"You want to tell him?"

"I might as well. He's scheduled back from Dallas tonight and he said something about dropping by my house. I'll tell him then." He paused. "Say, why don't you come over, too? Sally's going to her sister's for the weekend and we can get up a card game."

Kyle declined. "Another time, Dak. I've already got plans for tonight."

Dak's thin cheeks cracked into a smile. "Uh-oh. Those are dangerous words. I turned down a card game with the boys once to go out with Sally and look what happened."

Kyle laughed. "Don't start checking out the price of rice yet. We're not even to the tolerate stage."

"Sounds better and better. Who is this paragon of rare taste that can't stand you?"

"Didn't you say you had a circuit board to check?"

"I've been told by better men than you to mind my own business."

Kyle laughed again. "Go on. Get out. Go do your job. Catch whatever criminals may be lurking in the sagebrush."

"I think you mean scrub cedar," Dak corrected, thinking of the bane of the area farmers and ranchers.

"No, I mean sagebrush. This is beginning to get

more and more like a Hollywood 'B' movie all the time."

"Hummm. I think I'll grow a mustache. One of those long ones I can twirl."

"I thought only the bad guys wore that kind."

"Nah. You should go to Waco and see the Texas Ranger Hall of Fame. Some of those Rangers were mean-looking dudes, with fantastic mustaches."

"If you say so."

Dak left with a wave and Kyle resettled himself at his desk, wondering, if it were sabotage, who could possibly be responsible. As he had admitted, he was sure there were still people who blamed him for his uncle's deeds—Charmayne, for one. But would anyone's hate be so blind as not to see the good he was doing for the town? For so long he had wanted to make amends. Was it all going to be thrown back into his face, just when it was beginning to make an impact?

Kyle left his office early that afternoon, determined to put his work problems behind him. Something else had been playing games with his mind and it was a matter he could do something about. His Cadillac covered the distance between his assembly works and the mayor's office in a few short minutes.

At five minutes to five Charmayne was emptying her desktop of its clutter, always conscientious about leaving a clean-looking office. If the middle drawer was bulging with work needing attention, she wasn't haunted by it. It definitely wouldn't go away of its own accord; it would be waiting for her there the next workday. And it did her spirit a world of good to start the day with a clean slate. She liked to have control over some areas of her life, especially when other aspects of it were becoming so confused.

Then, rescuing her purse from her bottom drawer, she ran a hand over her hair and stood up. Today had to be a day for the record books, and she was glad that it was near to being over!

Maybe she would stop by Monica's on the way home. She hadn't seen or talked with her for what seemed ages, an unusual occurrence for two such close friends. But so much had been happening in her life recently.

When her thoughts again zeroed in on Kyle for the millionth time that day, Charmayne's lips firmed. Yes, she would go to Monica's. And they would talk about diapers and pacifiers and the merits of one brand of baby formula over another.

Ordinarily Charmayne listened to her friend with fond amusement because she could remember the day when Monica was adamant about not having any "brats" of her own, a view that had been formulated by the misbehaving children she had baby-sat with as a teen-ager. But now since little Michael's emergence, Monica had become Mother Earth and children had become her sole topic of conversation.

But today that was good, because Charmayne needed to become immersed in something—anything —that would quiet the proddings of her brain and cool the remembrances of her body. Her hand still tingled when she thought of touching Kyle, and her body burned. She wasn't sure if that emotion signaled embarrassment or pleasure. And that was what made her so jumpy, so on edge.

She paused to turn off the light switch before moving into the outer office that was emptying of people as well. Tina was covering her typewriter and Jane and Lois were speculating about a nighttime television soap opera that was scheduled to have an earth-shattering event take place.

"J.R. is going to get his comeuppance this time. I'm sure of it!" Jane was remarking.

"Oh, no. He'll find a way out of his troubles again. He always does!" Lois replied.

"One day he won't!"

"That won't happen until the series ends."

"But he deserves . . ."

The women left the room and moved into the hall, still deep in conversation.

Charmayne started to copy their departure, but as she did, she heard a familiar voice greet the two who had just left. Her instant reaction was that of a frightened rabbit. She spun around and quickly retraced her steps to her office, forgetting for the moment that going to ground would only result in her capture.

She was as far as her door when Kyle rounded the doorway.

"Hi," he greeted Tina.

She could feel his eyes fasten on her. Her body became still, her back to him.

"Hi," Tina returned, a wide smile coming to her mouth. Her gaze followed his and then returned. Her smile lessened. "If you've come to see the mayor, he's not here. He won't be in until Monday."

Kyle pulled his attention away from Charmayne. "No—" A knot of tension had suddenly closed off the passage in his throat and he had difficulty in speaking. All he could think of was how her body had felt pressed against him, the sweetness of her response, and the creamy smoothness of her breast.

"Mr. Richardson?" Tina prompted.

How much time had elapsed? Kyle shook his head. "No," he repeated and moved farther into the room. Outside the mayor's office he had been so confident, so cool. He would come in, bully Charmayne into going out with him again, and then he would . . . well, he would do what progressed naturally. But now he had suddenly lost all of his cocky assurance and felt little more than an absolute fool. If he could somehow disappear from the situation he would. But the laws of physics being what they are, he had to stand there and wait, hoping that something would happen to come to his aid.

Slowly Charmayne turned. She knew she couldn't pretend to be invisible forever. Her eyes unwillingly traveled the distance between them.

He looked so assured standing there, so heart-poundingly attractive. His red-brown hair curled just the right degree as it fell slightly over his forehead; his skin had just the right shade of tan to show his rugged features to perfection; his long, muscular form almost vibrated with virility even though, at the moment, it was covered in a suit. And his pale eyes were looking into hers with thoughts of seduction written all over them.

A veritable buzz of reaction shot through Charmayne, making every cell in her body spring into instant life. To combat her traitorous physical reaction, she forced herself to meet his gaze coldly. With an aplomb she didn't know she possessed, she glanced toward Tina and said, "I'm going now, Tina. If anything important crops up, let me know."

Tina blinked. Maybe it was because her voice sounded so strange, all tight and thin.

96

Charmayne ordered her legs to move and surprisingly they did. Kyle was between herself and the door, but if she pretended to ignore him . . .

It was Tina who stopped her before she was halfway to her destination.

"Oh—Charmayne . . . Charmayne, wait! I meant to give this to you before, but I forgot. And you might need it for the weekend."

Charmayne revolved like a statue on a pedestal. Why, oh, why, did Tina have to start becoming efficient now?

"Here." She bent to retrieve something from beside her desk. "I found this in your wastebasket the other day and I knew you wouldn't throw something so pretty and new-looking away. So . . ." She extended the much-despised powder-blue umbrella.

Charmayne stared at it as if it were something poisonous. She felt slightly sick. What could she say? What could she do? Oh, God! What a perfect mess!

Sight of the blue umbrella was all Kyle needed to snap him out of his altered state. With a return of his devilish grin, he stepped out from behind Charmayne and took the umbrella from Tina.

"Here, I'll take it." He reached for Charmayne's arm as well. "Charmayne, are you ready?"

Charmayne raised her blank gaze upward. Twinkling gray eyes laughed back at her. She could find nothing within herself to use in a fight. Now he knew what she had done with his gift, and although it shouldn't matter to her in the least, somehow she was ashamed.

Possibly it was her upbringing. Gifts, no matter how unwanted, were not to be spurned. They were to be taken gratefully, appreciation was to be verbally given, soon to be followed by a note.

When Kyle gave a gentle yet insistent pull on her arm, she followed his lead without making a sound. She did look back at Tina, though, as if silently pleading with her for help. All Tina did was look back at her.

CHAPTER SIX

Kyle's black Cadillac was parked next to Charmayne's gold Toyota in the rear parking area of the building. To get to them they had to walk across an expanse of crushed limestone, their feet crunching loudly on the whitish rock. Then Kyle was opening the passenger door of his car and motioning for her to get inside.

Charmayne gazed blankly at the expensive leather interior but made no move to obey.

"Go on. Get in," he urged, as if that would spur her on.

Charmayne did not move.

"Go ahead," he urged once more.

Again she remained still.

"Charmayne?" His questioning use of her name helped to snap her back to awareness.

"No," she answered slowly.

"Yes."

"No!"

Kyle shifted position and folded his arms, looking down at her with amusement.

"Why?" he challenged. "Are you afraid?"

How many times had he used that expression in the past as a more experienced thirteen to taunt her girlish eight into doing what he thought would be fun?

Charmayne decided the time for a mature answer had come. "Yes," she answered honestly, steadily meeting his gaze.

Kyle's smile increased and the afternoon sun caused the twinkle in his eyes to seem more intense.

"What are you afraid of?"

"I don't trust you." Again she chose honesty.

Kyle shook his head sagely.

"No, Charmayne. It's not me you don't trust, it's yourself."

Charmayne's mouth tightened. She hated him for using her own weakness against her.

"I'm not a glutton for punishment," she answered tightly.

"And I am?"

Charmayne looked away.

"Anyway," he continued, undaunted by her withdrawal. "I don't consider what happened between us as punishment."

"I don't want to talk about it."

"It happened."

"I still don't want to talk about it!"

Kyle sighed. "Am I just supposed to forget?"

Charmayne turned back. "That would be the gentlemanly thing to do."

Kyle laughed. "What century are you living in?"

Her cheeks flushed. "There are still some gentlemen left in the world today."

His eyes narrowed. "Do you have a particular person in mind?" Jealousy speared through him.

"Several!" she bragged.

Kyle absorbed her answer, then gave a devilish grin. "Well, I'm not a gentleman."

"I know that."

"You seemed to like it the other day."

Charmayne's eyes flashed as she fought to keep down the blush that wanted to cover her entire body.

"That was the other day."

Kyle smiled. He wasn't sure where this conversation was leading, but the possibilities were stimulating.

"Are you trying to tell me that if it happened again, you might not like it?"

His words were soft, causing an entire regiment of goosebumps to break out along the surface of her skin.

"I'm not trying to tell you anything, Kyle." She tried to move away from the car, but his arm came out and blocked her escape, trapping her between his form and the open door.

"If I kiss you right now, how would you react, I wonder?"

"Kyle . . ." She tried to move backward but was stopped by the car's metal frame.

He closed the space between them. "I love your freckles, Charmayne." His breath touched her skin as he bent close. "Every single one of them. Tell me, do they decorate all of you?"

Charmayne's face did flame at that intimate question because she couldn't help but imagine him finding out the truth for himself.

Kyle gave a satisfied smile. "Ahhh. They do."

He bent even closer and Charmayne had either to stay where she was and experience being kissed by him again or fold at the waist and slip into the passenger seat. She chose the seat. That might not be the wiser choice in the long run, but for the time being it would have to do. The long run would take care of itself.

Kyle's gray eyes danced at her decision. He had won! Then a little of the triumphant edge was trimmed from his victory when he wondered just where was he going to take her now that he had her. He didn't think she'd remain very calm if he suggested his home.

He wasted little time in getting into the driver's seat, afraid that she might change her mind and bolt. But she didn't and he breathed a sigh of relief as the car pulled away. He decided to let his subconscious direct him.

Charmayne began to question her sanity as the car rolled away. In town she could at least scream for assistance. Where he was taking her might be in the absolute middle of nowhere. And she couldn't count on another herd of cows to show up. Her lips parted to demand that he stop, but she decided against it, thinking that it might be interpreted as another sign of weakness. Not that she had exactly been the Rock of Gibraltar anyway. But she didn't need to add more proof.

Kyle flicked on the tape deck and the car came alive with the sound of a jazz ensemble. One of his fingers tapped lightly on the steering wheel in time to the beat. The music vibrated in Charmayne's soul.

He glanced across at her. She was sitting so still; she might have been a statue, except her breathing was disturbed, her small breasts rising and falling rapidly. A pang of desire surged through him, but he forced it down. He needed to keep some measure of control. He searched his mind for something to say.

"Kearney hasn't changed very much."

That gained him nothing. She remained silent.

"I'm glad that it hasn't, though," he went on as if she were vitally interested in every word that he had

102

to say. "Sometimes it's good to know that what you remember is solid fact."

She folded her arms.

He thought some more; then, as they approached a familiar area, he smiled.

"Do you remember the old Palmer place?"

That shook her loose, he saw with satisfaction. For years all the children living on the land surrounding the town had believed that the Palmer place was haunted. They probably still did.

"The Palmer place?" she questioned, catapulted instantly back into the emotions surrounding a childhood superstition. She made herself stop. She was an adult now. She knew that ghosts were only figments of people's imaginations. At least she told herself that she believed that.

"Sure. It's not too far from here, is it?"

Charmayne looked about them carefully. "No . . ."

"Let's go see it, then. I hadn't even remembered it before now."

Couldn't he have forgotten for a little longer? Charmayne wondered despairingly, then swallowed. "Okay."

A few miles drive down a graded road and a short walk across a field produced all that was left of the notorious Palmer place.

Charmayne approached it warily. On a surface examination it was merely a burned-out old house with a nearby barn that had fallen into disrepair, its gray weathered boards placed vertically to the ground as had been the custom of an earlier age.

But there was something more about the old place besides its dilapidated state; it had an eerie bleakness that reinforced the sense of loneliness and undoubtedly fueled the rumors about its being haunted.

Charmayne felt a nervous shiver run over her skin as her eyes dwelled on the barn with its witch's-hat shape and wide doors that were mismatched and hanging precariously from their hinges.

Somehow it looked incongruous with the scattered primroses and bluebonnets growing in the grasses surrounding it.

Kyle was looking at the barn as well. "Do you remember when we came here one night and went inside?"

Charmayne found no comfort in the memory.

"Yes," she answered. "I also remember that you made me come."

Kyle's mouth slowly curved. "Well, you kept daring me to come by myself. I thought the least you could do was tag along."

She suffered his derision. "Yes, well . . ."

"Do you remember the owl?"

"How could I forget?" A small smile tugged at her lips.

"I tried to act brave," he remembered.

"I knew you were just as frightened as I was."

"How?"

"I was shaking like a leaf, but when I let go of the old tractor's fender, it kept shaking. And I knew it was because of you."

Kyle's grin widened. "Then the owl hooted."

"And we both screamed and ran until we couldn't run anymore. You were practically dragging me."

"I pretended that I was helping you."

"You told me that you were."

"I did?"

Charmayne nodded. "And when I started to cry, you told me I was a stupid little girl and that we had to keep running or else the ghost would get me, that he only liked to eat girls."

Kyle laughed. "Of course he wouldn't have touched me."

"You seemed pretty sure."

"But I still ran."

Charmayne nodded. She hadn't thought about that night in years. For weeks afterward she had had nightmares and her mother had worried that she was watching too much television. She never told her what she and Kyle had done.

Kyle moved closer to the barn, and as Charmayne went with him she began to wonder about the original owners of the place . . . why they had left.

Kyle leaned toward one of the wide doors and shaded his eyes to look inside through a wide crack.

"The tractor's still here," he informed her.

He turned back around and her breath caught in her throat at how attractive he was. When he smiled, which was most of the time, he could not be compared with anyone.

Charmayne moved over to what remained of a split rail fence. She was trembling, but it was not from a fear of the supernatural.

Kyle followed her. He stopped beside a tree and leaned one hand against it for support.

"We had fun then, didn't we?"

He watched her nod of agreement. She didn't like to be reminded of her attachment to him as a child. He had been everything to her then. At least until . . .

"I didn't want to leave."

His soft words penetrated her soul. She had felt so betrayed! He hadn't even said good-bye! She remained silent.

"My uncle died, you know."

She lifted her gaze to his, trying to read what was left unsaid.

"I wasn't sorry." He spoke again, making the investigation easy.

"When?" she asked breathlessly.

"When I was seventeen."

"What—what happened?"

"He got drunk and drove his car into a tree."

Charmayne looked at the tree he was leaning against. He was talking so dispassionately. She had hated the man he was speaking of for years. Why didn't she feel any pleasure at hearing of his fate?

"Did you love him?"

"No."

"Not at all?"

"I tried to understand him, but I never loved him. He would never let anyone get that close."

"But you were his nephew!"

"It didn't matter."

She was learning some things she had never thought to question before. "Did he love you?"

"I don't think so."

"Then why . . . ?"

"Because he was my only relative. When my father died, my uncle took me. After that—" He stopped.

"Yes? After that?"

"After that things weren't so easy."

Charmayne was quiet for a time, absorbing all that

he had said. Then she remembered what he had told her yesterday.

"You really didn't know about the water wells?"

"No."

She looked down at the primroses growing beside the fence post. Should she believe him? Was he telling the truth?

A soft breeze made the wildflowers at her feet bend and sway and caressed her body with its warmth. Some of her hair swirled across her cheek and she reached up to push it away.

Kyle watched her graceful movement and wanted to take her in his arms. He wanted just to hold her—nothing more. At least for a time. It was a strange feeling, one he had never experienced with a woman before.

Charmayne's thoughts were conflicting. Listening to him now, she wanted to believe him. But if she did, she would be taking a step into the unknown, a leap of faith. And she wasn't ready to do that yet. She still wasn't sure. Her suspicion of him and his family had been too strong for too many years.

She moved away from the fence and started back to the car. Kyle followed.

When they reentered the parking area behind the municipal offices, they both were still silent. Kyle cut the engine and waited, one arm drawn across the steering wheel.

Charmayne felt his eyes touching her. She didn't look at him. She was afraid that if she did, she would give him the answer he so obviously wanted: that she believed him. Instead she reached for the door handle and stepped out.

"Charmayne," he called, stopping her from leaving him so easily.

She paused in the act of closing the door.

"I want to see you again."

She knew what he meant, but she stalled for time by saying, "I'll be in my office Monday morning."

Kyle gave her effort the disdain it deserved. He ignored it.

"Are you doing anything tomorrow evening?"

She wished she was! God, how she wished she was!

"I promised my mother I'd . . ." What? What could she say? Her brain worked furiously but could come up with nothing.

Kyle smiled slowly and her heart skipped an automatic beat.

"I'll be by about seven . . . and don't eat. This time I'm going to take you to Gibson's."

Charmayne drove home pushing the speed limit on the highway and then on the farm road to the maximum. If she could get away from her troubling thoughts as fast as she was covering ground, she would be all right. But her thoughts traveled with her; there was no escape.

When she glanced at her watch, she saw that she was an hour late, but still there was no sign of her father's pickup when she turned into the drive. Was he working late? Or had something come up after work that kept him away from home? Charmayne frowned, the weight of all her problems descending on her.

Her mother was in the living room dabbing at the painting of the schooner with a thin brush. She looked up when Charmayne came to stand next to her.

"That's coming along nicely, Mom," she encouraged.

Margaret Brennan smiled, but there was a shadow behind its curve.

"Yes, it is. I'm having a little trouble with the sails, though." She cocked her head to one side. "They look a bit flat."

Charmayne studied the painting. "What can you do?"

Her mother wiped her brush on a cloth and then swished it around in a jar of turpentine.

"Quit! At least for right now."

She dried the brush on a clean cloth and then stood up.

Charmayne went with her to the kitchen. Her mother poured coffee for each of them from the percolator that never seemed to be empty.

There was a question Charmayne wanted to ask, but she hesitated to voice it: Where was her father?

She spooned sugar into her cup and took it to the table, where she relaxed into a chair. With seeming nonchalance she glanced about the kitchen. Usually her mother would have dinner made. Tonight there seemed to be nothing even started.

Her mother sat in her favorite place and sipped her coffee. Her gaze rested steadily on the rear kitchen door.

Charmayne felt her stomach tighten as Lynn's words echoed in her ears. Could her mother and father be on the verge of breaking up? The idea appalled her. Not *her* mother and father. Other people's, yes. Her's, no!

She had to clear her throat before speaking. "How's dinner coming? Can I help with anything?"

Margaret Brennan seemed not to hear.

"Mom?" Charmayne urged.

Slowly her mother turned to her, a faraway look still in her eyes. Then the expression lifted and she gave a small start.

"Dinner . . . did you ask about dinner?"

Charmayne forced a tiny smile. "Yes. Do you need some help getting it ready?"

That was the best—pretend that nothing was wrong.

Her mother looked about and her hands began unconsciously to twist.

"Oh! Dinner . . . yes. Yes, if you don't mind . . ."

Charmayne's soul wrenched. She had never seen her mother in such a state before! She went to the refrigerator and checked its contents.

"Why don't we use this leftover roast beef? We can make a hash."

"Yes," Margaret answered briskly, too briskly. "That sounds good. A roast beef hash." She hurried over to the cabinet and withdrew a paring knife from a drawer; then, gathering onions, she began to slice and chop.

While she peeled potatoes, Charmayne keep one eye on her mother's activities. There was a bit more sniffing going on than was usual, even under the circumstances.

As she cubed the meat, her mother began to sauté the onions in oil.

Then an engine could be heard as a car made its

110

way down the drive. Her father? Charmayne peeked out the window.

"Dad's home," she commented, feeling the tension that had heightened in the room as if it were a ball of charged electricity just waiting for the signal of delivery.

Her words seemed to trip the wire. Her mother's stirring of the onions intensified. Then as the seconds passed and they heard the truck's door slam and the backyard gate creak as it was opened and closed, the large metal spoon Margaret was using clattered to the stovetop and she mumbled a broken "The onions," as an excuse and hurried from the room, tears streaming down over her cheeks.

Charmayne knew the problem wasn't the onions. Her mother just didn't want to see her father right then.

Feeling something like a waif left by the wayside, Charmayne felt the tears well up in her eyes as well, but she blinked them away with determination and took up her mother's previous position at the stove. Her father was coming and she needed some kind of control.

Raymond Brennan moved tiredly into the room, his exhaustion apparent even to the most undiscerning eye. His normally straight carriage was bent—his head drooping, his shoulders stooped—and he walked as if the entire weight of the world were resting on his shoulders.

For a moment he thought he was alone; then, when he saw Charmayne, he straightened and willed a lightening of his expression. Yet she saw.

"Where's your mother?" he asked, putting his lunch bucket on the counter.

Charmayne used the same evasion as Margaret. "The onion fumes were too strong. She had to get away from them for a little while."

Raymond grunted. Charmayne was not sure whether he believed her excuse or not. He stood by the counter as if unsure of what he should do next.

Charmayne moved to put the sliced potatoes and water into the cooking pot. Her father watched her in silence.

"Did you have a hard day?" she asked, using the old family standby.

"It was all right."

"You're late."

Raymond stirred. He didn't answer her question. "We had some trouble at the plant today. Some orders got confused."

"Oh?"

"Really put a bee in somebody's bonnet. Almost lost an account or two, I heard."

Charmayne was surprised by the amount of satisfaction this seemed to give her father.

"It must have been serious," she remarked tentatively.

"Serious enough."

"Did anyone get into trouble?" If it was that serious, someone may have been fired. The thought disturbed her as she projected what the loss of income might mean to a neighboring family.

"Naw. They kept everything under their hat, except for questioning everyone. Played it real cool."

"Thank goodness."

Her father merely shrugged. "Doesn't hurt to keep that bastard Richardson off guard a little."

Words of denial instantly sprang to Charmayne's

lips, but she clipped them off before they could be uttered. Now was definitely not the time to discuss Kyle's possible innocence concerning what had happened so long before. Instead, she observed, "That 'bastard' is paying your check."

"Don't remind me."

"I still don't think—"

"Stop it, Charmayne! You're beginning to sound just like your mother!" Raymond interrupted shortly, a frown darkening his features.

His immediate hostility had a feeling of repetition about it. Had her mother and father argued about that very thing? It seemed that they must have.

Charmayne turned away and stirred the potatoes. She didn't know what to say next. She didn't know how to defuse the situation between her parents. She couldn't even handle her father!

Raymond watched his daughter's withdrawal and saw it as rejection. Slowly another crack began to widen in his estimation of himself.

Without a word he turned away and reopened the outside door. Caring for the animals and the land was the only thing that kept him sane these days. At least they didn't pass judgment; they just accepted.

Charmayne heard the door close and knew that she was alone. God, she was so alone! She wanted to hurry after her father, go comfort her mother. But she couldn't do either. She couldn't take sides. She didn't know enough to make a decision about who was right or who was wrong. She didn't *want* to make such a decision. She put the lid on the cooking pot and resumed her seat at the table. Her coffee was cool now, but it didn't matter. Nothing mattered at the moment. Nothing at all.

Lying in bed that night, Charmayne felt no better. Her father had stayed outside seeing to whatever needed him most for at least an hour and her mother had not come out of her room until half that time had gone by. Her eyes were red rimmed, but the expression she turned to the world could only be termed one of forced brightness. She had gone back to her painting and jubilantly told Charmayne a short time later that she had the sails perfect now. The sails looked the same to Charmayne. But if her mother wanted to believe she had made a change, she wasn't about to tell her anything different.

When her father had at last come inside, a terse evening meal followed. Charmayne, for one, was too shaken by the preceding events to feel hunger even if it was much later than their normal dinnertime, and she noticed that her parents ate little as well.

Charmayne stared into the darkness of her room, thinking about her family, wondering what she could do. She needed someone to talk to, someone who could give her advice. . . . Then out of the darkness came a vision of pale gray eyes, eyes that asked for her belief.

She didn't want to think of Kyle now. She didn't need any more problems. Wasn't one at a time enough? Did disruption have to come in twos and threes?

His rugged face was rooted firmly in her inner vision. Had he told her the truth? Would he lie? What would his profit be in lying? A number of townspeople were seemingly already eating out of his hand, so why should she matter? Why should he care? They had been friends when they were young, but now . . .

But now, what? Did friends kiss as they had, touch as they had?

A fluid warmth washed over Charmayne's body and left her feeling weak and tingling. If he were here now, in this bed, she knew she would reach out and touch him again, just as she had before. Only this time she wouldn't want to be torn away. She would touch all of him, feel every strong, well-developed muscle. She would run her hands over his chest, his flat stomach, his thighs—every inch of his skin!—and want him to do the same to her.

A shudder ran from her head to her toes. If he were here with her now . . . She wanted him here with her!

Then, fighting against a drowning feeling of pure sensation, she struggled to sit up. No! She had to stop thinking that way! She couldn't let herself think that way! It was too dangerous, too . . . too . . . She couldn't find the right word, but she was well aware of the meaning.

She was much safer keeping up her guard of angry resentment. She had to remember what he had done to her family in the past, what he was doing now. Surely some of the problem between her parents had come about because her father was working at Orion Enterprises.

She didn't want to remember Kyle's confidences about his childhood; she didn't want to know. She didn't want to think kindly of him or in any way understand.

She wanted to be left alone. She wanted her family safe. *She* wanted to be safe.

CHAPTER SEVEN

Charmayne spent most of Saturday helping with chores around the farm. Because her father had to give the majority of his time to his job in Kearney, that left the weekend hours full. The day started early and would have lasted late, but a thunderstorm moving through the area brought them into the house a little after five and the continuing rain kept them inside.

While each was involved in his and her own jobs, the tension between her mother and father was less noticeable. But now that they were forced to remain in close quarters for a length of time, the strained silence was heartrending.

Charmayne felt it acutely, and she began to look forward to the time she would be with Kyle as a release. She had to get out of the house! Either that or start screaming or crying. Her nerves were jumping from worry; she had even caught herself slipping back into the childhood habit of biting her fingernails.

Again she didn't tell her parents whom she was going out with. She just mentioned the generic word "friend," and they were satisfied. Her mother barely looked up from her painting and her father merely rattled the newspaper he was hiding behind.

She was ready by fifteen minutes before the hour, because even though it was raining, she fully intended to meet Kyle at the fork in the road. Her reason for doing this still stood: He could not come to her home.

She was just slipping an arm into her raincoat, her feet already in rain boots, when the front doorbell rang. Her movements froze. Who? Oh, no! No! It couldn't be . . . ! Kyle wouldn't . . . Oh, yes, he would!

Charmayne dropped the coat and clomped quickly across the room, stopping her mother in the act of getting up.

"It's okay, Mom. I'll get it," she mumbled, a little out of breath. Her disturbed breathing did not come from her exertion. It came from fear. What was her father going to do?

Kyle stood on the porch, shaking raindrops from a collapsed baby blue umbrella. He looked up and a devilish laughter lighted both his eyes and his grin.

"Hi. I thought I'd save you some trouble and come get you this time."

For a moment all Charmayne could do was stare at him. She wanted to believe that this wasn't happening! But denying it had no effect. He still stood there, larger than life, dressed in dark blue slacks and a matching dark shirt, and looking heartstoppingly attractive.

She wanted to close the door in his face—keep the wolf at bay—but she knew from past experience that he wouldn't be content to let her do that. In fact, as she debated her course of action, he took a step forward and put a restraining hand on the doorframe.

"Aren't you going to ask me inside?" he prompted.

Kyle could see the conflict of emotions that warred within her and for a moment he wondered if he was doing the right thing. But he didn't want to see her on the sly. He didn't want to hide. If her parents disapproved, he would rather face their disapproval and deal with it. He knew that in the city, what a parent thought was not always heeded. But for the families of this small town, and especially for Charmayne, family approval and acceptance was important. He knew that without being told.

He didn't wait for her to answer. He leaned the umbrella against the outside wall and stepped inside.

Charmayne felt his eyes run over her, taking in the way her mint-green shirtwaist dress fitted her slender form. They stopped with amusement at her boots— he knew she had planned to meet him at the fork!— then they made a lightning-quick assessment of the room and settled on her parents.

Margaret returned his look with a frown. He was familiar, but she couldn't place him.

Raymond dropped the newspaper with a shocked clatter and stared at Kyle over the upper rims of his reading glasses as if he were seeing an apparition.

Kyle spoke first to her mother. "Mrs. Brennan."

Margaret lowered her brush. "I'm sorry, but I don't—"

"Richardson!" Raymond cut in.

Immediately her mother drew in a startled breath. Now she knew! She looked at Kyle with wide eyes. She had only seen him from a distance since his return to Kearney. But she should have known him. He still had the same looks he did as a child, only now they were stronger, more mature.

Kyle shifted his gaze to Charmayne's father.

"Mr. Brennan." He spoke carefully, showing respect.

That attitude surprised Raymond for a moment and he stayed silent.

Charmayne hurried into the breach. "I'll get my coat," she said to the room at large and moved as quickly as she could to the chair where she had dropped it. She put it over her arm and hurried back to Kyle's side, trying to escape the explosion she knew would eventually come.

"What the hell are you doing here?" Raymond demanded, finding his tongue again and squelching her hope.

She started to speak, but Kyle's answer overtook her.

"Charmayne and I are going out to dinner."

Raymond moved his disbelieving gaze to his daughter.

"Is that true?" he asked with deadly calm.

Charmayne had never felt so much like a traitor. She didn't want to go; she wanted to go. She was twenty-six. Her father couldn't tell her what to do anymore, who her friends might be. Yet, family loyalty meant a lot to her.

"I . . ." She wished she could disappear or make time run backward. She would have been waiting at the fork at six to avert a catastrophe like this.

"Is it?" Raymond asked shortly.

Margaret stood up, her hand touching her throat in a gesture of agitation.

"Raymond . . . don't . . ."

Her husband spared her a short glance. Unspoken words passed between them, then he turned away, remaining stubbornly determined to have an answer.

Charmayne saw her mother's pained look and knew another hurt had been added to what had been previously experienced. Momentary anger with her father made her answer taut.

"Yes, it's true." Her chin came up and she dared him to say anything more.

Charmayne and Lynn had always been model daughters. The Brennans were the envy of all their neighbors because of their family's mutually loving relationship. Now another part of that relationship seemed to be disintegrating.

Raymond held her defiant gaze, recognizing the same flare of anger in her green eyes that he had seen many times in her mother's. She was adamant. But she was his daughter! And she was spending time with a Richardson!

Raymond muttered an expletive and turned away in disgust. He didn't want to look at her anymore. His entire life was dissolving before his eyes and he wasn't sure how much more he could take.

Margaret took a step toward her husband, then stopped. She wanted to reach out to him, but she knew he wouldn't receive her gesture as she intended. Unconsciously she met her daughter's stricken gaze and a sad smile touched her lips. *Go,* she seemed to be saying. *Go ahead and leave. Everything will be all right. At least I hope everything will be all right.*

Charmayne was on the verge of tears. She didn't want this to happen. She didn't want to be the cause of more trouble between her parents.

Kyle sensed that the upset in the house was not solely because of his appearance. Something had been happening before his arrival and he had just stepped into it. He saw Charmayne's bottom lip quiver and instinctively reached out to protectively enclose her shoulders.

For a moment she stiffened. Then, as if needing his comforting strength, she allowed him to hold her.

Without another word Charmayne turned from the room and he went with her.

Snapping the umbrella into form, he saw her into the Cadillac, then moved smoothly around to the driver's seat. Before he started the engine he looked at her.

"Are you sure you want to do this?" he asked.

Charmayne nodded. The damage was done. Nothing she could do or say would change it. Her father wouldn't listen to her now, and she didn't know if she felt up to trying to explain.

The engine started and soon the car was reversing down the drive.

Kyle drove in silence, wondering about the Brennans. He knew Charmayne hadn't wanted him to come to her house; he had known that she would come to meet him as she had before. But he had arrived early and surprised her simply because of that fact. He had thought he could deal with any resentment Raymond Brennan might harbor against him. He had no idea that feelings would be running so high! Still, that was no excuse, and to make matters worse, because of his rash action he just might come out the loser of the entire situation.

His glance slid over to Charmayne. She was sitting there so quietly, her hands folded tightly in her lap, the pale green dress somehow making her look like a little girl. He didn't know what to say to her.

Charmayne felt his look and raised a hand to her hair, brushing it back from her forehead. She still was all trembly inside, but the beat of the rain and the steady rhythm of the windshield wipers as they strove to clear it helped to calm her. She wanted to

say something, but she didn't know how to begin.
. . .

As it was, they eventually chose the same moment to speak.

"Kyle, my father—"

"I'm sorry, Charmayne, I didn't—"

Both reverted to silence, waiting for the other to continue, but when each remained quiet, Kyle let out a long breath and laughed shortly.

"God, what a mess."

Charmayne wholeheartedly agreed.

"Look, Charmayne," he said. "I didn't mean to cause any trouble. I just . . . I just . . ."

He couldn't seem to get past the word.

"Didn't think?" she finished for him, words from the near past once again proving useful.

Kyle's darted another glance from the road. He couldn't gauge her motivation. Was she angry with him? Or what?

When he didn't reply she released a long-pent-up breath as well and said evenly, "I want to apologize for my father. He isn't usually so rude."

Kyle shrugged.

"He's been under a lot of pressure lately, and . . ." Her words trailed away.

"It's all right, Charmayne. I didn't expect him to greet me with open arms."

"No . . ."

Kyle thought for a moment, then asked, "Why is he working for me if he still feels so strongly?"

"He didn't know he was working for you when he took the job."

"But he stayed on after he found out."

Charmayne nodded.

Kyle didn't probe further. He didn't have to. He already knew the answer.

"Are you going to fire him?" Charmayne wanted to know.

Kyle was startled. "What?"

"Are you going to let him go . . . after tonight?"

A frown settled on Kyle's brow. "Do you think I'm that petty? I don't care whether the men and women who work for me like me or not. Just so long as they do their job."

Charmayne thought of her father's satisfaction at the trouble Orion had experienced. Was Kyle a better man than he? No! They couldn't be compared. Her father wasn't vindictive. He was just upset. That was all.

"I settled Orion in Kearney for one reason, Charmayne, and one reason only: I wanted to make up to the people of this town for what my uncle did to them. He took away their hope; I wanted to bring it back. And I don't want anyone's thanks. I'm not out to win a popularity contest. If some people still can't forget . . . well, I guess it can't be helped."

Charmayne sat very still. His words had the ring of truth.

She made no reply.

The dinner that followed was an anticlimax after the way the evening had begun. Neither Charmayne nor Kyle had any appetite and neither seemed in the mood to talk very much.

Charmayne's mind was reeling with all that had happened and at the secret Kyle had divulged to her. Like him or not, she didn't think he made a habit of broadcasting his reason for bringing his assembly plant to Kearney. Why he had told her, she didn't know, unless it was to underline the point he was trying to make about not holding her father's hostility against him, that if he did his job properly, he was safe.

Kyle himself was disgusted . . . with himself! Why in God's name had he told her that about his operation? Was he bucking for a halo? Saint Kyle! he thought derisively. She had accused him once of wanting a medal. It seemed that he was trying again. This evening wasn't working out as he had planned at all. He should have played his part as she expected and met her at the fork. Only when he took the screenwriter's job into his own hands had he bungled. In the future he wouldn't try to orchestrate their meetings. He would take things as they came.

When he walked her to her door, a heavy rain was still falling, and it was an accurate reflection of his mood: dark and bleak. His car, when he drove away, was his thunder.

Charmayne moved across the room and switched off the lone lamp her mother had left burning. It wasn't late, but the house was quiet. She knew her parents were already in bed. Had they talked? Or were they still at odds?

She stood for a moment in the hall, thinking back over the past several hours. And for the first time she remembered the protective arm Kyle had placed around her during the worst of the conflict. At the time she had been too upset to consciously notice. But now memory was clear and she marveled at his action.

The rain stopped during the night and the crowd

assembling outside the Kearney Baptist Church that Sunday morning was especially grateful. It had rained enough recently to give a body cause for reflection on the Great Flood. And for the sun to break through the gloom and look as if it was going to stay around for a while made everyone feel much brighter and more positive.

Kyle stood a little apart from the gathering of people and watched their happy faces. He didn't know why he was here. He wasn't Baptist. Really, he wasn't much of anything. Oh, he believed in God. But he didn't feel he needed to find him in a church.

His body straightened imperceptibly when he saw three figures getting out of a familiar gold Toyota. Now he knew why he was here.

Charmayne was dressed in white and the sun turned her shoulder-length hair into a brilliant orange flame. As he watched unobserved, he saw a smaller, rounder figure break free from the crowd and hurry over to give each of the three a hug. She had the same shade of hair as Charmayne. Lynn— Kyle remembered her name. Charmayne's sister. She had never been interested in tagging after his heels the way Charmayne had. She had spent most of her time in the kitchen learning how to cook at her mother's hand or in town taking piano lessons.

Now, from what he had heard, those piano lessons had paid off. From church organist she had become church first lady.

The tall, slender blond-haired figure of a man broke away from the crowd as well and walked over to place an arm about his wife's shoulders and pump Raymond Brennan's hand. He kissed Charmayne's and her mother's cheeks.

Unconditional approval. Kyle could see it from here. Charmayne's parents approved of one Pastor Robert Smith.

A wry grimace pulled at Kyle's lips. Well, he couldn't compete there. Bucking for a halo or not, he would never get one. He couldn't even keep a stupid promise to himself! He had said he wouldn't force a meeting between himself and Charmayne again. And here he was.

In the days of the liberated woman and man, did men have the prerogative to change their minds?

The crowd began to move inside and Kyle waited until most of them were through the door before he, too, went to join them. He slipped into position beside Charmayne. She wasn't aware of him until she slid into a pew and he followed. Her surprised intake of breath sounded loud in the small church.

Charmayne could scarcely believe her eyes! Kyle was here! Beside her! Was he crazy? What was her father going to say or do? Would he make a scene in church? A month ago she would have known. But today, with everything going topsy-turvy in their lives, she wasn't sure.

She directed a lightning glance toward her father and saw that he was unaware of who had followed them into the pew. He was calmly greeting a friend and didn't look her way. Maybe that was on purpose; he had been treating her coolly all morning. This was the first time she was glad.

"What are you doing here?" she demanded, hissing between partially closed lips, trying to whisper and yet show her disapproval.

"Can't a person go to church if he wants?"

"You don't belong to this church. I remember!"

"Maybe I joined."

"Maybe you didn't."

"I'm a visitor?"

"Kyle!"

Their intense exchange was stopped by the announcements of the day, followed by the first song. Kyle picked up a hymnbook and turned to the appropriate page.

Charmayne couldn't believe it when he listened to the first verse of the song and then joined in perfectly with the second. His voice was strong and musical.

Throughout the service Charmayne was as nervous as a cat. And her nervousness soon spread to her mother, who happened to glance over and see that Kyle was sitting beside them.

Of course he gave her a charming smile. She returned it weakly, then fastened her gaze on Charmayne. Both mother and daughter understood each other perfectly, and each let her eyes settle on Raymond.

His face was turned forward; he looked neither right nor left; his attention seemingly concentrating on what the pastor was saying.

For her part, Charmayne couldn't have repeated a word of the sermon, and she doubted if her mother could, either, although their reasons might not center wholly on the same responses. Charmayne was all too aware of Kyle's presence beside her. One of his well-muscled thighs was resting close to hers, his shoulder was touching hers . . . She could even feel his breathing! Like a sensuous arm, the spicy scent he used as cologne wove a path to her nose and the fragrance played with her senses.

Unbidden, a strong memory of what it was like to

touch him thrust itself into her mind, and she couldn't help it when her eyes made a reflexive survey of his body, moving over his arms and chest and stopping at his hips. She instantly forced her head to turn away.

Oh, God! This was wrong! She had to pull herself together. She was in church, for heaven's sake! Small beads of perspiration broke out above her upper lip and her breathing was unstable. Desperately her gaze clung to Bob. He could have been speaking Martian for all that she understood, but seeing him up there, in the pulpit, helped her to bring herself back under control.

Finally, what seemed millions of years later, they were standing for the hymn of Benediction. Again Kyle absorbed the first stanza and joined in with the second. He was a quick study.

Charmayne didn't wait for the last dying notes to be sounded. When the end of the song neared, she began to push Kyle out of the pew. She had to get him outside, away from her father's sight.

But Kyle was a large man. He didn't push quite so easily. And other people were starting to leave as well, clogging the aisle.

Charmayne knew she could count on her mother to delay the rest of the family, but she couldn't delay them forever. When a neighbor with three small children blocked their way because her youngest tripped and fell, she knew she was pursuing a lost cause. This was never more evident than when Kyle bent low to right the child on her pudgy little feet and kept hold of one small hand to assist her in leaving the church. Their pace became slow as a snail's. One quick glance over her shoulder, back toward the front of the church, showed that her family was filing out. Her mother sent her a worried look and Charmayne sent one in return. There would never be enough time now. Her father was bound to see.

On the outside Charmayne gave one last try. She took hold of Kyle's free arm and tried to direct his steps around the corner of the church. She had to talk to him; he had to be made to see. . . . But Kyle refused to come; instead he started to talk with the child's mother and made a production of giving back possession of the little girl's hand.

"Kyle!" Charmayne implored.

As a response Kyle drew her closer to him, entrapping her hand against his ribs.

She was forced into saying a few friendly words to the woman as well, for all the world as if she and Kyle were an old married couple passing the time of day with an acquaintance after a Sunday service.

That was the way her father finally saw them: standing close together and smiling. He didn't see that Charmayne's smile was strained.

Raymond's first impulse was to march right over and drag Richardson away from his daughter, then punch him straight in the nose.

Margaret saw her husband stiffen. She knew the possibilities of what might happen and looked around for help. She couldn't let Raymond humiliate himself, and that would be what he would do if she didn't intervene. But what could she do? She didn't seem to have any influence with him anymore. In her agitation she looked back toward the church doors and with great relief found salvation. Bob was standing there with Lynn, talking with a couple of new church members.

She caught Lynn's eye and motioned urgently. When Lynn started to break away from her husband, Margaret motioned frantically for her to bring him.

Raymond was about to take a forward step when Bob and Lynn arrived at their side.

"Raymond," Margaret called, her voice tight. "I believe you wanted to tell Bob what an interesting sermon he gave this morning."

Her husband didn't seem to hear her at first, but at the repetition of his name he halted and turned to face his son-in-law, who was also the family minister. It was then that the enormity of what he had been about to do hit him and he paled. If Margaret hadn't stopped him, he would have embarrassed all of them by attacking Richardson on God's doorstep! Margaret never would have forgiven him; neither would Charmayne or Lynn. A fine tremor shook his body. He swallowed.

"Ah . . . yes. Yes, it was very good."

"I'm glad you enjoyed it, Mr. Brennan." Bob sensed that something was wrong but was unaware of what it could be. He looked at his wife.

"Bob worked very hard preparing it," Lynn added, feeling just as adrift as her husband, unable to answer his silent query.

"Well, I thought it was wonderful," Margaret said. Thank God, her ruse had worked!

She looked across at Charmayne. She saw that she was trying to pull her hand out of Kyle's.

Kyle applied more pressure to keep it captive. He nodded to the talkative woman, who seemed relieved to be speaking with anyone whose vocabulary contained more than fifty words.

After what seemed hours to Charmayne but could

only have been minutes, the woman finally listened to her oldest child, who complained of having to go to the bathroom, and ushered her brood to their car.

The devil glint in Kyle's eyes had free rein as he looked down at Charmayne for the first time since coming out of church. She glared back at him as if she would like to tear him apart, bit by bit.

"Very cute, Kyle," she said angrily.

"I wasn't trying to be cute."

His innocent-sounding reply added to her anger. "Oh, no. Not at all." She paused for breath. "This entire fiasco was just an accident!" She glanced toward her family and saw her father turn around. She met his gaze and read a mixture of emotions in it. Finally it became one of accusation. Benedict Arnold no longer had the corner on the market of feeling a traitor. "Oh, no!" she groaned.

Kyle followed her gaze and released her hand, allowing her to hurry to her family. He followed at a more leisurely pace.

In his experience a state of war could only be continued if both parties wished it. He wanted to serve notice that as far as he was concerned, the past was the past and the sooner the entire Brennan family realized it, the better, especially Raymond.

He nodded to the older man, who woodenly returned his look and gave no sign of greeting.

His presence forced introductions. Kearney was a small town, but he hadn't personally met everyone yet in the month he had been back.

The response was subdued. The minister eventually held out his hand, doing his job.

"Mr. Richardson. I've been meaning to pay a call on you. I've heard a lot about you."

131

"All good, I hope," Kyle returned with a lazy smile.

Bob had moved to Kearney two years before. Charmayne was unsure if he knew of the past, or if he did, if he thought it important to today.

Bob smiled, his face looking more boyish when he did. "Good, yes. Especially about Orion Enterprises. I hope you realize what a godsend your company is to the people around here."

Kyle shrugged and the minister fell silent. He could sense the waves of tension from Charmayne, her mother, and her father. He glanced at Lynn for support.

Lynn could feel the tension as well and she determined to talk to Charmayne and get to the bottom of this little scene as soon as possible.

Margaret broke the silence that fell by telling Charmayne, "I was just inviting Lynn and Bob over to dinner, Charmayne. I thought we'd fry chicken and have mashed potatoes and cream gravy. You can make the biscuits. . . ."

The listed menu trailed to a halt. Margaret had been talking more to hear some kind of noise than to really inform.

"We'd love to come, Mother," Lynn agreed. That would give her a perfect opportunity to talk with Charmayne. She, too, had noticed how friendly Charmayne and Kyle had seemed earlier. She had also seen him sitting at the end of their pew. Her sister had a lot of explaining to do.

Another silence fell and this time Margaret realized how rude she had been. She had asked people to Sunday dinner and not included everyone in the group. There was one who had been left out and of all people he was her husband's employer!

Nervousness, embarrassment, and the strong remnants of southern hospitality she had been raised with prompted her blurt, "And you, Mr. Richardson? Would you like to join us?"

The blood in Charmayne's body ran cold. Was her mother going insane? Inviting Kyle to dinner? She shot a glance at her father to see how he was taking this. He looked as if he had been hit hard in the stomach.

Margaret's cheeks blazed when she realized the faux pas she had again committed. Please, Lord. Let him say no, she prayed.

Kyle knew he should politely decline the invitation that was so obviously unpopular. But something made him do the opposite. Call it perversity, call it stubbornness . . .

He summoned his most winning smile and inclined his curly head.

"Why, thank you, Mrs. Brennan. I'd be very happy to come."

Eleven little words. In some far corner of Charmayne's mind she counted them. Eleven . . . Could so few words change the course of events in a person's life?

CHAPTER EIGHT

In fiction large Sunday country dinners where family and friends gather to enjoy each other's company are happy joyous occasions, with good food, good talk, and goodwill.

Little about the midday meal at the Brennans that Sunday promised to meet those requirements. The chicken browned for too long—some unkind person might term it burnt—the gravy was lumpy, the biscuits didn't rise because Charmayne forgot to add the baking soda . . . only the mashed potatoes survived unscathed because Lynn was in charge of making them.

As for goodwill . . . it threatened never to appear. The discussion in the Brennan car as they drove home from church had been heated, her father had stomped off as soon as the car halted in the drive saying that he would be back when he was damn good and ready, and Margaret had burst into tears, just barely controlling herself by the time the others arrived.

Charmayne was ready to cry herself, her nerves stretched to the breaking point, and she had never felt less like partaking of a meal, much less preparing it. Hence the flat biscuits.

Through it all Kyle was unperturbed. If the chicken was slightly crispy, he didn't seem to notice. If the gravy could be chewed in parts, he chewed away. If the biscuits looked more like Frisbees than anything edible, it didn't bother him. And if the chair at the head of the table was empty, he seemed not to consider it unusual. The talk was subdued at first, but slowly Kyle's determined cheerfulness began to melt the most depressed spirit and even Margaret found herself laughing as she rose to serve dessert.

Charmayne thought the entire experience amazing. She couldn't believe the transformation! Bob was smiling, Lynn was relaxed, and she . . . she was suffering from a rash of conflicting emotions, her usual state of existence when around Kyle.

The conversation had been of many things during the meal, involving each of them, but now Bob was questioning Kyle about himself and Charmayne felt her breath shorten as she listened.

"You went to Southern Methodist University in Dallas, you say?"

Kyle nodded.

"What did you major in?"

"Business administration."

Bob smiled. "Did you always dream of owning your own business?"

"Not really. Oh, I can't say I didn't think about it. But I didn't really expect it to become a reality."

"You must have worked in computer technology before."

"Yes." He named a large technological corporation based in Dallas. "I worked for them up until the time I came here."

Bob leaned forward, truly interested. "It must have been a bit chancy . . . starting a new business now, the way the economy is and all."

"A bit. But printed circuit boards are the backbone of any computer. No circuit board, no computer. The demand isn't going to go down."

"Why did you pick Kearney?"

Charmayne's hand paused as she was sliding a dessert plate containing a delicious-looking piece of the lemon cake her mother had made yesterday into place in front of Kyle.

She knew the reason, but was he going to tell it to everyone else? Somehow, if he did, she would be disappointed.

Kyle evaded a specific answer. "A small assembly plant like Orion doesn't have to be located in a big city. In fact, quite a number of operations are locating outside of metropolitan areas."

Bob nodded sagely. He knew that for a fact. Hadn't his brother just been telling him about the number of high-tech agencies that were starting to spring up around Austin?

Charmayne eased the plate to the tablecloth and met Kyle's eyes. He had turned his head purposely to catch her gaze. For once they were serious. It was as if he were telling her that he didn't want the personal reason he had given her to be spread.

Her heartbeat increased. She didn't know why, but it was important to her that he remain reticent. She dragged her eyes away and moved to serve Bob.

When the meal was finally finished, Lynn took command, telling her mother and the two men to go into the living room and relax while she and Charmayne took care of clearing the dishes. This was the perfect time for the little talk she had planned to have with her sister and she wasn't going to let the opportunity slip away.

Charmayne rinsed the dishes and then, securing the plug in one side of the sink, added dishwashing liquid to the hot running water. Along with automatic clothes dryers, her mother detested dishwashers and wouldn't hear of having one in her kitchen.

Lynn finished putting away what remained of the meal, although she made a face at the flat biscuits.

"What happened to your usual flair with biscuits, Charmayne?" she asked. "A few of these could be glued together and used as a doorstop!"

"Humm? What?" Charmayne's mind had been miles away, or rather, feet—whatever the unit of measure was that counted the distance into the living room. She wondered what the others were talking about.

Lynn sighed. "Never mind. It wasn't important." She found a clean drying cloth and came to stand beside her sister.

They worked together in silence for a few minutes before Lynn again brought Charmayne from her reverie.

"Kyle has turned out to be a very handsome man. How serious is it between the two of you? And what are you going to do about Dad?"

The questions hit Charmayne like twin bolts of lightning. With the cracks seeming to remain echoing in the air, her first instinct was denial.

"I don't know what you're talking about. There's nothing between Kyle and me."

Lynn lifted a plate from the dish drain. "Sure. I believe that. Now are you going to tell me you have a bridge you want to sell me or a piece of swampland that would be a perfect setting for a home?"

Charmayne scrubbed on a nonexistent piece of hardened debris on a fork.

"I saw him sitting beside you at church this morning," Lynn continued. "And now he's had dinner with us. . . . Are you still going to say that there's nothing between you?"

"I didn't invite him to dinner, Mom did."

"But she wouldn't have done it if he hadn't been following you like Mary's little lamb!"

Charmayne stopped scrubbing. "He didn't do that!" she denied. Somehow the image didn't fit Kyle.

"He just as good as did. He couldn't stay away from you! And you may not have noticed, but at dinner he couldn't keep his eyes off of you, either!"

Charmayne's color rose. She had been aware of his attention during the meal, but she didn't think anyone else had. Maybe that was because she was too intensely aware of him herself to notice.

"There's nothing between us," she murmured firmly.

Lynn's blue eyes narrowed. Then a slow smile started on her lips. "Ahh. Now I see. It's too soon. Whatever it is is just starting!"

Charmayne's color deepened.

Lynn saw and laughed. "I'm right!" Then she sobered. "But, Charmayne, Dad will never—"

"I know! That's what makes it all so . . ." She lifted a hand in frustration, the fork still in her possession. Her stomach was tied in knots, just as it had been throughout the meal. And she felt just as confused. Was she beginning to feel something for Kyle? And if so, what? She plunged the well-scrubbed fork back into the water and began to wash it again.

"Are you falling in love with him?" Lynn asked softly.

Charmayne felt a jolt run through her body. Love? No. No. She didn't even know him!

"No!"

Lynn waited patiently for her to move on to another piece of flatware. She had run out of things to dry. "I remember when you were little and he lived here, you loved him then."

"I did not!" Charmayne returned hotly, a warmth covering her body.

"At the very least you had a crush on him. I remember, Charmayne. He couldn't make a move without you being right behind him. Talk about Mary's lamb!"

Charmayne's eyes flashed a warning as increasing discomfort made her snap, "I don't want to talk about it anymore, Lynn."

Lynn examined her sister's face. Deny it as she may, Charmayne's feelings were running much more deeply than she would ever admit at this time, or maybe even knew.

"All right," she agreed. "I won't say anything more. Except this: if you ever do need to talk, I'll be here. Don't forget that. Okay?"

Charmayne gave a quick assenting nod, then finally rinsed the fork and gave it to her sister. Lynn looked at it in amusement for several seconds before drying it and putting it away. If it shined a little more than the others in the drawer, it certainly had good cause.

When the kitchen was back to its usual clean state, Charmayne and Lynn joined the others in the living room. Kyle was unknowingly sitting in her father's favorite chair. Charmayne glanced at her mother, who gave an imperceptible shrug.

Bob was leaning forward on the sofa. He glanced

up when Lynn settled at his side, but the gesture was made unconsciously. His real attention was on Kyle, who was speaking.

"Who did you hear that from?" Kyle asked.

"It's just a rumor. I also heard that there was some trouble recently with a couple of orders."

"That didn't take long to spread."

Bob smiled. "One of the hazards of living in a small town."

Kyle's smile was tight. "The first is a total falsehood. I'm not going to close Orion."

Charmayne sat on her mother's art stool and couldn't take her eyes away from Kyle. Every time she saw him, she was amazed at what an attractive man he was. And it wasn't just his face, it was everything about him. She moved uncomfortably, all too aware of the discussion she had just left in the kitchen.

"The second, I'm sorry to say, is true," Kyle went on. "We did have a little problem, but everything came out all right in the end. The accounts weren't lost, which is the main worry taken care of."

Bob frowned. "Yes, I suppose so." He thought for a moment, then said, "As I mentioned earlier this morning, and as I'm sure you're aware, Orion Enterprises means a lot to the people living around here. Without it some of them would lose their land. The added income helps them keep afloat."

"Yes, I know."

Bob hesitated. "Could what happened the other day have been an accident, or could it have been something else?"

Kyle became still, his eyes fastened on the minister.

"Have you heard something that makes you think that?"

Bob met his gaze and a silence stretched between the two men. Then, as if suddenly becoming aware of where he was and that possibly he had said too much already, Bob shook himself free of the moment by laughing shortly and saying, "A man of God always hears things." Then he attempted to lighten the situation by joking, "Sometimes more than he wants to hear. Brother Whitman, the pastor before me," he added for Kyle's benefit, "told me there were days when he wished someone would just call him and wish him a good day, and not expect him to keep it that way!"

Polite laughter followed, but each person in the room was involved in his own private thoughts.

Kyle felt that the minister knew more than he was saying and resolved to have a much more private and revealing conversation with him at a later time. Lynn looked at her husband and resolved to do the same thing. Margaret was thinking of Raymond, hardly having heard any of the last comments made. She was wondering where he was and about the difficulties they would experience if he lost his job at Orion. Since, by acting so rudely to his employer, he certainly wasn't going out of his way to insure that he kept his position, he might not have it for much longer. A spark of anger lighted within Margaret. Raymond was behaving like a fool!

Charmayne was sitting completely still, a frightening idea beginning to take root in the back of her mind, one that she rejected but found that it stubbornly would not be turned away.

Her thoughts took her back to Friday afternoon

when her father had come home from work. He had told her of the mixup in orders and he had seemed so pleased. Oh, God, her mind skipped ahead at a dizzying pace, was her father the person responsible for the accident? Was that what Bob was hinting at? Sabotage? It sounded like something out of a novel. Suddenly she began to tremble. Surely Bob didn't know how her father felt. If he had, he wouldn't have said anything here, in his home. He wouldn't have said anything at all! Was he just speculating? Yes, that was probably what it was. The rumor about Orion's closing having added to his suspicion—

The rumor! A knot tightened in Charmayne's stomach. She had heard it first from her father! Now she remembered! Could it be that he was the person responsible for spreading that lie as well? Did his hatred run so deep?

The more Charmayne thought about the possibilities, the more upset she became. In order to stop her rampaging worry, she forced herself to her feet and mumbled something about taking a walk.

That her decision was sudden was more than evident to the people of the room. But she pretended not to notice their surprised looks. She excused herself and hurried through the kitchen, letting the back screen door close behind her.

When she was outside, the heat of the April sun shone down upon her and she took several deep breaths of the warm dry air. She didn't know where she was going, what she was going to do.

The screen door closed for a second time and when she looked around she saw that Kyle had followed her. His presence was not welcome.

Eleven little words . . . words that could change a

life. She had thought that earlier, only she hadn't known exactly in what direction they would influence her or even if they would. Now she was beginning to find out, and she wished they had never been uttered.

She should have ignored Kyle at church. She should have frozen him out of her life, right then and there. If he hadn't practically forced her mother into inviting him to dinner, the conversation between Bob and himself would never have taken place, and she would never have had to experience the misery she was now facing. But then he had done nothing but cause trouble for her her entire life. She wished he had never come back to Kearney. Why couldn't he have stayed in Dallas?

When Kyle moved down the steps and continued to walk steadily toward her, Charmayne gave a soft cry and turned away. She moved rapidly through the gate, into the farmyard, past the pigs, past the barn. Her flight was the repeat of an earlier one, but at least here every inch of ground knew her footsteps. There would be no hidden stone ready to impede her flight.

Kyle fought against the instinct to hurry after her. He didn't understand why she had rushed from the room as she had; and there was no other way to describe her action. She had been sitting quietly in her chair one moment, then the next, she was up and nearly running out of the room as if all the devils in hell were at her heels. And just now she had looked at him as if he were the leader of the pack in the flesh!

Kyle watched as she rounded the corner of the barn, and he could resist no longer. He started to run after her, his progress restricted somewhat by his snugly fitting jacket. He arrived at the barn in time to see Charmayne disappear over a gentle rise. If he let her get much farther ahead, he might never find her! Stripping off the jacket, he threw it over the top rail of the corral and set off once again in pursuit. He loosened his tie as he ran and this time his way was easier.

Charmayne knew that Kyle was closing the gap between them and she increased her speed. Her only problem was her shoes. They definitely weren't made for running. Still she ran on, her lungs beginning to hurt from the effort.

She struggled past one of the fenced-in fields that her father had planted in wheat, past a flock of the sheep they owned, past an occasional white-faced cow that looked away from a solitary contemplation of empty space, past a watering hole that because of the amount of rain they had received was now completely full.

She was almost to a thick growth of cedar her father had left for the animal's protection in winter, when Kyle gave a lunge and pulled up next to her. His fingers instantly closed on her arm.

"No!" The word tore from her lips as she protested the touch of the man who had caused her so much pain. Tears were slipping down over her cheeks as she tried to pull away.

Kyle had no intention of letting her go, and when she continued to fight for freedom, his free hand came out to take hold of her other arm. The battle was over before it really began.

Heat radiated from both of their bodies, and both of them were heaving for breath. Charmayne's hair was in wild disarray, mussed by both her run against the wind and her frequent checking of his progress.

Her color was high, her cheeks darkest of all. Her mouth parted as she gasped for air.

Kyle's gray eyes moved over her distraught features. He knew she hadn't approved of his coming to dinner, and he had been painfully aware of her father's disappearance. But that still didn't explain.

"Let go of me, Kyle!" she cried, mustering another attempt at escape.

"Not until you tell me what happened . . . why you ran away!"

"I won't tell you a thing. Not a thing!"

"I could make you!"

"How?" she challenged, her green eyes like living jewels.

Kyle stared down at her. He could come up with one method without wasting further time on thought! Her parted lips and straining breasts invited his invasion. But he knew that would gain him nothing except momentary satisfaction. And he was coming to realize that he wanted more than just a moment's coerced pleasure from Charmayne.

He eased the grip of his fingers and strove to make his voice gentle.

"I want to help you, Charmayne," he replied simply.

His choice of words unsettled Charmayne even more. Help her! He wanted to help her! She didn't hear the genuineness of his tone.

"Then go away!" she cried. "Just go away and leave me alone! Leave *us* alone!"

"I can't do that."

"Why?"

"Because . . ." He stopped. What could he say? He didn't really know.

Charmayne was trembling with anger.

"You just like to torment me, don't you?" she accused. "Can't you see when you're not welcome?" She used any defilement that came to mind. "You might come back to Kearney with your money and your company . . . and people might let you. They might even accept you, to a degree! But you can't buy your way into people's hearts, Kyle. Money and fancy reasons for spreading it around just can't make you friends!"

Unconsciously Kyle's fingers began to tighten again. She was hitting him on a tender spot.

"If you want to live in Kearney, no one can stop you. It's a free country," she continued. "But don't ever expect to become one of us. You're not, Kyle. You never were and you never will be."

As her hurtful words ended, the pressure on her arms increased until she thought the bones were going to snap. Kyle's face was as hard as the granite stones that could be found in the area. His eyes held the coldness of an icy spring.

Echoes of past years spun through Kyle's mind. Years in which one humiliation had followed another. Barely had he and his uncle settled in a town before they were hurrying away, sometimes accompanied by the local sheriff who saw them to the town line with the warning not to come back. Then when his uncle had died, he had tried so hard to forget. He had gotten a job, any job. He had worked as a delivery boy, as a waiter, done outdoor gardening for people with too little time or inclination to do it for themselves, then later he had found summer employment in the Texas oilfields—he had taken any job that would give him enough money to get through college. He was determined to find respectability. And all this time there had been one dream he had set above everything else: one day he was going to come back to Kearney to repay the people who lived there. At the time it was happening he hadn't known what his uncle was planning, how he was going to steal their money. But since this had been the most successful con game his uncle had ever tried, he had eventually bragged to Kyle. Told him everything . . .

A wall of hurt seemed to encase Kyle. Emotions from childhood churned with those of adulthood. For a moment he forgot where he was. Then as some of the stinging suffering faded, his gaze focused on Charmayne and a bubbling anger rose up to take its place.

Hours ago he had wanted to kiss her; he had wanted to overwhelm her, storm her emotions until she gave him everything that he could possibly ever ask. But he had quelled the desire, telling himself that he wanted more from her than instant gratification.

Well, to hell with waiting! She was never going to give him more than the time of day without a fight. So fight they would! If the only kind of pleasure he could get from her was to be taken by coercion, then coercion it would be. He had the Richardson name; he might as well live up to the Richardson fame. She already thought he was on the road to hell anyway . . . he might as well give her more cause!

With a harshness that was alien to his better nature, Kyle jerked Charmayne to him. He paid absolutely no attention to her gasp of surprise or the fleeting look of fear in her eyes. He molded her body to his, crushing her breasts against his chest, her hips to his hips, her thighs to his thighs, and he kissed her, his mouth devouring hers in a mindless determination to ignore anything but the erotic sensations such an intimate act could bring. His mouth burned, pillaged, destroyed. . . . His tongue tasted the softness of her lips, the silkiness of her inner mouth, the smoothness of her own tongue. He wanted to draw her very soul from her body! He wanted to make her respond!

Charmayne was startled by Kyle's reaction to her words. He'd grabbed her just as she was experiencing her first twinges of regret. She was angry with him, but she didn't need to destroy him! He had dragged her against him and was kissing her so fiercely, allowing her no chance to think further. A fleeting thought passed through her mind a second later that she should resist, but then his hand began to massage her lower back, moving over her waist, over her hips, finally drawing her even closer against him so that she would have no trouble feeling his body's instant response to hers. Her hips were melded to his hardness. As he moved against her, a sweet heat like none she had ever experienced before slid through her, making her wholly aware of each and every molecule of her body. It was as if she were alive for the first time! The dry heat of day seemed to crackle in her lungs as it mixed with his scent. Her fingers, flexing across his ribs, seemed to vibrate with his warmth.
. . .

When he released her mouth, her head fell backward, exposing the delicacy of her throat. He didn't hesitate to answer her unspoken plea. His lips moved along the sensitive skin, exquisitely sensual as they

148

skimmed from one pulse point to the next, his breath warm as it made its own feathery trail.

Then he brought one hand up between them to cover her breast. The thin material of her dress lent little protection, the telltale hardness of her nipple springing into instant response.

Charmayne gave a soft murmur. Within half a heartbeat his mouth came back to cover hers, and again she experienced the physical drugging of her senses at the intensity of his demand. Her reactions became purely instinctive as his hands continued to caress her. She ran her palms over his back, her fingers kneading the strong muscles, feeling the contours, pulling him to her. She willingly pressed her body to his.

The sudden explosion of desire his embrace elicited seemed to take precedence over everything else. She couldn't think of anything but the bursting need he had caused to erupt within her.

Then, just as suddenly as he had pulled her into his embrace, he released her, and Charmayne teetered, his abrupt withdrawal leaving her unbalanced. Only his firm retention of her arm kept her from falling.

With passion-dazed confusion she looked at him, not understanding why he had broken them apart.

His face still seemed to be sculptured from stone, but this time his smokey eyes were shimmering with something other than cold anger. A fire was smoldering in their depths and their touch was like an intense flame that licked at her sensitive skin.

"At least the two of us agree about one thing, Charmayne." His voice was low and hoarse-sounding. "Even though I may not fit in, I sure as hell have my uses!"

Charmayne had trouble translating his words into meaning. His anger, his hurt, his flaring desire had all combined in an assault that left her reeling. And coming in tandem with the onslaught of her own burgeoning emotions, it took her several seconds to respond.

"I don't—" she began. *Understand* was the word she was going to use, but he intervened with "Care? Well, neither do I. But I'll be around."

"But, I—"

"Call me. I've lost the inclination now. But whenever you're in the mood, let me know."

Charmayne raised her hand to hit him; not slap, as some women might have done. But hit. Her balled-up fist was barely deflected from contact with his nose.

He held her wrist inches from his face, and his expression was closed.

"I taught you how to fight when you were eight, remember? You were a good pupil, you learned fast. But you haven't had much practice lately, have you? Well, now there's something else I can help you learn. And as with everything else, practice makes it perfect, too."

Charmayne's mind was now clear. Anger had driven out any other emotion. She knew exactly what he was referring to.

"Just what makes you think that I haven't already had a few lessons?"

Kyle gave a short laugh. "Maybe you have. But your partners were amateurs."

"And you're much their superior, I suppose."

A slow smile curved his lips. "I don't think I'll let you down."

Charmayne had had enough. She jerked her arm away and took a step back. She wanted distance between them. Up close her riotous senses refused to behave.

"I'd rather go to hell first," she declared.

"Heaven, hell . . . what's the difference?"

Impotently Charmayne wanted to stamp her foot. Really, she wanted to do more than that, but she controlled herself nobly, sensibly. She would never win in a physical battle with him. She never had and she never would. And she was beginning to doubt her ability to do better than break even in a verbal sparring match.

"Maybe one day you'll find out," she settled on saying sweetly.

Kyle shrugged, his face relaxing more into his normal expression, his aggravating smile increasing.

When he said nothing else, Charmayne spun on her heels and began to walk away in the direction she'd been headed before he stopped her. Kyle stayed where he was.

No further words were exchanged between them.

Charmayne remained outside until she was sure he would be gone from her home. She rested beneath the shade of a scrub oak and waited. Only she didn't let herself think. Not about him, not about anything.

When she finally did return, her mother was alone, and she didn't look in any more of a mood to talk than Charmayne did. Both women retreated to their rooms and neither came out until much later, Charmayne only doing so to brush her teeth in the bathroom and get ready for bed.

Yet once she was lying in bed, she couldn't find

rest. She heard her father come in a little after ten, then, for the first time in her life, she listened as her parents argued. The words were muffled, but she didn't need to hear any to know that the scene was one of anger.

A silent tear escaped the corner of her eye and ran along the upper edge of her cheek to fall on her pillow.

Her entire life was coming apart at the seams and Kyle wasn't helping in any way. Why, oh, why did he have to come back into her life now?

The hours she had spent in her room earlier had been useful in getting some of her anger released. She had written a wonderful poem of whose sarcastic verse Kyle was the butt.

But now, with the anger burned nearly out, she faced the time of questioning herself.

He hadn't made her respond to him when he kissed her. No person can *make* another do that. Either an attraction is there, or it isn't. And with her, she knew that it was. She might fight against it, but when he decided to take matters into his own hands to prove a point, she had little protection against him. Her best bet would be to stay away from him. Then the danger would be reduced. If he came near, she wouldn't let him touch her. And she would definitely keep their conversations limited to business or the weather. Nothing personal.

At that thought her conscience twisted. She didn't like to think that she had tried to hurt him earlier. But she had. And she wasn't very proud of herself for doing it. It was just that he had made her so angry because he had made her suspect her father!

Again, the word *made*. In all honesty, and as little

as she liked to admit it, he hadn't made her do that, either.

Charmayne gave a silent groan and turned on her side, curling a section of her pillow over her face.

She had to stay away from him! She had to. For her own survival.

CHAPTER NINE

The beginning day of the new workweek gave Charmayne little time to think, and she was grateful for that fact. Besides the usual requests for and complaints about city services, a water department truck had crashed into a city councilman's brand new car, and the man had gone nearly berserk, alternately crying and swearing his insistence that the driver of the truck be put in jail. Charmayne had done her best to calm him, explaining that the accident had happened because the truck had swerved to avoid a dog in the road and that punishing the driver was a little harsh. But the crushed fender that had so recently been a smooth pristine red was hard to discount. The city's insurance was an answer, but it did little to console the councilman.

Then the mayor had come back into the office from another minor emergency which had cropped up, and they had exchanged information. The mayor's story was the better of the two.

He leaned back against her desk and passed a hand over his face, wiping away his tears of laughter.

"I wish you could have been there, Charmayne. Otto didn't exaggerate when he called. That blamed horse of his was standing just like he said: right in the middle of the cattle guard with all four legs buried up to his fetlocks between the pipes. Lord only knows how he got in there, but he sure wasn't getting out without some help!"

The mayor paused to laugh, the picture vivid in his mind. "When I got out there Otto and Mel Foreman were just standing there scratching their heads. And the horse was just kind of waiting, you know. . . ." He paused to collect himself. "We thought about every possible thing we could do to get him out without hurting him and then decided that the only way was to cut the pipes.

"Well, Mel went to his place and brought back an acetylene torch. Then we were ready. Mel turned on the gas and struck a spark to light it. There was a loud *pow*—you know how it sounds, like a crack of thunder—and the next thing we knew that fool horse was standing beside us! He must have levitated straight up like he had springs on the bottom of his hooves, because there he was!"

Tears came to the mayor's eyes again and his body shook with laughter. "We couldn't believe it! I had heard about that happening—about horses being able to jump straight up—but I had never seen it. Neither had Otto or Mel. We were almost rolling on the ground!"

Charmayne was laughing as well. From his description she had an accurate idea of what it must have looked like. She could just see the horse and the three men.

Finally she asked, "Was the horse hurt at all?"

"Only a few scratches and maybe a little injured dignity. But I don't think he really cared. And Otto was saved the expense of rebuilding his cattle guard."

They commiserated companionably for a few moments before the mayor said, "Lord, what a day!"

Charmayne nodded, then confided, "I would bet you can expect a visit from Councilman Thompson. He's probably going to complain about the leash laws not being enforced."

"Probably. But we do the best we can. If he'd like to volunteer to help us out personally, I'd be glad to let him."

"I don't think that that's what he has in mind."

"No." The mayor smiled. "I doubt that it is, either, but it's the option I'm going to give him. Put up or shut up, isn't that the term?"

Charmayne nodded again, a dry smile on her lips.

The mayor started to leave, then paused. "Oh, Charmayne. I almost forgot. I know you've been extremely busy, so I've tried to keep most of the preparation for the Centennial out of your hair, but now . . . Well, now, since it's coming up so soon—just a couple of weeks away—and things are really beginning to jump, I was wondering if you wouldn't mind . . ."

She had known it was going to happen. If she had been a betting person and could have found some other sap to take her up, she would have wagered all she possessed that she wasn't about to get out of the Centennial celebration so easily.

"Mind what?" she asked warily.

"Serving on a committee."

"Which one?"

"The Coordinating Committee."

Oh, no! The biggie! The one that oversaw all the others!

The mayor rushed on. "As president of the Chamber of Commerce, Mary Roberts was heading it, but since her baby came early, she's had to resign, and—"

"And no one else will take it on," she finished for him.

"No." The mayor shook his head. "Someone did.

156

But only on the condition that he have another person added to the two he already has."

"And you volunteered me."

"Well, no . . . actually he requested you."

Charmayne began to experience a dread feeling. "Who?" She was reluctant to learn.

"Kyle Richardson."

Charmayne groaned. It was a spontaneous reaction and she could do nothing to hide it from the mayor.

He pretended not to notice, but privately he wondered at her reaction to the name when just the day before he had seen the two of them sitting together in church. His interest didn't lie in meddling in other people's business, though. He had one objective and one objective only.

"So, you see, you won't be chairing the committee. You're just going to be one of the assistants."

Charmayne regained her professionalism. "I'd rather not, thank you."

"I've already told him you would. I gave him my assurance this morning."

"Then you can just unassure him."

The mayor put on his marine drill sergeant look from long ago. "Do you have a particular reason for not wanting to help?"

The ring of duty began to strangle Charmayne. What would he say if she told him yes? He would want to know her reason, that was what, and she wouldn't be able to tell him. But if she gave in, she would be doing exactly the opposite of what she had decided last night.

She tried to stall for time. "Could I think about it?"

The mayor's lips firmed. "No. I don't know if you're aware of this or not, but Kyle has donated a nice sum of money to our Centennial fund. I'm not going to offend him. Think about this as an extension of your job."

But the mayor's office wasn't supposed to get involved with events the Chamber of Commerce planned, except in a support capacity. And this would certainly be more than mere support! As well, it would be on her free time! She wanted to say those words in protest. But Mayor Cliburn didn't put his foot down often, and when he did, he expected to be listened to.

"All right," she finally agreed. "I'll do it."

Maybe she could manage to miss most of the meetings.

"Good. I'll tell Kyle."

The marine sergeant look disappeared and in its place was his usual ugly teddy bear.

Charmayne stared at the door after he'd closed it.

Kyle sat at his desk and unconsciously twirled his pen. His secretary had left several letters for him to sign, but he was ignoring them. He was waiting for a call, and when he finally received it, he smiled. Then, after replacing the receiver on its rest, he twirled his chair around and looked through his window at the wide expanse of blue Texas sky, the letters totally forgotten.

When Charmayne arrived home from work that evening, it was to find her mother seated in the living room, her rocker creaking back and forth, her eyes red-rimmed and hollow from crying. She could see that little had been done about the house that day:

the comfortable chaos was more disorganized than usual, the breakfast dishes were only partially done. Her father's truck was absent from the drive. She didn't know if he had been home already and left, or if he had yet to make an appearance.

She dropped her purse onto a chair and moved to her mother's side.

"Mom?" she prompted, dropping to her knees and putting her hand on the wooden arm. This morning her mother had been quiet, yet she had shown no other ill effects of the argument the previous night. Was this a delayed reaction? Or had something else happened?

Margaret sniffed but kept her face turned forward. A tissue was being mangled in her hands.

"Mom . . . Is there anything I can do to help?"

Charmayne had rarely felt less capable of giving aid, but if her mother needed her, she would find strength from somewhere.

Margaret gave an audible sob and buried her face in her hands, her body beginning to shake with tears at the gentle concern in her daughter's voice. Charmayne's arms came out to encircle her and she remained in that position for some time, soaking up the loving protection, for the first time becoming the daughter to her daughter—feeling the warm love and support, yet knowing that her child was incapable of solving her problem.

Then she straightened, and Charmayne's arms fell away. Margaret dabbed at the moisture around her eyes.

"No . . . it's nothing. I just—"

"Mom," Charmayne contradicted. "It's more than nothing. You're upset."

Suddenly Charmayne was hit with the idea that possibly her mother knew! Did she suspect her father as well? Did she have proof? Her heart cried a protest. No! Not her father! She looked closely at her mother. Had that been the problem all along?

"Is . . . is it about Daddy?"

Never would she be able to explain to someone how difficult that question had been. It concerned one of those problems that you hoped would go away if you pretended long enough that it wasn't there. But it didn't. It only got worse.

Margaret jumped to her feet, leaving the rocker in motion. She moved over to the front window, crossed her arms over her breasts, and looked outside. But Charmayne could tell that she was seeing nothing. Her entire body was still; her vision somehow turned inward, to the troubled visions in her own mind and heart.

Charmayne stood up and followed her mother. She didn't want to press the issue, but if her father was involved in some kind of trouble, they needed to talk about it.

"I've been worried about Daddy myself." She stated this softly, hoping that if her mother knew of her own suspicions, this would open an avenue of mutual confidences.

"I don't know who she is, Charmayne."

Her mother's reply was low and intense, and it took Charmayne a second or two to understand. Then she stood riveted to the spot. What was her mother saying?

"It would be easier somehow if I did." Margaret paused. "I know that probably sounds crazy to you, but it doesn't to me. If I knew, I could fight her. As

160

it is . . ." Her mother turned, agony in her expression. "As it is, I feel as if I'm doing battle with a ghost!"

Charmayne's shocked gaze met her mother's. Her mother thought her father was seeing another woman? Was that what she was saying? But no! That wasn't it! He couldn't . . .

"I shouldn't be talking with you about this. I know that. But I . . . I just can't take it any longer without . . ."

An agitated hand ran through her richly silvered hair. She turned back to the window and remained silent.

Charmayne's mind was racing, trying to assimilate what she had heard and put it together with the picture she already had formed. The two didn't match.

"But, Mom," she began, then had to swallow to continue. "Dad wouldn't—"

Her mother twirled around. "Wouldn't what?" she demanded. "He's changed, Charmayne. He's changed so much over the past month or so that he's like a different man! He doesn't talk to me anymore . . . he doesn't touch me. . . ."

Margaret tried to collect herself, then she went on, "I tried to ignore it at first. I made excuses. But I can't do that anymore. Not and keep my self-respect."

Charmayne's insides were flopping around like so much Jell-O that had just been hit by a giant fist. Who was right? Her mother or herself? Or were they both right?

"Have . . . have you talked with him?"

"No," her mother answered, her lips firming. "When he's ready, he'll tell me."

161

"But, Mom, you could be wrong!"

"I don't think so."

"Do . . . do you think it might be something else?" That was as close to her suspicion as she was going to get.

"Like what?"

Charmayne held Margaret's gaze. She could see the hurt, the confusion, the pain . . . and she merely shrugged. Her mother already had enough to worry about; she wasn't going to add more problems to her already overfull basket.

The sound of a truck turning into the drive had her mother peering outside.

"That's him," she said tightly. Then she dropped the curtain and said, "I can't see him now. Tell him . . . tell him I have a headache." She started to walk stiffly away, then stopped, again turning to Charmayne.

Her face softened a degree and a sad smile attempted to move her lips.

"Anything's possible, Charmayne. Maybe I'm just getting old and letting my imagination run away with me. But I truly don't feel very well. Would you mind finding something for your father and you to eat?"

Charmayne swallowed. Candy coating for a bitter pill? "No, I don't mind at all. You go lie down and rest."

The heartbreaking smile faltered. "Yes. I will."

She moved into the hall just as the back screen door opened and closed.

Raymond saw the untidy remains in the kitchen and a coldness clutched his heart. Was Margaret ill?

He put his lunch bucket on the counter and started to move into the hall. He was just in time to meet Charmayne coming into the kitchen. He backed up a space to let her inside.

Charmayne glanced up at her father's still hand-some face and looked quickly away again. She couldn't meet his eyes! Not after what she suspected; not after hearing what her mother thought. It was too soon. She knew they would need to talk, but she wasn't ready yet. What if he admitted it? The thought filled her insides with ice.

"Is your mother sick?" His gruff voice broke the still air as he motioned toward the sink.

Charmayne hurried over toward the dirty dishes. "She's not feeling very well," she replied tightly, trying and failing to make her tone normal.

"What's the matter with her?"

"A headache, a little fever . . ." she fabricated the fever on the spot and began to let the cold water out and refill the sink with hot.

"Sounds like a cold."

"It probably is."

"I'll go see—"

"No!" Charmayne turned, her plea sounding urgent. At her father's surprised look she came up with another fabrication. "She's asleep."

Raymond's dark eyebrows creased together. She felt his eyes run over her keenly but tried to keep her movements natural. She was washing the dishes for her mother, who was feeling unwell. Nothing more, nothing less. Then finally, he turned away.

"Dinner will be a little while, then?"

"Yes. Do hamburgers sound all right to you?"

"Sure. Sounds good."

"Then that's what it will be."

"And some French fries?"

"Yes."

She heard her father take a step away. "I'll go see to the stock. Let me know when it's ready."

"All right."

Charmayne's hands were trembling when she was once again alone, and tears spurted to life in her eyes. She didn't know what to think anymore. She loved her father. He was a good man. Hard, to a degree. But good! She had never known him to harbor any ill feeling except toward one family: the Richardsons. They were his Achilles' heel, his one major flaw. And that was probably because he had been the prime contributor to Martin Richardson's scheme and had suffered most at the loss.

She watched her father's strong back as he moved through the gate. He was still a relatively young man at fifty-eight. Was he having an affair with another woman as her mother thought? Was that all there was to the explanation?

Charmayne was torn. She didn't know which story she wanted to believe—if either.

After their dinner Charmayne was once again plunging her hands into hot soapy water when the telephone rang on the wall beside her. She rinsed them, and made an attempt at drying them, but they were still damp when she picked up the receiver.

"Hello?" she responded, trying to wipe first one palm and then the other on her jeans.

"Charmayne?"

If Kyle hadn't recognized her voice, she knew his. She started to hang up, and then thought better of it.

He would just call back. At the moment her father was back outside, finishing his chores, but it would be dark soon and he would be coming in. She didn't want to have to deal with Kyle then.

"Yes."

The tone of her reply was not promising.

"This is Kyle."

"I know."

She heard a small chuckle and experienced a prickling along the hairs of her arms and neck.

"And you didn't hang up?"

Charmayne remained silent, her memory of how they had last parted keeping her quiet.

"You must be tired," he decided.

"Why?" Was he just going to pretend that yesterday hadn't happened?

"I've come to expect a fight from you."

"Well, you're not getting one this time."

"I'll be right over."

"No!" She was afraid that he would.

Again the chuckle tumbled along the nerve centers of her skin.

"Don't worry. I can't. Otherwise I wouldn't be calling. I've got a lot of work left to do before I can get away from the office." He stopped, waiting for her to say something; then, when she didn't, he offered, "I understand that you've been told about the committee."

Charmayne's fingers tightened on the receiver. "Ordered is more like it."

He ignored her comment. "We're having a meeting tomorrow night at eight."

She didn't miss a beat. "I doubt that I'll be able to make it."

"Oh?"

"My mother isn't feeling well. I think she has the flu or something." From a headache to a simple cold to a flu. This alleged illness kept getting worse.

"That's too bad."

"Yes."

"Your father can't take care of her for a few hours?"

Charmayne's stomach plunged.

"No." She refused to give a reason.

"We'll put the meeting off a night."

"No . . . I don't know how long—"

"I'll hire a nurse."

"Don't you dare!"

"Then you think you can make the Wednesday meeting?"

"I'll try," she said through gritted teeth.

"I guess that's all a chairman can ask."

Chairman, Schairman! Charmayne's temper finally snapped. She couldn't confront her father, so she struck out at the one person who so richly deserved it.

"Don't push it, Kyle. You may have gotten your way with the mayor, but you're definitely not going to get it so easily with me!"

"I didn't think I was."

The calm reply to her hot outburst had the effect of deflating Charmayne somewhat.

"See you Wednesday, if not before," he said pleasantly, a smile in his voice. Then he hung up.

Charmayne stared at the dead instrument. She had the distinct feeling that he was laughing at her. And she didn't like it. Not one bit.

She replaced the phone on its hook and thrust her

166

hands back into the water. She had washed two glasses before his *if not before* sounded again in her mind. What had he meant by that?

The next night she found out. As had happened before, he appeared at their door without warning. Only this time, instead of the hated umbrella, he was carrying a bouquet of flowers.

Charmayne stared at them, then looked into his laughing twinkling eyes.

"For your mother," he explained.

"My mother?" she asked, slightly dazed.

"She's ill, I believe?"

Quickly Charmayne glanced over her shoulder at the woman who was busily cleaning a brush, preparing to apply another shade to the developing painting. Her father had gone out after dinner and her mother had determinedly involved herself in her artwork.

Charmayne turned back to see that Kyle had a view of the living room as well.

A smile crept along the sides of his mouth, starting first at one corner and then spreading until it involved the other.

"She's better?" he asked. The dry question was stated with tongue firmly planted in cheek.

"Yes." Charmayne thought furiously but could come up with no better answer.

"Then we could have had our meeting."

"Yes . . . no . . ." Charmayne felt as if she had her back to the wall. Drawing herself up, she asked tightly, "What do you want, Kyle?"

"To give these to your mother. I've already told you that."

"I'll give them to her. Thank you." She made as if to take the bouquet and readied herself to close the door immediately afterward.

Kyle held the flowers just out of her reach, his increasing smile showing the evenness of his teeth.

"I'd rather do it myself."

Charmayne played with the idea of saying that her mother's illness was seriously contagious, but if she did, the entire town would soon hear about it and be at their door, wanting to help.

Still she held her ground.

"I thought I made it plain the other day that we don't want to be involved with you in any way."

Kyle's eyes twinkled in the light spreading out onto the porch. "Oh, you made a number of things plain, all right. But noninvolvement wasn't one of them. Just the opposite, in fact."

Charmayne's breath caught in her throat. She willed herself not to blush.

"If I remember correctly," she countered, "we left off at something of an impasse. You told me to call you. . . . Well, I haven't, and I'd appreciate it if you would wait until I do."

He tipped his curly head. "Were you planning to call?"

Charmayne's face did flame at that. To keep her mental balance, she tightened her fingers on the doorknob.

"I think you know better than that!"

Kyle took a step forward, making her give an instinctive step back. "That's what I thought. And that's exactly why I'm here."

From behind her, Charmayne's mother called, "Who is it, dear?"

Kyle took the necessity of a reply from her hands. He stepped forward again and crossed the threshold.

"Kyle Richardson, Mrs. Brennan."

Margaret gave a small start and then relaxed.

"Oh, Mr. Richardson . . ."

"Call me Kyle. I feel a little strange hearing you call me Mr. Richardson when I can remember coming into your kitchen for bowls of warm peach cobbler."

He presented the yellow and white daisies to the seated woman.

"I heard that you weren't feeling well," he explained again.

For a moment Margaret was mystified; then, after a look at her daughter's stricken face, she took the flowers.

"Well, I haven't exactly been feeling my best. Thank you."

Kyle turned back to Charmayne.

"Is your father home?" he asked.

Charmayne had remained at the door, unable to close it. She had left it open on the hope that she would be able to rush him back through the instant he'd finished delivering his gift.

She shook herself and slowly closed the door; clearly her wish was not to be realized.

"No." Then, on a sudden thought: "Why?"

"I'd like to talk with him."

"What about?"

"Charmayne—" Margaret admonished, shocked that her daughter was acting so rudely.

Charmayne paid her mother little mind, her thoughts dwelling on only one cause. She didn't remove her eyes from Kyle.

Kyle met her gaze and wondered at her sudden intensity. There had been strong emotions flowing through the air since she had opened the door to him, but this was something else. This was more like fear.

He frowned. "I'd rather not say. It's something private between the two of us."

That answer frightened Charmayne even more. Did Kyle suspect her father's actions as well?

"Well, he's not here and we don't know when he'll be back."

Kyle studied her tightened features. Was she trying to protect her father? From him? And why would she be doing that? If she had merely been trying to avoid a confrontation between the two men, she would not be so desperate. No, this was something more.

"I'll catch him tomorrow during the day, then." He decided to test the water. When he saw her uncontrolled start, he knew he was right. She was afraid of something.

Busy trying to keep her father away from his grasp tonight, she had forgotten that he worked for Kyle! Her heartbeat quickened.

"Charmayne." Her mother's voice brought her from the depths of her despair. "Why don't you offer Kyle some coffee?"

Reminded of her manners, Charmayne accepted the reprimand and stiffly asked if he would like some refreshments.

When he refused, she breathed a silent sigh of relief.

"Thanks anyway, Mrs. Brennan," he was saying. "I can't tonight." He twisted back around to Charmayne. "You will be at the meeting tomorrow?"

Charmayne gave a jerky nod of her head.

"It's at my house. Do you know where that is?"

She passed it every day on her way to work. Again another jerky nod.

"Okay, then I'll see you at eight."

His smile included Margaret. "I'm glad to learn that you're feeling better, Mrs. Brennan."

"Oh . . . oh, yes. I am. Thank you. And thank you for the flowers. They're beautiful."

Kyle's eyes crinkled as well. Then he repeated, "See you tomorrow, Charmayne," and let himself out the door.

For a time neither woman spoke. Charmayne avoided her mother's gaze. Finally her mother commented inquiringly, "I was supposed to be ill?"

"With the flu," Charmayne admitted unwillingly.

"I made a quick recovery."

"That's probably what Kyle is thinking."

Her mother gave a slight smile. "I'm a fast healer."

Charmayne met her mother's eyes, so like her own. "Thanks for not giving me away."

Her mother shrugged. "What was it you wanted to avoid?"

"A meeting."

"The one Kyle talked about being tomorrow?"

"It was supposed to be tonight, but he moved it."

"To accommodate you?"

Charmayne nodded.

Her mother was silent a moment. Then she said, "I think he likes you, Charmayne."

The observation was met with silence.

Her mother spoke again. "How do you feel about him?"

171

The softly stated question galvanized Charmayne into action. Ever since Kyle's appearance on the doorstep, she had reacted with all the animation of a statue! She moved back over to the chair where she had been sitting and took up the letter she had been in the midst of writing.

"I don't!" she said in reply, hoping that the matter would be done with. She didn't want her mother questioning her now, adding to the questions already besieging her brain.

"Are you sure?"

"I'm positive."

Her mother's expression became wistful. "I was positive about your father, too."

Charmayne murmured a reply and pretended to become involved in her writing.

Yet deep within her, several small voices were vying to be heard, each with a different message. Eventually, though, one emerged stronger than the rest. It was the one that would not allow her to deceive herself. Because no matter how many times she told herself, or anyone else, that she felt nothing for Kyle, it simply was not true. She felt something, only she wasn't sure exactly what.

CHAPTER TEN

Dak Stevens sat in a chair across from Kyle's desk, his fingers drumming on the metal arm. The travelers being changed while in production had been a problem. But the act of sabotage they faced today had a more ominous connotation because they could no longer contend that it may have been an accident. Contamination of the chemicals used in cleaning the circuit boards was not something that could happen without premeditation. Someone was definitely intent on harming them, and was going about it with seeming ease.

"Is the entire batch ruined?"

Dak nodded. "The soldering joints are broken on all of them."

Kyle grunted as if in pain.

"We didn't notice what was happening until it was too late."

"Any idea how it happened?"

"You know what I think."

Kyle was silent a moment then asked, "Do you have any idea who might have done it?"

Dak shook his sun-streaked blond hair. "Nope."

"Does Tony?"

Dak shook his head again.

Kyle sighed.

After a thoughtful moment his partner continued, "Tony and I kept a good eye on everything, but obviously we didn't keep it well enough."

"Don't blame yourself; Tony shouldn't, either. We

probably would have had to post a twenty-four-hour security guard to keep it from happening."

"Not a bad idea."

Kyle's eyes met Dak's steadily. "Do you think it calls for measures that strong?"

Dak did. "If we don't, we may not have much of a business left."

Kyle hated the idea, but it seemed the only option left to them. Yet reporting the incident to the police force in the small town would probably cause more disruption than help. No, for the time being it would be better to handle the situation themselves.

"I think you might be right. Maybe if we hire a guard it will scare off whoever is doing this."

"Maybe."

"You don't sound very positive."

"I'm a realist."

"So am I, but I still contend that the people here are basically good."

"All it takes is one bad apple."

Kyle was forced to agree. He couldn't go on being a Pollyanna believing in the goodness of everyone in Kearney. Undeniably someone was not, and it was someone who didn't care if he destroyed his neighbors in the process.

"I have a friend in the security business in Dallas," Kyle stated. "I'll give him a call this afternoon. Maybe he can suggest someone."

"Good." Dak uncoiled his slender frame from the chair. "I'll sleep a little better knowing someone's here."

"Yeah. I guess I will, too."

"There's no telling what might happen next."

* * *

174

Dak's parting words stayed with Kyle for the rest of the afternoon. They were like a warning that knotted in the pit of his stomach. As he watched the men and women file from the building into the parking area for the return to their homes, he couldn't help wondering which of them was responsible.

Then he saw the lean, rangy form of Raymond Brennan as he moved slowly across the cemented area toward his blue pickup truck. Unlike the others Raymond seemed in no hurry. His steps were slow, as if he wasn't particularly eager to reach his destination.

Kyle watched him from his eagle's eyrie, watched as Raymond opened the driver's door and perched on the seat inside, one booted foot still on the cement, the other drawn up on the running rail. A cigarette sparked into life.

Kyle made an immediate decision. From almost the first day he had returned to find his business humming in the little town, with Raymond working in it, he had wanted to speak to him. As a boy he had looked up to the redheaded giant. He still did, if the older man he had become would let him. But he hadn't wanted their conversation to take place here, on his ground. He didn't think the older man would appreciate the status that their employer/employee relationship placed him in. But anywhere else seemed impossible. Raymond never stayed around long enough for him to begin. He would take advantage of the time he had now.

Raymond was still sitting in his truck when Kyle approached, the cigarette running to ash between his fingers.

When he looked up and saw Kyle, he started to

175

turn away—his foot lifting, the door slamming shut —as if he was now going to leave.

"Mr. Brennan. Wait," Kyle called.

At first he thought the man was going to ignore him. Then those pale blue eyes that he remembered so well—eyes that looked as if they could see straight through you—turned on him.

"I'm late getting home, Richardson. Make it quick."

Raymond Brennan was not an easy man to tame. He might be doing the job of a city man, but he wasn't yet up to playing by anyone else's rules.

Kyle was unsure of just what he wanted to say. There were so many things.

"I want to apologize about the trouble I caused last Sunday." Nothing like jumping into a situation in the middle!

Raymond said nothing.

"I didn't want you to feel as if you had to leave your own home."

"I didn't feel I had to."

"But you left because of me."

Raymond did not deny it.

Kyle didn't let his gaze falter.

"Your family was upset."

Again Raymond said nothing.

Kyle held on to his patience. "Doesn't that matter to you?"

When Raymond finally spoke, the words burst from him. "It matters a hell of a lot if you really want to know, Richardson! You shouldn't have come. You knew you weren't wanted."

"I know that."

"Then why did you do it?"

"Because none of us can continue to live in the past! What was done back when I was a boy, was done. I can't change that. But I can try to change the present."

"By nosing into my home and chasing after my daughter."

"Let's leave Charmayne out of this."

"Let's not! I don't like the idea of you having anything to do with her."

Kyle took a deep breath and let it out slowly. He might bring up the idea that Charmayne was a grown woman and free to choose her friends herself, but that would get them nowhere. He changed the subject.

"I just wanted you to know that I regret what happened."

Raymond again accepted his statement without comment. Then, after an uncomfortably long minute had passed, he asked, "Is that all?"

Kyle nodded, his mouth grim.

Raymond turned away.

When the truck's engine started and the wheels began to turn, Kyle stepped aside.

Charmayne dreaded this night. She didn't want to go to a committee meeting. She didn't care if the town was three hundred years old! What use was it to celebrate? If it had been Christmas, the way she felt now she would have made a perfect Scrooge. She would rather be anywhere but here.

When she pulled her Toyota into the drive behind Kyle's Cadillac, she was relieved to see that Hilda Morrow's car was parked there as well. For a time she had wondered if Kyle had gotten her to come to his home under the pretext that the other committee members would be present, when in fact they would not.

Still, even though she was now assured of not being alone with him, her pulse rate speeded up as she slid out of the bucket seat and closed the door.

The walk up the short flagstone pathway seemed long, and by the time she had arrived at the door, her palms were damp and her breathing was erratic. She didn't know what was the matter with her! He was just a man. An ordinary male of the species. What was she getting so worked up about? She was here to do a job, nothing more. Mayor Cliburn had practically ordered her to do it. So why was she trembling?

Was it because she was coming to his home? No, don't be silly, she admonished herself. One house was the same as another. Yet that wasn't quite true. The interior and exterior structure might be basically the same, but it was the personality of the person residing within that stamped a house with its distinctiveness. Was it this that she was afraid of: seeing Kyle in his own domain? Was it because she found it hard enough to resist her unsettled feelings about him under normal conditions without having to share the more private aspects of his life?

Charmayne swallowed before pressing the button that rang the doorbell. Then, straightening her shoulders, she waited for her summons to be answered.

Kyle didn't make her wait very long. Within seconds he was opening the door, and Charmayne's hard-won resolve to keep herself under firm control immediately received a death blow. Her breath caught in her throat and her blood gave a responsive leap. He was laughing at something that had been said to him and she was almost overwhelmed by the force of his virile good looks. His curly hair showed to a burnished bronze in the late evening light, the strong features of his face looked as if they could have been carved by the loving hands of a sculptor, his smile could have lighted up half the world, and his casual navy corded jeans and pullover shirt could have come straight from the pages of an exclusive men's fashion magazine. Charmayne had to fight down a feeling of panic. She wanted to turn around and run. As on earlier occasions, she felt the need for escape! But today there was no cause except the tumult of emotions within herself. And she couldn't run away from herself.

"Charmayne . . ." Kyle's smile had changed. There was a subtle difference, but it was there. It was not just her imagination. A tenderness, a special kind of joy . . . it was there!

Charmayne's heart was now pounding. What was happening to her? To them?

"Come in." The invitation was issued softly enough to make her wonder if he was just asking her into his home.

Charmayne felt rooted to the spot; her legs wouldn't move. But after a second's pause the directive from her brain was received and she stepped forward.

She wondered what would happen next. But in some crazy way, because it was something she would have prayed for before, she was disappointed when the illusion of intimacy was shaken by Hilda Morrow's crackly voice.

"Ah, another person to help in our insanity!"

179

Charmayne found a smile in herself somewhere. She still felt as if she were drifting on the edges of a fog, as if the answer to all her questions was just a hand's reach away, but she could not quite lean far enough outward yet to touch it. . . .

Willie Morrow, Hilda's husband, spoke from his relaxed position on the couch. Willie was the exact opposite in appearance to his wife. Thin, frail, he looked as if he might be taking his last breath at any moment. In addition he was quiet and seemingly ineffectual in contrast to his wife's booming confidence and "let's stop standing around and get the job done" attitude. She outweighed him by close to a hundred pounds and was at least a foot taller. But Hilda was in love with her scrawny husband and when he felt firmly about a subject, she listened respectfully to his viewpoint. She might not always agree, but at least she listened.

"Glad you could join us, Charmayne," he said. "We need your help." He turned to give Kyle a weak smile. "Kyle's, too. Hilda and I couldn't do all of this ourselves."

"My God, no!" Hilda agreed. "It would kill us!" Then she laughed. "Might as well spread the pain around, I always say."

Charmayne took a seat in a chair that was part of a living-room grouping placed around a low glass-topped table. Kyle offered her a choice of a variety of drinks from coffee to liquor, but Charmayne didn't agree to any of them. A fine trembling was still in possession of her body, and she wasn't sure she would be able to complete the process of bringing the glass to her mouth without giving herself away.

Kyle took the chair next to hers and guided the

discussion immediately to the Centennial celebration.

Charmayne stayed silent for a long period of time, listening as Kyle did to the reports Hilda and Willie were giving them concerning the status of preparations. Only occasionally did her attention stray. While Willie was talking about the amounts of food the Food Committee had ordered and about the post-celebration chores the Clean-up Committee were marshaling themselves for . . . her gaze was drawn to Kyle, and the foggy feeling of unreality surrounded her once again. Only when she forced her eyes away did she absorb some of her surroundings.

Kyle's taste in decor was impeccable. He had blended country comfort with city smoothness of line and the result was warm and exhilarating. The colors he had chosen were earth tones, from the long rust-colored sofa Willie and Hilda were sharing to the light forest-green of the curtains. Teak bookcases filled most of one wall and a slow-moving ceiling fan stirred the air above them. And nothing was out of place. Magazines were stacked in a brass holder, the day's newspaper was folded on an end table, and any memento used for decoration was positioned with care.

Charmayne's thoughts were brought back to the business at hand when a question was put to her about the planned parade. A permit had been requested from the mayor's office, but so far there had been no reply. She assured everyone that it soon would be received. Then the talk moved to the planned rodeo. A company that specialized in supplying stock for the event had been contracted with, and the agricultural teachers at the local high school as well as the county extension agent had agreed to oversee the amateur showing of animals for prizes. Plans had been formalized for booth construction for the bazaar and a contest was being planned for competitions there: best homemade preserves, a chili cookoff, best dessert at the show, a sewing competition . . .

The list of activities went on and on and after several hours, Charmayne could see why Mary Roberts had decided to have her baby early. She had probably driven up and down on the roughest road she could find just to induce labor!

Finally the conversation moved to plans the Decoration Committee had decided upon—red, white, and blue bunting which would be used on each booth and in the rodeo arena, and would be stretched at intervals down the town's main streets; then they talked about the plans the Publicity Committee had already instigated. The members had put notices in all the state magazines and had arranged for publicity in surrounding towns as well as Dallas–Fort Worth, San Antonio, and Houston. If even a few people from all the areas reached came, Kearney would have a very successful hundred-year celebration!

Hearing the plans caused even Charmayne to become involved in the excitement. And she joined in with Kyle as he congratulated the original members of the Coordinating Committee for a job well done. Everything seemed to be coming along perfectly.

"But there's always a hitch that pops up unexpectedly," Hilda warned. "Mary's motto was to be ready for anything."

Kyle smiled and leaned forward, his elbows resting on his cord-covered knees. He took one of Hilda's hands and the woman actually blushed. Charmayne saw the reaction and knew that she wasn't the only one who felt Kyle's attraction. She had indeed been the last holdout. She knew that. Yet seeing a person as strong in character as Hilda fall prey to his charm, she wondered if she had ever really had a chance.

"Hilda, with you on our side"—Kyle's voice was warm and sincere—"nothing would dare go wrong. But if you think we should be prepared, then we will be."

Hilda's blush deepened just as Willie's grin grew wide. He was proud of his wife and her ability to get things done.

"Well, I do think we should. Just in case," Hilda said gruffly.

Kyle patted her hand and released it.

"Then I guess that's about all we need to cover tonight. I think we should get together again over the weekend. Does Saturday night sound good to everyone?"

"Fine for us," Willie agreed.

Kyle turned his head to look at Charmayne, and she gave a quick assenting nod. She could invent a date, but it would do her no good. He would discover her lie, ferret out the truth, so she might as well agree.

"Why don't both of you come out to our place?" Hilda asked. "Kyle, there's no use in you having the meetings here all the time."

"Sounds good to me. Charmayne?"

Charmayne met his gray gaze and again experienced his magnetism. If he had asked her to try a leap over the moon right then, she might have attempted it. She forced her eyes away, knowing that she had to keep some kind of control.

"Sure. At the same time?"

"Yes," Kyle decided, then looked apologetically toward the Morrows. "If that's convenient for you—"

"Eight is fine," Hilda concurred. Then she rocked to her feet and held out a hand to her husband. He took it the more easily to escape the depths of the couch. "If anything else comes up, we'll let you know."

"Fine," Kyle agreed, standing up. He saw the middle-aged couple to the door and then, after saying a last good-bye, he turned to find Charmayne directly behind him, intent on leaving as well.

His head tipped a little to one side. "Do you have to go now, too?"

The warm intimacy of his voice caused its usual red alert along all the nerve endings of her body.

"Yes."

"Wouldn't you like something to drink? It's been a long evening."

"No, I don't think—"

"Some coffee? You have a long drive."

Charmayne was standing a step away from him. She was extremely aware of the short distance between them. In fact, she imagined she could feel the heat emanating from his body. It left her breathless.

"Come on," Kyle decided in the face of her hesitation. "One cup can't hurt."

Oh, yeah? she wanted to say. But she allowed herself to be led back into the room proper.

"Have a seat. I'll make some fresh. What's out there can probably get up and walk in here by itself!"

His smile set off fireworks.

Charmayne sank onto the sofa. She didn't think her weakened knees could make it back to the chair she had been using earlier. She knew she should leave. What in the world was she thinking about, staying like this? She looked at the door to freedom. Could she make it before he heard her? Her fingers tightened on her purse and she started to shift forward. Then Kyle came back into the room, his easy strides making short work of the distance from the kitchen to the couch. He sat beside her and the only thing that kept her from bouncing up like a frightened jack-in-the-box was that he immediately laid his curly head back on the rear cushion and let out a deep sigh.

"This has been a day!" He stared at the ceiling for a moment and Charmayne stared at him. It was like cobra and flute; she couldn't resist his fascination. He rolled his head to look at her and caught her rapt attention.

He smiled softly. "You look tired, too."

Charmayne had rarely felt less exhausted, but she shook her head in agreement.

"I'm glad we're coming in on this at the end," he continued, and she knew he was referring to the celebration. "Mary had the right idea."

Charmayne allowed herself a small smile. "I thought that earlier myself."

Kyle shifted his head, but still remained in a position to watch her.

185

She felt his eyes run over her face, touching her hair, her chin, her lips. . . .

He reached out to slide a finger along the curve of her cheek. He said nothing.

Charmayne closed her eyes. She couldn't have said anything if she had tried. Her throat seemed closed, her blood pounding at her temples. The sensuousness of his touch was awakening her memory.

Then his hand moved away and her eyes slowly fluttered open. He was looking steadily at her, his expression serious.

"I've always thought you were beautiful, Charmayne. Even when you were a little kid, you were beautiful."

Did he really mean that? She looked deeply into his eyes. He did.

Kyle wanted to tell her so much more! He wanted to tell her that suddenly, at this moment, he knew that he loved her. All along there had been something . . . from childhood there had been a thread of feeling that never completely left him. Maybe that was why he had felt the need to come back to Kearney. Maybe it wasn't purely to help the people his uncle had cheated. Maybe it was because Charmayne and her family had been hurt as well. Maybe he had loved her then only he hadn't understood, and now . . . now he understood.

Yet he held himself in check. He was afraid of her reaction. He knew that she didn't hold him in good stead. Oh, he could make her respond, but as he had felt before, he wanted more than that. Now he wanted her love. But was that too much to ask? He already had so many strikes against him.

Charmayne felt Kyle's sudden tensing and her

186

body tensed as well. She sensed that he was about to tell her something.

Then, much to Kyle's relief, the telephone rang, shattering the shimmering air between them. He reached for it as he would a saving lifeline. It was resting on a table at his side.

"Hello?" He would gratefully kiss whoever the caller was at their next encounter.

"Hey, buddy!" Charmayne heard the masculine greeting as Kyle fumbled momentarily with the phone. When he got the receiver back under control she heard nothing more except his side of the conversation. Which was just as well. It was more than enough. From tingling awareness she plunged into abject fear. The call concerned the acts of sabotage at Orion Enterprises.

"No . . . no. It's okay," Kyle was saying. "I tried to call you earlier, but you were out. I'm having a little problem here. Some unexplained accidents." To himself Kyle was quickly erasing the promised kiss. He wasn't about to kiss Mark Lester. He didn't think either of them would get a thing out of it.

"No, nothing tremendously serious yet, but . . . annoying. I was wondering if you would recommend someone who could come out and help us for a time." He was quiet as he listened to what his friend had to say. Being in charge of security for one of the larger department stores in Dallas put Mark in contact with just the kind of person Kyle needed for Orion.

"Well, we had a mixup in some paperwork that gave us a bit of trouble, and today some chemicals were contaminated." He listened again. "No, at first I thought that, but I'm beginning to lean more toward the idea that someone is deliberately trying to harm the business."

When he said that, Charmayne's soul cried out. Please, no! Not my father!

"Yeah. Okay. You check around and see who you can come up with. I'll trust your choice."

Whom was he talking to? Charmayne wondered frantically. The police? A detective agency? Would the trail lead straight to her father?

"Let me know who you settle on. Okay? Thanks, Mark."

He hung up. He was still a moment, leaning forward, before he turned back to Charmayne. A small smile turned up the corners of his lips.

"That was a call I'd been waiting for."

Charmayne nodded stiffly. Her entire body seemed turned to ice. She had to talk with her father. Make him see reason.

Kyle frowned when he saw the difference in Charmayne. Fear and pain were once again in her eyes and he wondered at the cause. Had he done something, said something?

"Charmayne?" he began when she suddenly jumped to her feet.

"I've got to go," she murmured distractedly.

Kyle's frown deepened. "What is it, Charmayne?"

She didn't answer him; she just hurried toward the door.

"Charmayne . . . Your coffee . . ." He tried again to stop her. But either she didn't hear him or she chose not to. Either way she was gone and he was left to stand alone.

Later that night as he lay staring into the darkness,

the firm mattress cradling his long form, his arms folded beneath his head, Kyle couldn't get the vision of Charmayne as he had last seen her out of his mind.

She had looked so afraid.

His newly discovered love had urged him to go after her; make her confide. But the love was all on his side. She felt nothing for him, except maybe contempt. And contempt didn't invite confidences.

Kyle's jaw tightened at that thought and his inner resolve became fixed. No matter what it took, he vowed to himself, he was going to make her love him. If it was humanly possible . . .

CHAPTER ELEVEN

The nervous fear Charmayne had experienced the night before remained with her the next morning. Only now it had increased, if that were possible. She had left Kyle's home with the intention of talking with her father, confronting him, making him see reason. But she had been unable to satisfy any of her needs. Her parents had been in bed upon her return, and this morning, for the first time in several days, her mother had risen early and helped prepare breakfast as had been her custom before all the trouble began.

She had been forced to be subtle when she wanted to be direct and the result was increased frustration. When she mentioned casually that she had heard about another accident at Orion, her father had remained close-mouthed. But it wasn't the silence of innocence. After having lived with him for twenty-six years, she knew when he was attempting to hide something. And she knew that he definitely was now.

She arrived at her office with a headache, which only increased in severity as the day went by. It was not helped by the mayor's growing worry over the upcoming election, or by the rumor that she already knew to be true concerning trouble at the town's newest business.

That night she was too ill to protest when her mother insisted, immediately after Charmayne had come home from work, that she go to bed. Her stomach had become involved in the headache and the upset left her no choice. She knew her illness was a reaction to stress, but the way she felt right then, she didn't care. All she wanted was to go to bed and pretend to be a child again. When her mother brought in a bowl of warm chicken broth, she tried to eat it; then she kissed her father good-night when he came in to see her, not saying a word about anything but her love for him.

Only when she was alone did a lone tear appear from nowhere to trace a path from the corner of her eye.

When Saturday arrived she still had not confronted her father. One cause after another had delayed her doing so, and the one time she did have an opportunity, she couldn't find the appropriate words. How did a daughter ask her father a thing like that? She felt so disloyal! The moment passed.

It was late afternoon and she was on her way to the henhouse to gather eggs when her mother's voice caught her attention.

"Charmayne . . . Telephone!"

Charmayne waved an acknowledgement and turned on her heel, retracing her steps to the farmhouse.

She put the basket used for collecting eggs on the counter and moved the few extra steps required to retrieve the receiver her mother had left dangling from its wall mount.

After she had given her usual greeting and received one in return, Charmayne's fingers flexed on the hard plastic molding. The caller was Kyle, and his voice sent chills of both excitement and apprehension throughout her body.

"I'm calling to remind you of the meeting this evening. Eight o'clock at the Morrows'."

Charmayne had not forgotten. Mixed in with her anxiety about her father was her heightening confusion over her feelings for Kyle. She couldn't get that tender look he had given her out of her mind.

"I remember."

"Good." Kyle paused. "Why don't you let me pick you up? I have to drive by the turnoff to your house to get to the Morrow place. It seems silly for the two of us to come in separate cars."

Charmayne's stomach did a good rendition of a flip-flop. It still had not completely settled from its upset of two days before.

"And, Charmayne," he added, "I do mean your house."

Charmayne hesitated. If he suspected her father, would he want to come to their home? And if he didn't . . . could she get her father to cooperate enough to make it easier on him if he was discovered?

"All right," she agreed.

Kyle was silent a moment as if surprised that she had agreed so easily. Then he said, "I'll be by around seven thirty." When she consented again, he hung up.

Charmayne looked at the now humming instrument that remained in her grasp. Had she done the right thing?

In his living room nearer to Kearney, Kyle was looking down at his now silent telephone as well, his hand still covering the receiver on its cradle. He had expected more resistance. He even had alternate persuasions ready to use if she declined. But she had agreed so easily. . . . A troubled frown creased his brow. It had been too easy.

* * *

Charmayne and her parents waited in the living room. There was another strained silence between them, but this time it was directed at her. Her father had not approved when she informed him that Kyle was coming by to take her to the committee meeting. And when she had insisted that he be present when his employer arrived, his disapproval of her idea had increased.

"I don't see why it's necessary, Charmayne," he had said stiffly.

Charmayne held her ground. "It is because we've got to stop living in the past! Once and for all, the bitterness has got to end!"

"I don't like you seeing him. He's trouble."

"You don't know him, Dad. All you see is the Richardson name. He's not like his uncle. If you'd give him even half a chance, you'd learn that for yourself!"

"You're defending him? To me?" Her father had sounded deeply wounded.

When she started this conversation, Charmayne had not intended to champion Kyle. But since her father asked that question, she saw that she was.

"Yes. I guess I am."

Raymond had grimaced in disgust. "My own daughter . . ."

Charmayne still could not make herself broach the subject she had been so intent on facing. She continued to use a back-door approach.

"What will he have to do to convince you, Dad? He brought Orion Enterprises here, to Kearney, when he didn't have to. He could have opened it anywhere. There are lots of small towns in Texas. But no, he chose Kearney. And why do you think he did that? For all the thanks he'd get?" She paused for effect. "No, I guarantee you he didn't! He knew that the people here would resent him. That he might be treated badly at first. But he did it anyway. And it's due to his willingness to take abuse that a number of our friends, not counting ourselves, are still here . . . living on their land, working their land."

Her green eyes had held her father's pale blue. "Dad, there are very few people left who still feel strong resentment for him. And it's not only because of the jobs he brought to us. It's because of Kyle himself! He cares, Dad. He cares about the people, about the town!"

She could think of nothing more to say, so she lapsed into silence.

Her father had turned his gaze to the horizon, his piercing gaze burning inward. Then, his voice low and vibrant, he said, "I hope you're right about him, Charmayne. Because you must love him an awful lot to feel that way."

Charmayne had given a quick gasp. She started to deny what he had said. Instead, she remained silent. Her father had a way of cutting through issues to get to the truth. And this time, to her startled perception, she knew that he might be right again.

No further words had passed between them, but later Charmayne was not surprised to find her father already in the living room when she walked into it. He didn't give her a word of greeting and her mother was silent as well.

Now, they waited. For what? Fate?

Kyle remained seated in his car for some seconds before starting the motion to get out. His arms were folded on the steering wheel, his gaze steady on the frame house a short distance away.

Every time he came here, he felt waves of negative emotion. Would it never end? Would he ever be allowed a place among them?

He drew in a deep bracing breath and opened the door. Maybe he did have a little of his uncle in him after all. He was willing to challenge the odds, to fly in the face of sanity . . . just to achieve a goal. Did it really make a difference that his goal was Charmayne and his uncle's had been money?

Charmayne's features were schooled as she opened the front door and motioned for him to enter.

Raymond and Margaret watched his approach. Again, Kyle could feel the undercurrents of suppressed tension.

"Mrs. Brennan. Mr. Brennan," he acknowledged courteously.

"Hello, Kyle," Margaret answered and then had to suffer her husband's suprised look because she had addressed his employer by his first name. She kept her face forward, pretending to be unaware of his disapproval.

Raymond's lips thinned. Was Margaret betraying him as well? He allowed only a small, quick duck of his head for a reply. It was as if his neck were stiff and it hurt him to move.

Charmayne nervously tried to keep control of the situation.

"Would you like to sit down, Kyle? We have a few minutes before we have to leave. The Morrows' place isn't that far."

Kyle's gaze swept over her features. What was she trying to do? Force the issue?

He took a seat on the sofa and tried to look comfortable.

Into the pause created by the two women racking their brains for what to say next, Kyle came to the rescue by observing, "You look as if you're feeling better, Mrs. Brennan."

Margaret gave a small start as memory failed her, then she smiled tightly and answered, "Yes . . . yes, I do. But I think mainly I was just tired."

Margaret shot a glance at her husband. His brow was furrowed.

Raymond leaned forward and unconsciously cracked a knuckle, a habit he sometimes fell into when he was perplexed. Lately, although he wasn't aware of the fact, he could have been a one-man percussionist in a symphony orchestra. Richardson had seen his wife when she was ill? he wondered. Just how often had he been here? Did he come around every time he himself was absent?

Raymond's second knuckle cracked. The sound was loud in the taut atmosphere of the room.

Charmayne knew the time had come to leave. So far her father had been taciturn in the extreme, but at least he was here. That was quite an accomplishment, really. But the strain he was under was growing, and she didn't want what little good he had managed to achieve to be destroyed. She reached for her purse.

"I think we should leave now, Kyle." She slid the strap onto her shoulder. Since she had never taken a seat, she waited for Kyle to relinquish his. When he was at her side, she told her parents, "I'm not sure what time the meeting will be over. It could take only

196

a few minutes, or it could take a few hours. Don't wait up."

Her mother nodded; her father remained still. She knew she needn't have told them not to wait up. They hadn't done that in years. But somehow, tonight, the cautionary seemed appropriate.

Kyle was silent as he showed her into his car and then got inside himself. The starting engine sounded loud in the night. Then they were reversing out of the drive.

Instead of decreasing as she had hoped, the knot of tension in her stomach only got worse. She should have known that it would, though; she had merely exchanged one kind of hell for another.

She stole a quick glance at Kyle's profile. He looked so handsome in the late evening light. All of his features were so distinctive yet fitted together so smoothly, the effect pleasing to the eye but at the same time showing the strength of his character. Her lashes lowered, her gaze transferring to his lean yet powerful body, remembering what it was like to be held close against him, to feel his muscles straining her to him at the height of his arousal, remembering his touch.

Charmayne took a deep gulping breath, feeling precisely as a swimmer would who had gone too long and too far out of her depth. Was her father right? Was she in love with him? Or was what she felt for him only a sexual response? She had to consider that it was. She was a mature woman with all that included in emotional and physical needs. Was it just his body that fascinated her with its promise? Or was there something more?

Kyle's fingers were tight on the steering wheel. He

loved her. It should be easy to start a conversation with her. But what could he say?

In the end the journey remained silent, both too caught up in private emotional upheavals to do more than mentally reach out one to the other.

Being in the company of Hilda and Willie eased the situation a good deal, but still an underlying tension pervaded the time spent at the meeting. Possibly the older couple did not feel it, but Kyle and Charmayne did. A taut wire of tingling awareness seemed to be stretched between them. Kyle's gray eyes, deep and unfathomable, were unable to stay long away from Charmayne's leafy green ones.

Charmayne tried to concentrate on what was being said, but little more than a sporadic sentence got through ungarbled to her brain. If she had been called upon to give an account of the meeting, she embarrassingly would not have been able to do so.

For Kyle the time passed no more easily. He was aware of Charmayne's every move: of the way the soft material of her cream-colored dress clung to her slender shape, how it emphasized the curves of her small breasts and narrow waist, how it made her skin glow with life and complemented her bright hair. His eyes traced the freckles that she seemed to disdain. To him each and every one was a beauty mark; they were a part of her, therefore he loved them. It was all he could do not to humiliate both of them by jumping across the table that separated them, drag her into his arms, and start to kiss and touch her, uncaring of their hosts' presence. The need within him was beginning to border on the uncontrollable.

When finally, an hour and a half later, the meeting ended, the strain of suppressed emotion was beginning to tell on each of them. Kyle knew he had to partake in some kind of physical activity immediately or he was going to explode, and Charmayne felt as if she were suffocating. She had to get outside, get away from a situation she no longer felt able to handle. They both declined an invitation to a final cup of coffee.

Again, the car ride began in silence, with Charmayne overwhelmingly aware of Kyle's continued presence. Her torture was not yet over!

And Kyle was struggling to contain his slipping control for just a while longer. He would limit himself to a kiss, just one kiss. . . . She probably wouldn't even willingly grant him that. She had been so quiet all evening. She probably wanted to be anywhere but there with him. Once before she had hinted at being experienced in lovemaking. Was there someone special now? Someone she would rather be with? A shaft of jealousy pierced his chest. It burned like a mortal wound.

Kyle's fingers crushed the wheel and his mouth tightened.

Charmayne felt his sudden increase in tension and again her breathing became difficult. It was like the calm before a storm. One moment, an electric silent tension; the next, the wild exuberance of nature's fury.

Her hands tightened their grip on each other.

She felt Kyle's long glance before it swung back to the road. She kept her eyes forward. Then he glanced at her again and the speed the car was traveling decreased. Her heartrate increased correspondingly. She shot him a nervous look.

In the inky darkness of night that surrounded

them, the only light coming from the country sky, Kyle met her wide gaze. And he could stand it no longer. Almost like a robot, he directed the car to the side of the road and shut the engine off. Then he turned to her, and without uttering a sound, he reached forward and let his fingers slide into position around her neck. A low groan escaped his throat as he urged her toward him, leaning forward at the same time to taste her sweet lips.

Charmayne remained docile in his embrace for a paralyzed second. Then, as the warmth of his devouring mouth broke through her surprised state, her body awakened to a return of passion and she immediately surrendered to it. Her mouth opened to his and the kiss deepened and intensified. When Kyle's tongue thrust intimately into her mouth, her own tongue made a delicate parry. When his hands stroked her back, massaging, caressing, hers did the same to him. She loved the feel of his strong muscles straining beneath her fingers, loved his warmth and smoothness.

Kyle no longer had even a small measure of control. When he had reached for her, he hadn't cared if she fought against him or not. He had to touch her! Then when, unbelievably, she responded—it was as if she, too, had been holding herself back!—what little sanity remained to him had evaporated. He was functioning purely on instinct now. And his instinct demanded only one thing.

Charmayne was panting when Kyle's mouth left her lips and began a descent. His kiss had been like a dam bursting; all of her studiously constructed walls against him had instantly crumbled. She didn't care if he was a Richardson, if his uncle had treated her family badly, if he himself had coerced her into doing things she, at the time, thought she didn't want to do. Now, none of that mattered. She gasped his name as the buttons of her dress parted and his face became buried between her breasts.

The thundering in Kyle's bloodstream increased, his body having attained a driving, pulsing life. Her breasts gleamed white in the partial light and his lips closed around one delectable curve.

Charmayne arched her back as a surge of both weakness and strength coursed through her. She wanted him. All he had ever had to do was touch her and she wanted him. Only now, this time, the desire was a torrid flame. If he didn't take her soon, she felt as if she were going to die in his arms.

Kyle's tongue was smooth on her skin as it darted across her nakedness; his hands were hot as they touched her.

She drew one leg upward as his fingers trailed along her thigh. She cursed the panty hose that kept them from full contact.

Kyle loosened her belt as she did his. She pulled his shirt free of his pants and unbuttoned it, wanting to feel the hard warmth of his chest against her. Then her hands dropped to his waist, running along the flatness of his stomach. She felt him give an involuntary quiver. The evidence of her potency delighted her.

Her dress was nearly off her shoulders by now and the waistband was free. All it would take would be two flicks of the wrist to remove it completely. Yet Charmayne was more concerned with Kyle at this moment than with her own stage of undress. Her palm cupped his male hardness through the material of his pants.

Kyle's hand covered hers and kept it there. Their breathing was mutually erratic.

"God, Charmayne . . . I want you!"

The first words spoken between them were a masterpiece of understatement.

Charmayne's pulse leapt and a pleasurable heat engulfed her body. She gave a nervous little laugh.

"I know."

Kyle laughed as well, but unsteadily. Conversation, far from lessening his desire, had, if anything, strengthened it.

"Do you want me to make love to you?" His words were clipped.

"Yes!" Her reply was short as well, and her fingers tightened a degree.

Kyle groaned in response and buried his mouth against her neck, sweeping aside her hair.

Charmayne reluctantly removed her hand. She didn't want to stop touching him, but in order to complete their union, she must.

She met his mouth once again when he prompted her to do so, and in her mind she felt her soul come to meet his. Nothing could be more right than the two of them. This was just an extension, on another level, of their childhood. She had always loved him. Her father had been right.

Kyle pulled away and even though she couldn't see his eyes clearly, she could feel their burning gray flame.

"I have a blanket in the trunk. Are you willing to chance the field?"

The field sounded like heaven. She nodded quickly.

Kyle kissed her soundly again and then released her. When he stepped out into the night, she felt as if a part of her was missing. Then he was opening the door on the passenger side of the car and reaching for her. Charmayne didn't hesitate. She placed her hand in his and allowed him to help her out beside him. He lowered his head to her fingers and kissed each one. Then, flashing a quick self-mocking smile, he pulled her with him.

The fence along this section of road was not in as good repair as the one they had crossed what seemed such a long time ago. This time she could have clambered over it easily herself, but Kyle didn't let her. Again she was lifted up in his strong embrace, the blanket folded beneath her on one of his arms, and they crossed together.

Charmayne rested her cheek against his chest, one hand stroking the crisp dark hair at his nape. She loved him. She loved the boy he was and the man he had become. She loved everything about him.

Kyle examined the field before them, the light of the moon giving faint guidance. He saw no livestock, which he had learned was important to check for—he'd never had to worry about a cow coming along and interrupting an intimate moment in Dallas!—and with the fence being in such disrepair, he doubted that there were any. He lowered Charmayne to her feet when they were on the far side of a gently rising hill so that he could spread the blanket. Then, when he was done, he turned back to her.

Her face looked small in the mass of hair that framed its gentle lines, and even in the starlight he could see that her eyes were wide and tonight they looked as deep and mysterious as dark forest. He waited for a moment, unmoving. Had she changed her mind? Had the time taken to leave the car given her the opportunity to have second thoughts?

His brow was creased slightly until he saw the first glimmer of a shy smile. Then, when she compounded her action by taking a step forward to run her fingers along his naked stomach and chest, he knew, without a doubt, that she was still willing. He drew her to him and bent down over her, kissing her, caressing her, giving her his love.

As with one will they stretched out on the blanket and the kiss continued. Within a few seconds, though, that contact was no longer enough. They helped each other with the task of taking off the rest of their clothes and when they were finally free, their bodies once again came close. Charmayne thrilled to Kyle's touch, and he reveled in her softness. He wanted to touch all of her, kiss all of her, know everything there was to know about her . . . take his time. . . .

But at this moment a slow loving was not to be. His body was alive to only one objective: that of possession. He shifted above her, and with her compliance, achieved the purpose he had been born for. He entered her in one smooth motion. Then he had to be still. If he was not, his excitement was so great that everything would be over instantly.

The stars shining down from the heavens into Charmayne's eyes were nothing to the internal starbursts that she was experiencing. Kyle's entry had brought her to the brink of a tingling fulfilment. And she wanted more . . . much more. . . . Her arms were curved around his back and her breasts were pressed to his chest. She arched upward once again, to add to her pleasure as well as his.

Kyle felt her movement and shuddered. Then, mindlessly, he reacted—rocking, thrusting, his long lean body giving and receiving the promise of gratification until neither could stand the torture any longer. Responding to a blinding burst of light, Kyle pushed farther into Charmayne and then his body took over its involuntary mission, completing, perfecting, fulfilling.

Charmayne responded with all the enthusiasm of her youth. She wanted everything that was happening. Her own excitement had increased to fever pitch. Then, only a few seconds after she felt Kyle's release, her own pleasure climaxed.

Soon, Kyle lay spent against her, their hearts' labored beating matching the deep, ragged breaths they took. Then Kyle shifted some of his weight; he had tried not to rest against her too heavily.

Charmayne lifted her hands and ran her fingers through his curly hair. It was so soft to touch.

Kyle turned onto his side and kept her close by, bringing her with him.

Charmayne felt no shame at what they had done, only joy. She loved him. And she had an idea that he cared for her as well. She still had not forgotten the way he had looked at her the other day. And she knew that if she could see his face clearly now, she would see that look again . . . knew that, if anything, it would contain even more tenderness.

Kyle's eyes were soft and filled with his love as he looked across at her. Her arms were entwined about his neck and he could still taste the sweetness of her breath and her kiss. He leaned forward to experience it again.

Charmayne returned the pressure of his lips, a happiness growing within her. Finally, when the kiss broke, she buried her face in the curve of his neck and whispered, "Thank you, Kyle."

"For what?" he asked huskily.

"For not making our first time be in the back seat of your car."

His arms closed about her more tightly. His voice was huskier when he replied, "We outgrew that a long time ago. I wanted this to be special, Charmayne."

"It is."

They were quiet a moment, appreciating each other and what had happened between them.

"Had you planned this, Kyle?" she asked curiously at last.

She felt his smile. "Not exactly."

She pushed up on an elbow and looked down at him, at his beloved features revealed by the stars and moon.

"You just happen to carry a blanket in the trunk of your car. . . ."

"You could say that. I put it in this morning."

"In case you might need it," she teased.

"I like to be prepared."

She settled back against him. "I'm glad you brought it."

"Me, too."

The sound of a cricket chirping nearby filled the air.

"Kyle?"

"Mmmmm?"

"Are you happy?" Suddenly that he be happy seemed important to her. He had been through so much in his life. She wanted him to be happy now.

"Right this minute? Of course I am."

"No . . . well, yes," she stuttered, then corrected herself. "That's not exactly what I meant. I'm talking about being here . . . in Kearney."

Kyle thought of the woman in his arms. What more could a man ask?

"Yes."

"The people treat you well?"

Kyle thought back to the first stunned reactions of his employees and then of the acquaintances he had made when he was a boy.

"Yes, most of them do now."

She was quiet a moment; then: "Kyle?"

"Ummm?"

"Why did you come back? Was it just to help the people here?"

Kyle made no reply at first. Then he decided to be honest.

"I wanted to help them, yes." He hesitated. "But I also wanted to come back and see a certain little girl with red braids and huge green eyes who had at least a million freckles. Do you remember her?"

Charmayne smiled. "Yes." She plunged on. "Why did you want to see her?"

His arm tightened. "Because I couldn't seem to forget her. I might have aged eighteen years and had a lot happen to me after I left, but she was always there, in the back of my mind, even when I didn't know it."

She knew she was pushing her luck; he had said nothing about his feelings for her. And the discovery of her love was so new. But Charmayne was the type of person who liked to have things straight if it was within her power to make them that way.

She took a breath and asked, "And why do you think that was?"

During the time when Kyle didn't answer, her breathing stopped and her heart pounded.

At last he asked softly, "Would you believe me if I told you that it was because I loved her?"

"As a friend?" Charmayne probed.

Kyle smiled and ran a finger across her exposed breast.

"I don't feel like this about my friends—even my close ones."

His huskily spoken words, along with his touch, caused a resurgence of the fire in her veins.

"I don't think of you as just a friend, either."

Kyle's teeth flashed white. "Thank God!"

Charmayne smiled in return, but fragilely. "No." The smile flickered. "I don't mean that. I mean . . . Kyle, I know I shouldn't say this. But . . . Kyle, I think I love you, too."

Could a man hear more precious words? Kyle's heart somersaulted within his chest. This was a night to be remembered for all time! Charmayne loved him! But wait . . . she'd said "think." He calmed down a degree.

"Don't you know?"

Now it was Charmayne's turn to make him wait. Seconds seemed like hours to him.

"It's all so new. . . ." Her eyes searched his. "Do you?"

"Do I what?"

"Love me."

Kyle hugged her slender body against him. If he told her how much, would she believe him? The glitter in his eyes reflected the pinpoints of the thousands of lights shining down from above. He closed them to help keep himself in check.

"I've already told you that I do."

Charmayne shook her head. Her nose was tickled by the fine hairs that grew on his chest.

"No. You said you loved a little girl."

"That's true."

"But she grew up!"

"So did I."

Charmayne struggled to raise her head. "And you still do?"

Wordlessly, Kyle nodded.

Charmayne's spirit began to sing. He did! He loved her! Then suddenly some of the clouds they would have to weather began to crowd out the happiness of her smile.

"But, Kyle, what about my—"

He let her get no further. "Hush," he interrupted. "Not now. We'll worry about everything else later. Right now we have other things to do."

With unfailing direction his mouth covered hers and she lay fully back onto the blanket. Then, soon, as again the heat of their passion turned to molten need, his body rose to cover hers.

CHAPTER TWELVE

The events of the evening before seemed as if they had happened to someone else, Charmayne thought upon awakening the next morning. Kyle loved her! She loved him! It didn't seem possible! But it was. Her mind immediately went back to the lovemaking they had shared, to the shadowy beauty of his body —all she could see in the partial light—to the magic of his touch, to the ecstasy of his possession. . . . She remembered his husky voice filled with tenderness and caring.

A happiness like none she had ever experienced before took possession of Charmayne's body. An illumination of spirit. She crossed her arms over her chest and hugged herself. She couldn't believe something like this was happening to her! She peered into the mirror hanging above her low chest of drawers. Did she look any different? Was there some sign of the magnitude of her self-discovery?

Glowing eyes looked back at her, set in a face that radiated with love. Yes, the change was there. Anyone who looked at her would be able to see.

Slowly the radiant glow began to fade. Anyone who looked . . . Yesterday Kyle had said they would face the problems that confronted them later. Well, she was going to have to face one of them in just a few minutes: her father. What could she say to him? He had already guessed how she felt about Kyle. But did she have to confirm it? And did she have to do it now? Wouldn't it be best to let the situation ride, especially while everything else was so unsettled?

Charmayne ate breakfast with her parents and then drove in to Kearney for church services, all the while hiding the swelling gladness within her. Her discipline received a thorough jolt, though, when she saw Kyle waiting for them outside the church's door.

He looked so big and strong and wonderful with his hair glinting chestnut in the sun and his smile warm and welcoming. He didn't try to hide the way he felt about her, not from anyone.

When they approached, he pushed away from his leaning position against a side pillar and fell into position beside her. He tipped his head to her father and mother.

Margaret was startled by his presence at first, then when she saw the special look that passed between her daughter and this man, she knew, and she breathed a fateful sigh.

Raymond's lips firmed and his jaw set, but since there was nothing he could do to change the situation —if Charmayne loved him, he was helpless to object —he nodded coldly in response and stepped inside the church.

All through the service Charmayne was aware of Kyle. Had only a week gone by since last Sunday? So much had happened, so much had changed.

Kyle went through the motions of taking part in the worship service, but in reality his thoughts were wholly concerned with Charmayne. The lightly scented perfume she used tempted his nose and the occasional brush of her arm felt like an electrical spark. He should have stayed away today. Last week his presence had only caused trouble. But asking him to stay away from Charmayne now was like asking a man dying of thirst to refrain from drinking water.

He had to come; he had to see her. He had to reaffirm in his own mind that she was his.

His hand reached out to cover hers on the bench seat. Her fingers turned and curled into his.

After the services Kyle filed out of the church behind the Brennan family after having met Raymond's unrevealing blue gaze and held it. Eventually the man had turned and walked before him.

Once outside, the family paused as it had last week, waiting for the minister and his wife to join them.

Being in the same situation again recalled to Kyle's mind that he had meant to talk with the pastor of the church. But with everything that had been happening, he had forgotten. He once again made a mental note to speak with him. He wanted to find out who was causing the trouble, and if the minister could shed some light . . .

Kyle was brought to an awareness that he was not paying attention to what was being said when Charmayne shyly touched his arm and repeated a question that her mother had just asked.

"Mom wants to know if you would like to come to dinner today, Kyle."

She wanted him to accept. She didn't want to be parted from him for any longer than was absolutely necessary.

Kyle gazed down into her beloved face and ached to kiss her. The feeling was very strong, but he contained himself. He considered the invitation. If he went, he wasn't sure how much control he would have at being so close to Charmayne yet unable to touch her. And he didn't want to alienate Raymond more than was absolutely necessary. His game plan was a long-term one. He wanted to win Raymond's trust and respect. Manhandling his daughter right in front of him when he disapproved of any association between them would not be the wise thing to do. So, calling on all the maturity he had won during his thirty-one years of life, he answered softly, "No, I don't want to intrude again, Mrs. Brennan. Anyway, I have some things I need to take care of this afternoon. But thank you for asking."

Charmayne felt crushed. She looked quickly at the ground.

Words passed over her head: polite words of contradiction that he would not be intruding and disappointment that he would not be able to come.

Charmayne hadn't realized that everyone had moved away leaving Kyle and herself alone until his finger came out to tilt her chin upward. He smiled down at her moist eyes.

"I love you, Charmayne," he murmured huskily. "Remember that."

No more appropriate words could have been spoken to restore her failing will.

"You won't come?" she breathed, still hoping that he would change his mind.

He shook his head. "No, I don't think I should."

She wanted to kiss him; she wanted to throw herself into his arms and beg him never to leave her again. But a quick look at her family standing a short distance away gave her pause. Yes, it would be best to continue with this charade. At least today when they met, her father hadn't looked as if he would like to kill Kyle. That was some measure of progress.

"All right," she whispered, agreeing with his reasoning.

She started to turn away, but he reached out to capture her arm, unable to let her go so easily. "Can I see you tomorrow?"

Her eyes began to shine.

"When?"

"Lunch?"

That was forever! "All right," she repeated.

Kyle's fingers tightened momentarily on the smooth flesh of her upper arm. Then, reluctantly, he released her.

With a wildly thumping heart, Charmayne moved into the circle of her family and their friends, feeling as if a part of her remained somewhere else—with Kyle, wherever he might go.

Kyle extended the roughly put-together note he had found lying on his desk early that morning to the man sitting across from him. It was a collection of words selected from the pages of a magazine and glued onto a single sheet.

"Not very original," the man observed, after taking it from him and reading it quickly.

Kyle's lips tightened. "No."

The security man's brown eyes lifted from the paper and went directly to his new employer.

"Mark filled me in on the trouble you've been having. This doesn't surprise me very much."

"No, I suppose it doesn't me, either. Do you think it means what it says?"

"Possibly."

"Then we shut down. I don't want anyone hurt."

The security man's eyes narrowed. "I don't think you should. You'd be doing exactly what he wants you to."

"I don't want anyone hurt!" Kyle repeated.

"Neither do I," was the quick comeback. The note fluttered onto the surface of the desk that separated them.

Kyle took a deep breath. He was holding on to his patience with difficulty. The man was so cold. "Then what do you advise?"

"Go on with business as usual. Let me have a chance to get to work. That's what you hired me for. Only, I don't want to advertise the fact that I'm an agent; I'd rather come on as a new employee. That will let me dig in and find out what's being said."

The man would never win a popularity contest, Kyle decided wryly. He looked a real Caspar Milquetoast type: pale skin, nondescript features, a small wiry build. Nothing like the brawny athlete he had expected. It was only the quick intelligence behind the dark brown eyes that made the man in any way unusual. Luckily his arrival had coincided with a letter from Mark extolling his record as one of the top men in his profession; otherwise Kyle might have thought someone was playing a joke on him. The thought went through his mind that this was another case of not judging a book by its cover. Then he said, "Do you think this might be a bluff?"

"That's possible, too."

Kyle sighed and picked up the letter once again. He reread it for what had to be the twentieth time. *What happened before isn't half of what will happen again if you don't leave town. Kiss your building goodbye.*

"But if it's not, I have a responsibility to see that no one suffers because I ignored it."

"I think we have a few days. Whoever sent this

isn't going to do anything immediately. He probably wants to watch you squirm. Let me get on the line and see what I can pick up."

Kyle held his gaze steadily, trying to read the man's mind. Then he glanced over toward Dak Stevens, and Tony Campo, who had remained quiet all through the interview. Silently he asked their opinion.

Dak was the first to speak. He cleared his throat. "I don't see where we have much choice, Kyle."

Tony concurred. "Me, either. If we shut down, it won't solve the problem. It will just make it worse."

Kyle made the decision. "Can you get in the line and fit in? Not make anyone suspicious?"

The security man smiled and a light chill ran down Kyle's spine. The smile held both confidence and a cold kind of determination. "I never promise anything I can't deliver," the man said. "I'll fit in."

Without another word the meeting broke up. When he was alone, Kyle swiveled his chair to look out the window. But his gaze registered nothing, his mind's eye still concentrating on the letter resting behind him on his desk.

Charmayne had looked forward to lunch with Kyle that noon as a child anticipates a trip to the circus. She could barely wait. So when he called to cancel their date, her spirit plunged.

He had sounded so distracted when he told her something had come up. Was it the truth? Surely he wasn't trying to avoid her! Momentary misgivings rose up to overwhelm her. Then, remembering the warmth of his gaze yesterday and the touch of his hand as he told her once again that he loved her, she relaxed into a floodtide of feeling. If he said something had come up, she could believe him. She was long past the point where she doubted him anymore and even a flickering uncertainty was unworthy of either of them.

She continued with her day exactly as she had the morning: dealing with all the minor emergencies and irritations in the lives of the townspeople of Kearney.

As the days went by, the major topic of conversation on everyone's lips seemed to be the town's upcoming Centennial. Almost everyone had a part to play and when the grapevine revealed that Charmayne was on the Coordinating Committee she received just as many calls on that subject as she did on the running of the town—more, in fact, as the weekend neared. It seemed that the more involved the people became in their town's celebration, the less energy they devoted to grievances among themselves.

Everyone was preparing for the great event. Excitement was contagious. Even Charmayne's parents forgot their strained bickering and began to take part. Raymond offered his services to the Clean-up Committee and Margaret became involved in deciding what was the best batch of peach preserves she could enter in the fair competition.

Charmayne dealt with the furor as best she could and went to bed exhausted each night.

Then on Thursday the telephone rang and Kyle's deep, husky voice vibrated the nerve endings throughout her body.

"Charmayne?"

Charmayne closed her eyes and allowed the sparks

that shot through her full freedom. She had missed hearing from him so much during the past two days!

"Kyle—" Her fingers tightened convulsively on the receiver.

She heard him give a deep sigh, then murmur, "God, I've missed you."

She managed a shaky smile while her throat automatically closed. She had to force her voice to burst through. "I haven't been anywhere. Just here."

"I know. And it's been driving me crazy that I haven't been able to . . . Charmayne, things have been a little wild around here, but I need to see you. Can you make lunch today?"

Could she? She would like to see someone tell her she couldn't! "Yes."

"I'll pick you up in about ten minutes."

She checked her watch. That would give her time to comb her hair and put on some fresh lipstick. "I'll see you then," she agreed.

After replacing the receiver, she jumped from her chair and hurried into the women's room a short distance down the hall. She moved so quickly she didn't see the puzzled looks that were exchanged by the women in the outer office. They were wondering at the beaming smile she could do little to contain. It was so different from the expression of tension she had been wearing almost continuously for so long.

Charmayne was waiting with time to spare when Kyle came slowly into her office. Instantly she saw that there was a change in him; as if he, too, was now living under a great strain. His eyes had a haggard look that only worry can put there and his face had a few more lines in it.

Charmayne stood up and automatically moved

218

around her desk to meet him, her expression one of concern.

"Kyle?" she questioned briefly before continuing into his outstretched arms.

Kyle hugged her to him, needing her warmth, the feel of her body against his. Ever since receiving the note he had been unable to relax. It didn't seem to matter that he had the knowledge of an agent working daily to discover who had made the threat; the responsibility of his employees' safety rested heavily on his shoulders and he was only hoping that he was doing the right thing in going along with what the agent said. If something happened and someone was hurt, he would never be able to forgive himself.

His arms tightened against Charmayne even more, feeling her softness. Almost as a penance he had stayed away from her.

Charmayne buried her cheek against the material of his dark jacket. She wanted to cry out her joy in being held by him, but instead she kept it to herself. She knew that something was wrong. But what?

She lifted her face to pose a question, only to be stopped by the immediate pressure of his lips.

For Kyle the kiss was a rejuvenation. He drank from the sustaining fount of her lips and felt life seep back into his veins.

Charmayne raised herself on tiptoe and molded her body to his, her arms reaching up to enclose his neck. Instinctively she had felt Kyle's need of her, and she reacted with a desire to be whatever source of comfort he required. If he needed to hold her, he could hold her. If he needed to kiss her, he could kiss her. If he needed to love her, he could love her. Her love was strong enough to share itself.

219

Within a moment of her offering, the pressure of the kiss increased, and his lips, firm yet sensitive, buried themselves against her own, moving, enjoying, demanding, giving. . . .

Finally, after a soul-wrenching space of time, Kyle broke the kiss and cradled Charmayne's head into the curve of his chest and neck.

Again Charmayne's cheek was snug against the dark material of his jacket, only this time the beating of their hearts was marking the height of their arousal with near syncopation. She could hear both her own and Kyle's thundering in their chests.

Drawing a trembling breath, Charmayne brought her arms down to wrap them about his waist beneath his jacket. She loved the feel of his warm skin beneath his shirt and the hard muscles she found there.

Kyle dropped his chin to the top of her head and held her close, wanting to do much, much more than they had, and yet knowing that now was not the place or time.

After some moments passed and the quickened pace of their heartbeats became somewhat more subdued, Charmayne pushed away and tilted her head back to look at him. The lines she had seen earlier were still there, but some of his haggard look had disappeared.

Holding her chin between his forefinger and thumb, Kyle dipped his head once more and placed a short sweet kiss on her parted lips.

"I've needed that for days," he murmured softly, his lips crooking into a smile.

Charmayne's eyes were warm with her love. "As I said before, I haven't been away."

Kyle's smile disappeared for a moment, then came back. "I know. But in a way, I was."

Charmayne frowned slightly. "I don't understand."

Kyle released his hold on her and rocked back a short step, running his fingers through his hair. "It would take a lot to explain, and I'd rather forget about all of that right now." His eyes narrowed. "Can you be away from here long?"

Charmayne would have given almost anything she possessed to be able to answer in the affirmative. But with the way the day had gone, she was going to be lucky if she didn't get attacked at the table where they eventually chose to eat. One question seemed to breed many more. She had even heard from people who normally caused no ripples in her day, just went about being good, hardworking citizens. Only now, they had questions and suggestions about the celebration as well. Kearney might be having its one hundredth anniversary, but if it didn't hurry up and have it, Charmayne decided that she might not reach her twenty-seventh!

Kyle saw the regret she could not mask, and fighting down the disappointment he felt, he decided to make the best of the time they did have and said soothingly, "Well, never mind. How long do you think you can take?"

"A half hour, if I'm lucky."

"Things are that bad?"

She nodded grimly.

"Is it the Centennial?"

She nodded again.

"I've had a few calls myself, but not many."

Charmayne smiled wryly. "They probably don't

want to bother you. People are used to calling me, so they do."

"Hilda Morrow called me today. She says she thinks we need to have another meeting. Sort of a last-minute affair to be sure everything is ready."

"God," Charmayne half-prayed, half-wailed.

"I told her tonight was fine with me. How about you?"

Charmayne shrugged, but she was fast overcoming her first aversion to more work and was beginning to realize that if there was a meeting, she would therefore be with Kyle. The idea looked more promising as the passing seconds took shape.

"Sure. Why not? Since Saturday is the big day starting the big week."

Kyle nodded shortly, then became silent. Charmayne withdrew her purse from the lower drawer of her desk, all the while watching him as his attention drifted from what they had been speaking about. She knew he was thinking of something else as surely as if she had been privy to his private thoughts.

"What is it, Kyle?" she asked quietly, clutching her purse before her.

Kyle started. Her question had brought him back abruptly.

"Ummm? Oh. Oh, nothing."

"You're worried about something."

He pushed back his jacket and buried his fist in his pants pocket. "There's always something to worry about when you run a business, Charmayne."

An icy finger touched Charmayne's spine. His business! Were there more problems in his business? Had she really expected everything to disappear just

222

because her father had seemed a degree more accommodating, even if it was just bare toleration?

"Something has happened at Orion?"

Kyle took his hand out of his pocket and let his jacket fall loose again. He forced a smile. "Hey! I said I wanted to forget about all of that for a while! Anyway, it's nothing for you to worry about."

Yet, Kyle thought, her father worked at Orion. Right at this very minute he might be in danger!

Charmayne absorbed Kyle's words, but they did nothing to alleviate the concern she felt. Had something more happened? Was her father involved? Had the man she had overheard him hiring already arrived and started his job?

The cold hand of fear took possession of a part of her soul, but she didn't let it have access to all. A section was reserved for Kyle and herself. The love they shared would not be completely usurped.

The lunch that followed was short yet enjoyable, neither allowing themselves to be the object of the other's depression of spirit.

Only when Charmayne arrived back in the office did she at last flag, the smile disappearing from her lips, her eyes losing some of their shine.

For Kyle a return to his office was like reentering a tomb. In one way there was some security about doing so—at least it was still standing—and in another, he was on tenterhooks to know if and when the threat would be realized.

The meeting that night was a letdown for Charmayne. Kyle called at the last moment and told her that he would be unable to make it. Once again something had come up, he said. His voice was worried.

Charmayne accepted his apology for putting the brunt of the work on herself and the Morrows, but she assured him that everything looked as if it had been taken care of. The meeting tonight could only be a safeguard against any annoying little last-minute inconvenience.

Charmayne drove to the Morrows and again entered their house to find that, as she had suspected, Hilda had things firmly in command.

Kyle drew the blinds to his office window closed to shut away the darkness outside. Dak and Tony were seated in chairs waiting for the security agent to appear. It had been the agent who had called this unexpected meeting.

The three men sat together in silence, none wanting to voice the fears that had haunted each of their moves all week.

Finally, at the exact minute he had told them he would be there, the security man arrived. He tapped once on Kyle's door and waited for permission to enter.

His thin, pale face was exactly the same as Kyle remembered, and so was the dark intensity of his eyes.

Kyle motioned with his head toward the remaining empty seat.

The security agent took it and then looked from one man to the other before refastening his gaze on Kyle.

"Well?" Kyle asked at last, unable to refrain from questioning him any longer.

The man crossed his legs, one ankle coming to rest over the other knee.

"I've found something. It may be important, it may not."

Kyle spoke for each of his partners. "Let's hear it."

The security man took a deep breath, then said, "Some of the people of Kearney don't care very much for you, Mr. Richardson. It has something to do with your past."

Kyle nodded. This was not news to him.

"There's mainly one person, though, who might dislike you enough to want to harm you, and consequently your business, and who would also have access."

Kyle was silent, but Dak was not. "Who?" he asked quickly.

"A man by the name of Raymond Brennan."

A thick silence fell over the room as each man considered the name.

"No." Kyle was the first to speak.

The security agent's lips thinned. "I'm not mistaken. His name is Raymond Brennan."

"And I'm not mistaken, either," Kyle countered. "Raymond Brennan is not the kind of man who would do these things."

Kyle felt his partners' eyes swing from him to the agent and back to him. Kyle met their gazes steadily, each in turn.

The security man remained silent. It was no skin off his nose if they didn't believe him. He had done his job to the best of his ability.

Dak cleared his throat again before he spoke. "Raymond doesn't seem the sort—"

"He's not," Kyle cut in. "I guarantee it. I've known him for a long time."

The security agent inserted himself back into the conversation. "That's where the trouble stems from, I understand. The past. I've been told the man can't stand anyone named Richardson. Something to do with an uncle of yours."

Wisely he said no more.

Kyle knew a moment of frustration. Would he never be able to live down the reputation of his uncle? Then he shook himself free of the thought.

"I've known about this for a long time. You've come up with something, all right, but not the right something." He paused. "You've learned nothing else?"

"Nope. Just that about Brennan."

"Then keep at it. There's got to be more."

Dak and Tony exchanged glances. Finally Tony spoke. "Kyle, we'd like to speak with you . . . privately." He looked pointedly at the security agent, who got slowly to his feet. "But first," he asked the man, stopping him, "how much time do you think we have if this person does mean business?"

"Well," the slender agent answered, "in my business, no news doesn't necessarily mean good news. But then again, since he hasn't done anything yet, he might not be going to. Some people just like to imply that they'll cause trouble, just to make trouble."

"And you think that might be the case here?"

The man pursed his lips and slowly shook his head. "Nope. I didn't say that at all." Then he moved easily to the door and let himself outside.

It was only when the partners were once again alone that they realized what was so strange about the agent. He made no sound when he walked. It was as if he were floating on a cushion of air.

Dak gave an unsettled laugh. "God, he gives me the creeps! I'll be glad when he's gone."

Tony agreed. "A regular 007!"

Kyle leaned back in his chair and privately agreed with them. He would be glad when the little man left, but now it would be for more than one reason. He didn't want Charmayne's father involved in this. *He* knew Raymond couldn't possibly be the person responsible for the damage and the threat, but how could he convince the others?

"All right. Out with it," he directed Tony.

Tony folded his blunt-cut fingers and stared down at them contemplatively before speaking. "This is a bit of a ticklish subject, Kyle. But I feel I have to say something. Dak agrees."

"Yes?" A knot of tension tightened in Kyle's stomach. He had an idea what his friends were going to say and he didn't want to hear it from them.

"It's about Raymond Brennan."

"What about him?"

The other two men exchanged another glance and Dak took up the cause. "Or more exactly, his daughter."

Kyle let out an expressive breath of air.

"All right. What about her?"

"Kearney is a small town, Kyle. We know about you and Charmayne Brennan. Everyone does."

"So?"

Dak hesitated, then forged on. "So, we're wondering if you're letting what you feel for the daughter affect the way you feel about the father. The man we

227

hired to find out who's causing our problems thinks it's Raymond Brennan. Why can't you accept that?"

Kyle's teeth clamped together and he held himself firmly under control. What his friend was suggesting was dangerously close to treason.

"Charmayne has nothing to do with this. Neither does her father. Yes, he dislikes me. He probably always will. He's stubborn that way. But I tell you, the man is not the type to take his revenge like a coward. He wouldn't hide behind an anonymous note and petty little pranks. He would do it the way he considers is a man's way: he'd come over and beat the holy shit out of me."

Dak gave a tight smile. What Kyle was saying was his impression of Raymond as well.

Tony looked unconvinced but said nothing. If Kyle felt that strongly, possibly he was right. He had trusted Kyle enough to follow him from his job in Dallas to become a partner in the firm. And so far things had worked out . . . if only they could straighten out this "little" problem. Tony swallowed and remained quiet.

Kyle spoke again. "None of what we've discussed this evening is to get out of this room. I don't think I have to remind you that we're talking about a man's reputation, here."

"Of course," Tony agreed.

"Right." Dak nodded.

Some of the tension in Kyle's shoulders and neck relaxed. He knew he could trust their word.

The two men shuffled out of the room after calling a subdued good-bye. There was still a problem. Nothing had been solved.

Kyle ran a distracted hand through his hair, disturbing the loose brown curls. He had been doing that a lot lately; he would probably end up bald if he didn't watch out. Did pulling on hair hasten its loss?

He gave a hollow laugh that exactly matched the hollowness of his eyes.

CHAPTER THIRTEEN

Friday seemed to fly by for Charmayne and everyone else in the mayor's office. Mayor Cliburn had each of them listen to the speech he was going to present at the opening ceremonies the following day, and he wanted each of them to give input as to how it sounded. Of course, he didn't want to hear anything derogatory, but luckily the speech was good enough that no one had to hedge.

Hilda and Willie Morrow were in town all day, and so, it seemed, was half the countryside. From the high school football field the band could be heard practicing a final time for its duties as chief music maker at the parade and all events requiring music thereafter, while the banging and clanking of last-minute construction of fair booths blended in. Very little day-to-day work was accomplished.

Saturday started out as every new day should: the sunrise was a spectacular display of clear sky and bright beginnings. Not a single cloud was on the horizon and several hundred souls breathed a united sigh of relief.

Charmayne was up and moving early that morning. Hilda had requested her appearance in town at seven o'clock and she was there with time to spare. So were a number of her fellow workers. Tension and excitement only gained momentum as the minutes ticked by and more and more people began to arrive —some familiar and others strangers, the first guard of the many visitors they hoped would arrive that weekend.

Kearney's Centennial was more than just a celebration by the town of its incorporation. It was hoped a gathering of this sort would give a much-needed boost to the merchants of the area. If every visitor who came spent a few dollars in town, the event would be a success and everyone would be happy: the visitor because he had gained pleasure from coming, the merchant because of the exchange of business, and ultimately the town because its economy would prosper.

Primarily, though, Charmayne hoped for the celebration's success because of the amount of work that had been done. So many people had given so many hours. . . .

All during the last-minute preparations for the parade: assisting in seeing that the mayor was mounted properly on the horse he was to ride, that the visiting dignitaries—the governer's representative, the locally elected official to Texas House—and the town's judge and the town's police chief, were each in line and their cars in proper order, Charmayne kept a partial eye out for Kyle. But when she failed to see him, she became so involved with what she was doing that she eventually had little time to look.

Finally the parade got under way with the band in the lead, and Charmayne could relax a degree. But Hilda soon found something else to call to her attention and she was quickly involved in another project.

That was the way her time was spent during the next few hours, lending a helping hand in first one area and then another.

It was well after noon before she received her first break. And still she had not seen anything of Kyle.

Charmayne sank into the chair behind her desk and gave a long exhausted sigh. This was the only place she could think of to rest. The town was flooded with people, the nearby fairgrounds was packed, every available space seemed to be taken up by someone. Her office was her only escape.

She unfolded the crisp tissue from around the hot dog she had purchased for lunch and took her first bite of food for the day. The aroma and the taste made her stomach snarl with hunger.

A short time later, having devoured the entire sandwich along with the salty contents of a bag of potato chips and a heavily iced soft drink in a paper cup, she crumpled the tissue into a ball and deposited it in the nearby trash can. She was finished with her meal . . . still she did not hurry. She knew the moment she stepped back outside, Hilda would be sure to find her and she would be immediately caught up once again in the behind-the-scenes action.

Determinedly she retained her seat, putting the cup to her lips and shaking it slightly so that several pieces of chipped ice fell into her mouth. The coolness on her tongue was wonderful. She moved it from place to place, sucking on the melting liquid.

Yet while she enjoyed the refreshing sensation, her mind did not remain on the pleasant experience for long. As they had been wont to do with ever increasing frequency over past days, her thoughts moved to Kyle. Where was he? What was he doing? Why hadn't he been with them this morning when he knew his presence would be needed? The only excuse she could think of was that his reason again concerned Orion Enterprises.

The cup Charmayne was holding poised in the air slowly settled onto the top of her desk blotter as an overwhelming feeling of guilt rushed over her. She should have talked with her father by now. She should have confronted him. If she suspected him, no matter how unwillingly and with little proof beyond a strong fear, of being the person responsible for the acts of sabotage at Orion, she should have spoken with him. She should at least have warned him. She knew that Kyle was hiring a security agent to check into the matter. She had been present when he had done so. But she had not. She had used the excuse to herself that she wasn't ready yet to confront him; she couldn't find the words. Was it that? Or was it that she was torn? How did she choose between the father she loved and the man she loved? No matter what her decision, she would be hurt. As a result she had taken the path of least resistance and tried to pretend that there was no problem.

Charmayne thought of her father as she had last seen him. Of how, even though a short time before he had seemed at least mildly enthusiastic about volunteering his services on a committee, yesterday and the day before he had been more distracted than was his usual condition of late. His temper had been short and he had snapped at her when she mentioned anything about the upcoming events of the weekend. Then she thought of Kyle and her heart twisted. If her father was discovered as the culprit—she experienced even more guilt at thinking that—how was Kyle going to react? Would he expect that she should have confided in him, told him her fears?

Charmayne pushed to her feet with a sudden motion, feeling as if her world, a world that over the past few weeks had been slipping quietly out of her control, was at last about to complete its final thrust. Events were happening, or were about to happen, that she could do little to affect if she merely continued to wait for them to come about. She knew this in the deepest recesses of her soul and the idea frightened her.

With a muffled cry of protest she hurried away from what had once been the sanctuary of her office and returned to the streets outside. Yet she didn't go back toward the fairgrounds or the rodeo arena. She had to get away. She had to find either her father or Kyle.

Kyle was embroiled in an increasing tension-filled frustration as well. Late last night he had received a call from the security agent, who reported a conversation he had overheard between two workers. The men had thought they were alone, but the agent was there, well hidden.

They had been talking about something that was to happen this weekend at Orion. One of them had been Raymond Brennan.

Kyle wouldn't believe it! He couldn't believe it. Not Raymond Brennan. He wouldn't suspect him of wrongdoing even if he had not been Charmayne's father. The man had too much integrity, too much pride!

But the agent seated before him now was coldly impersonal. A man's vouched-for personality made no difference to him if he was a suspect.

234

"Who was the other man?" Kyle asked, hoping to be able to lay blame elsewhere.

"James Drayton."

Kyle frowned. James Drayton was a relatively new addition to the work force. He had been with Orion only since Kyle's own return to Kearney.

"Have you checked him out?"

The agent nodded. "As far as I can tell, he's clean. He has no reason to want to harm you or your business."

"But he was talking with Raymond Brennan. . . ."

"Brennan was asking him about dynamite."

"They were probably talking about using it on their land. The farmers and ranchers do that occasionally around here, you know, to remove tree stumps."

"I don't think it's stumps Brennan has in mind."

"What makes you say that?"

"He said something about bringing the place down."

Place down . . . Orion? Kyle cleared his throat and leaned forward, folding his fingers together on the top of his desk, trying to keep himself calm.

"What more did you hear?"

"Wasn't that enough?"

"No, I still say they might have been discussing something else. That's not enough evidence to ruin a man's life."

"It's your building."

The grim reminder wasn't needed. "I know that." Kyle repeated, "Did you hear anything else?"

For the first time the security man shifted uncomfortably in his chair. "No, there was a noise and they moved away."

"A noise?"

"I almost sneezed. It was dusty where I was."

So the man was human after all! Kyle's fingers loosened a moment and then reclamped together.

"So what do we do, just in case?" He had to be a realist about this.

"There are a lot of people in town this weekend, but most of them will be at the fairgrounds. And since it is the weekend, no one will be here. I say we wait and watch. I'd feel better about this if I had some kind of backup, though."

If, against his judgment, Raymond was involved, Kyle definitely didn't want his name given to the police. He had Charmayne to think about.

"No. I still don't want to call in anyone else."

The agent kept his eyes narrowed on Kyle. "Then if we continue to handle it ourselves, I'll need a little help. The building should be watched day and night."

"My partners and I will help."

The man nodded. "I think we should get out of here now . . . let this look like it's any other Saturday."

"Yes." Kyle stood away from his desk. "I'll take first watch with you. Just let me make a call to Dak and then we'll leave."

Again the man inclined his head.

Kyle made the call, arranging with Dak to notify Tony, and then set up the time they would meet.

When he left the office, he took one last look around. Would it still look the same on Monday?

Would it even be here then? He felt as if he was leaving a friend to an unknown fate.

Raymond Brennan was troubled. He didn't know if he had done the right thing. Maybe he should have told someone, warned them. He didn't like Richardson, but more was involved here than just Richardson. And he had the added complication of Charmayne's feelings for the man.

Raymond left the farm and drove into town. He had to see Drayton, talk with him again. Maybe do more than talk if he wouldn't listen to reason.

By late afternoon Charmayne was becoming frantic. How could people just disappear? Kyle was nowhere to be found. She had checked his home; his car was gone. She had even gone to Orion to see if he was there, but he wasn't. The building was locked and no one was about. Then she had driven back to her home. No one was there, either. She knew her mother was planning to come into town later with a friend, but her father had made no mention of leaving after he finished his morning's chores. Thinking that she would find them somewhere at the fair, she drove back into town. Only her mother could be found, and she didn't know where Raymond might be.

Charmayne wanted to scream. The intuition that something was on the verge of happening had grown as the hours of the day passed by.

Raymond pushed his way through the crowds gathered around the various attractions. He moved past the booths and children's games without really

237

seeing them. He was searching for one man. He had been told that he was somewhere on the grounds.

Kyle waited in the position where the agent had suggested that he stay. He was beginning to get a little bored. If detective work involved so much staying in one place waiting for something to happen, he was glad he had changed his mind when he was ten years old. Then he had wanted to be a policeman. Now he much preferred being what he was. Maybe the job wasn't as glamorous sounding, but it was definitely more interesting.

So far the only break in the monotony of his wait had been when Charmayne drove up to the building and tested the front doors. He had watched as she walked along the side of the building toward the rear. Not realizing that he was holding his breath, he waited for her to reappear. With some relief he saw her immediate return. She was looking for him, he knew that. And he wanted to go to her. But he couldn't. He had to stay where he was. When Dak relieved him in a few hours, he could put in his first appearance at the fair that day. He wasn't sure how Charmayne or Hilda and Willie would receive him— he had certainly shirked his duties of opening day— but he would just have to suffer their disapproval. God knew he was good enough at doing that. He had had a lot of practice.

As the afternoon sun began to slide lower in the western sky, the fair was still going strong. But as time drew nearer for the rodeo to begin, a number of the throng of people started to migrate toward the arena to find their seats.

Charmayne stood outside the arena gates and looked from one face to another. She was supposed to be making sure that the ticket office's supply of change for large-currency bills met the demand—Hilda had at last found her—but instead she was checking the crowd for her father and Kyle. She didn't understand their continued absence.

Then, as a reward, she saw her father. He was walking with a group of people who were approaching the area where she stood, yet he was not really with them. He, like herself, was looking for someone.

"Dad!" she called, raising her voice to be heard over the noise of the people. She stood on tiptoe and waved.

Raymond didn't seem to hear her. He stopped, gave one last look around, and then started to turn away.

Charmayne dropped all pretense of checking with the ticket sales counter. She placed the empty cigar box she had been carrying on a nearby cement block and hurried after her father.

"Dad!" she called again, "wait!"

This time Raymond heard her. His large body stiffened and he looked around as he came to a stop.

"Charmayne . . ." He seemed to be coming out of a dream. A distracted frown furrowed his brow.

Charmayne gazed up into her father's pale blue eyes. Almost the entire day she had been searching for him, and now that she had found him, she was determined that she wasn't going to let him get away without speaking to him.

"I have to talk with you," she said hurriedly.

"What is it? What's wrong? Is it your mother?" His hands came out to grip her arm. Charmayne saw the worried look he couldn't prevent from showing in his eyes and knew a moment's relief that he still cared. If nothing else, she didn't have to worry about her parents' loss of feeling for each other. Her father still loved her mother, and she knew her mother was still very much in love with him. Whatever differences they had could be worked out.

"No . . . Mom's fine. I saw her just a little while ago. She's over at the quilting booth." She took a breath. "I have to talk with you about something else. Something important."

Raymond's hands lightened their grip on his daughter's arms. For a moment he thought his soul had been pierced.

His voice was husky when he answered, "I can't now, honey. I have to find someone."

"But, Dad, I—"

Raymond didn't let her finish. "I said, I can't now, Charmayne. Listen to me."

Charmayne stood her ground. "No, you listen to me! I know something is wrong. And I think I know what it is! I know you hate Kyle . . . but, Dad, you can't continue to do what you've been doing!"

At first he almost asked what she was going on about. Then gradually the meaning of her words penetrated his consciousness. She thought that he was the one responsible for all the mischief that had been happening at Orion. If the fact hadn't hurt so much, he would have laughed. It was so ironic!

The pain reflected in his eyes made Charmayne bite her bottom lip. Had she made a mistake?

"I don't have time for this now, Charmayne." His voice had become that of an old man tired to death of living. She had wounded him in a way that few others could. "We'll talk about it later." That she thought him capable of doing someone harm!

Charmayne swallowed tightly and her eyes began to swim with tears. "Dad, I—"

"Not now," he cut in, recovering himself. "I have to find someone."

"Let me help!" Suddenly she wasn't sure of anything anymore. She just knew that she had to make amends. How could she have been so foolish as to suspect her father?

"No. You stay here. And don't leave these grounds. Find your mother . . . stay with her. Promise me."

A sliver of jagged fear went through Charmayne, leaving in its wake a certain numbness. She had been correct in her premonition of trouble. "Dad, what is it?"

Raymond didn't answer. He merely dropped her arms and walked away.

Charmayne stared after him, wanting to call him back, wanting to follow, wanting to warn him not to step in what might be harm's way.

Kyle went to the fairgrounds after he was relieved of duty outside Orion. He wanted to find Charmayne. He needed to be with her. He needed her softness, her touch. But, as she and Raymond had found earlier, it was difficult to find someone in this crowd, especially when the stands at the rodeo arena were packed with people.

His eyes went over the sea of faces. As far as he could tell, she wasn't here. Possibly she was at home. He sought out Hilda. She was beneath the stands in a small back room usually reserved for storage but which had been cleared out for use as a temporary fair office. She had not seen Charmayne for at least an hour, she told him. She was too busy to question him about his absence and he ducked out of the room before she was able to take a break.

Outside, a warm evening breeze tickled the back of his neck. Reflexively he ran a hand over his hair. If she was at home, he wouldn't bother her. His need of her was great, but how could he go to her home even partway suspecting her father of wanting to do him harm? No, it was impossible. Until this was cleared up, it would be best if they remained apart.

Kyle decided to go to his own home and get some rest. He had to be up early to relieve Dak. Tomorrow was going to be another long day.

Tony Campo ran a weary hand over his face, concentrating the massage on the area around his eyes. He was exhausted. He had gotten little sleep the night before; his two-year-old daughter had been suffering with a high fever that wouldn't seem to break. He and his wife had stayed up all night with her until finally, just before the morning light began to turn a section of the night sky a pale pink, the fever peaked and started to recede. Still they found little rest because their youngest, at six months, started to come down with the same illness as their first child and she became increasingly fretful. He had managed to catch a few minutes of sleep during the day, exchanging an hour or so with his wife, but that had not been enough. He had counted on making up some of his lost sleep tonight. But here he was, standing guard outside Orion.

Tony shifted position, trying to straighten his

cramped legs. It was hard forcing a six-foot frame into such a small area, but the security agent had been adamant that he be well hidden.

Lisa had not been exactly pleased to have him absent from home tonight. She was just as tired as he and now had the responsibility of the children all to herself. But at least the baby had been sleeping peacefully when he left. He only hoped she stayed that way, or else Lisa was going to have his hide for breakfast when he returned.

Tony grimaced and laid his head back against a metal support. His eyes felt as if sandpaper had been installed on the inside of his eyelids. They ached each time he blinked.

He forced them open. He was supposed to watch the rear of the building. A light in the parking area before him switched on just as it always did at dusk for security's sake. He looked at his watch. Eight o'clock. God, it felt as if it should be midnight!

His eyelids wavered shut, but he instantly opened them again. No. He couldn't go to sleep. He had to make himself stay awake. It was important.

Charmayne didn't know what to do. Her father had been gone for a half hour and during that time she had done nothing but worry. What was he doing? Why was it so important to him that she stay on the fairgrounds? Was there danger if she didn't?

She thought of Kyle. Where was he? Could he be the one in danger?

A shaft of near physical pain shot through Charmayne's body. Once, a long time before, she had wished Kyle ill. She had wished he had never returned. It had been an unworthy thought, one that did little to enrich her character. But she had been so upset with him, so confused. Once thought, though, it could not be erased and she burned with shame now at the memory. She hadn't meant it. She hadn't! She loved Kyle. She didn't think she could stand living if anything bad were to happen to him.

She could remain still no longer; the rodeo held no appeal. She hurried away from the edge of the arena and made her way to her car.

She would find Kyle if it was the last thing she did that day.

Raymond was afraid he would be too late. He knew Drayton wanted the explosion to be timed perfectly so that it would get the utmost attention. And the darkness, combined with the crowd in the rodeo arena and fairgrounds, was perfect for his purpose.

Raymond moved stealthily across the back parking area of Orion. He knew Drayton would come this way as well. If he wasn't here yet, he would wait. He had to stop him.

It took Charmayne some time to squeeze her car out of its parking spot. A number of people had double-parked and she had to use the best of her driving ability to gain escape.

Her hands gripped the steering wheel, worry about Kyle and her father uppermost in her mind. She wanted neither of them to be hurt.

She would drive to Kyle's house once again. Surely, this time, he would be there.

Kyle awakened with a start from the dream he'd been having. He sat up in bed, his breathing heavy, his heart thumping strongly, his mind alert. Had he heard a sound?

He listened with greatly sensitized hearing, but there was nothing.

Still, he had a feeling of unease.

He threw the sheet away from his legs and reclaimed his slacks from the chair next to the bed where he had left them a few hours before.

Then he pulled on a shirt and fastened it as he traveled the few steps into the bathroom.

He knew he was probably being overly cautious. Dak and Tony were watching the building. But he felt as if he should be there. He didn't know why, he just did.

Raymond found the door unlocked. He frowned. That meant Drayton was already here. In a way he should be grateful; but the fact worried him. That meant he was definitely going to go through with his plan.

Raymond stepped forward and slipped into the lower hall. Where would he be? Where would he think it would be to his best advantage to set the explosive?

He moved along the passageway toward the assembly area. That was the logical place. Dynamiting a broom closet would do his cause little good. Drayton wanted Orion to be put out of business . . . at least for a time.

Raymond hurried his steps.

Tony jumped out of sleep, startled by he knew not what. His first question to himself was "Where the hell am I?"; then he shook his head vigorously, trying to clear it of the fog that kept him from thinking.

When he had gained a measure of success, he was furious with himself for having fallen asleep. Kyle and Dak had trusted him. He had known it was going to be difficult when he agreed to stand watch, so there was no excuse for what he had done.

He peered intently at the parking area. Everything looked the same. No one was about. He continued his careful surveillance for some time before satisfying himself that his lapse had done no harm.

Then he resettled his position and once again took up his wait. This time he would not go to sleep. He vowed this with positive determination.

Raymond moved through the darkened hall, knowing the building's setup without requiring light. He gained the assembly area and paused. He could see the subdued beam of a small flashlight. Drayton was there. He was right.

Taking a deep breath, he moved into the large room.

The man a short distance away from him jumped and swung around at the evidence of intrusion. The flashlight beam arced upward and caught Raymond directly in his face.

Raymond blinked at the blinding rays. The man studied him for a moment, then some of his fear lessened and he lowered the beam.

"Brennan! You scared the living hell out of me!"

Raymond forced himself to be calm. His heart was beating heavily in his chest and all the moisture in his mouth had dried, but he held on to his determination.

246

"Drayton, I don't think you should do this."

The younger man positioned the flashlight onto a work station. The reflecting light showed his tight features.

"If you've come to preach to me again, Brennan, you can forget it. I'm doing what I have to do."

"But you're wrong! You're not going to hurt just Orion. You're going to hurt the people of Kearney, too!"

"You said that before." The slits of his eyes narrowed even more. "Just why are you trying to protect Richardson? I didn't think there was any love lost between you two."

"There's not," Raymond confirmed as he took a step forward. "I'm not trying to help him. It's all the jobs that will be lost if you do this." He stopped speaking for a moment as he came nearer. "I'll level with you, Drayton," he began again. "I need this job. If I didn't have it, I would go under."

The man shrugged and withdrew a slender stick with a long fuse attached from a bag beside the flashlight.

Raymond's stomach contracted, yet he continued, "So would a lot of the people here—your friends, even people in your own family."

"So?"

"So why don't you put that away?" He motioned to the stick of dynamite. "Come with me . . . we'll have a beer . . . talk a little. . . ."

"I'm all talked out."

He searched in his pocket for his lighter.

Raymond followed his movement with his eyes. His blood slowly froze.

247

He took another quick step forward and reached out. The man evaded his grasp.

"Don't do it, Brennan. Don't try to stop me," he warned.

Raymond didn't listen. He lunged forward again, but he was too late to stop the contact of flame and fuse. A sizzling sound seemed to fill the building with its forecast of what was to come.

James Drayton held the explosive away from Raymond's straining reach and then flipped it into a corner of the room.

"We have about a minute and a half to get out of here, Brennan. What's done is done. You can't change it now."

Raymond looked from the heated glow of misguided intent in the man's eyes to the section of the room where the charge was lying. If he could get to it, he could tear the fuse away.

"I wouldn't try to be a hero if I were you," the man advised.

A look of aversion passed across Raymond's strong features. Over the past weeks he hadn't thought very much of himself. He felt as if his entire life had been a failure. He had let down his children, his wife. . . . They had trusted him to care for them and to keep the heritage that had been in his family for so long. And he was barely able to do it. He wasn't very much of a man. But now, here, was an opportunity to redeem himself.

His blue eyes hardened as his jaw jutted stubbornly. "I'm not you, Drayton. And you're not me."

He started to brush past the staring man, but a hand shot out to stop him.

"Don't be crazy, Brennan. I don't want you to be hurt."

"I won't be hurt."

Seconds were ticking away and perspiration began to bead on the man's forehead. He was becoming frightened of the time. It wouldn't be much longer.

"Come on, Brennan. We've got to get out of here!"

For an answer Raymond jerked on his arm. But the man's hold was surprisingly strong.

"I said come on!" the man yelled. He gave Raymond a tug and his age as well as his physical condition gave him the upper hand. Against his will Raymond felt himself being pulled backward.

Drayton started to run as best he could, dragging the older man behind him. They were almost to the door before Raymond summoned enough strength to break away. Without really thinking, he turned back to the large room. James Drayton did not try to stop him again. He was now consumed with merely one goal, his own survival. He threw the door back and dove outside.

Raymond did not take a full step before it seemed as if all the gates of hell were opened in front of him. There was a flash—he never heard any sound—and debris started to fly through the air.

Before his brain had truly taken in what had happened, something hit him full force and he was knocked flat to the floor. After that there was nothing but darkness.

CHAPTER FOURTEEN

Charmayne both saw and heard the explosion. She had just passed the entrance to Orion Enterprises when the terrible sound buffeted her car. At almost the same instant she gave an involuntary cry. It had happened! What she had feared had come to be! With her entire body trembling she rammed her car into reverse, then directed it down the entryway and into the parking area.

A man ran past her, away from the building. Another pounded after him. Yet another was running toward her. Charmayne felt her companions of the night more than she consciously saw them. She was aware of only one thing: she had to get inside the building. She had to see if anyone was hurt. She had to find out!

The force of the blast had blown the heavy door shut and what must have been debris within made opening it difficult. Charmayne pushed against it, her fingers clawing at the wood, a primal sound of desperation coming from her throat. Soon another pair of hands was giving her aid. Then a strong shoulder was pushing as well.

Charmayne spared a glance at the man beside her. She had seen him before. He was one of the men who had brought Orion to Kearney before Kyle made his appearance.

The door finally gave, and with added pressure it opened enough to let them inside.

An acrid smell mixed with dust and smoke greeted their nostrils. The explosion had started a fire. The man pushed in before her, rushing toward a chemical extinguisher that was positioned on one wall. Acting quickly he moved to direct its spray onto the flames.

Charmayne surveyed the scene before her with widened eyes. This was the first time she had been in this building. She saw that she was in a hall and that the greater destruction was in a room farther away, where the main part of the fire was located. But, with the lone light of the parking lot shining in through the opened door, she could also see that this area had not escaped unharmed. Rubble was everywhere. Her gaze moved over the floor while her mind tried to deal with what had happened, with what she should do next. She wanted to find Kyle, but suddenly she seemed unable to make herself move. . . .

Then her eyes fastened onto a long form partially buried beneath a mound of rubble. Kyle? Oh, dear God, Kyle?

Moving like a frozen image of herself, Charmayne inched forward until she was standing above the unconscious form. Slowly she bent down and began to remove pieces of wood and dry wall. Her soul was screaming for her to hurry, but she couldn't move any faster. As if in slow motion, her muscles obeyed the frantic directives of her brain.

A roaring was sounding in her ears and her heart was beating at double its normal rate when she was at last able to identify the person at her side. The light wasn't perfect, but she didn't need more to see that this man was not Kyle. Instead, he was her father.

Instinctively, Charmayne reached out and brushed a bit of dry wall away from his cheek, her mind numb.

From somewhere deep inside herself she was aware of all that was going on around her. She knew when the man who had helped her open the door came back to stand at her side, panting from his efforts. She was aware of a faraway shout and the racing of a car's engine followed by a screech of brakes. Soon there was a hard thumping of shoes against concrete. Then she was aware of the arrival of a man in the doorway. He seemed suspended there, unmoving.

His very stillness caused her to raise her face. Her eyes ran over his silhouette. She knew him.

Slowly she returned her attention to her father and bent down over him, protecting him, loving him . . . loving both of them.

She thought her heart was going to burst.

Kyle stared at the chaos before him, at the fallen figure, at the girl by his side. Then, giving his head a determined shake, he forced himself into action. He met Tony's tormented gaze as he went down on one knee beside Charmayne.

"I must have dozed off, Kyle. God, I'm sorry." Tony was crushed.

Kyle merely grunted. How the situation had occurred wasn't important to him now.

"See if the phones still work. We need a doctor. Keep calling until you get through to him. He's probably at the fairgrounds."

Tony seemed glad to have something to do. He hurried away.

Kyle's fingers closed about Charmayne's arms. She straightened easily, as if no longer master of her own physical actions. Her neck was bent, her red hair making a curtain over her features.

Kyle couldn't help himself; he moved a section of soft hair away from her face and leaned forward to brush her lips with his. She didn't respond. He might have been kissing a living statue.

He steadied her, then turned his concern to her father. He felt for a pulse and experienced relief when he found evidence of the surge of Raymond's strong heart.

He was just sitting back on his heel when Dak moved into the doorway, pushing a man before him. Using a primitive form of coercion, he had the man's right arm bent high up on his back, forcing his fingers past his shoulder blades.

"Kyle! You're here!" Dak exclaimed.

Tony moved back into the room at the same instant. "The doctor's on his way." He paused to flick a switch. If the telephone worked, maybe some of the electrical wiring survived as well. No illumination answered his speculation. He dug into his pocket for his flashlight. In the excitement he had forgotten that he had one. He aimed it at the ceiling, giving the room a faint source of light beside that streaming in from outside.

Kyle regained his full height and looked across at the man Dak was holding. His questioning frown moved to his partner.

Dak's eyes held more than a glimmer of triumph. "I caught him running away from the building just after the blast."

Kyle's gaze swung back to the man. James Drayton. He spoke softly, yet with a thread of steel to his words.

"Tony, I think you need to make another telephone call. This time to the police chief's office. They may already be on their way, but just in case . . ."

The rest of the sentence hung in the air among the occupants of the room.

Beads of perspiration stood out in stark relief on James Drayton's face. He was experiencing both fear and pain. At mention of the police he tried to jerk himself away, but the grip on his arm only increased and he cried out incoherently. Then, in an attempt to save himself, he followed a weak man's course.

"Brennan did it!" he accused, his voice high-pitched and squeaky. "It was his idea. He thought it up, bought the dynamite . . . he did it!" He paused for breath. "I tried to talk him out of it, but he wouldn't listen. He's had a grudge against you for years, Richardson. For years—"

Kyle's lips thinned. "Shut up, Drayton," he snapped.

"But he did!"

"I said shut up!"

Both Dak and Tony were unsurprised by Kyle's adamancy and the violence that was barely contained beneath it. Dak advised the man he was holding that for his own protection he'd better listen.

The sound of sirens cut into the silence of the night and soon the police chief's car along with Kearney's only ambulance came to a halt in the parking area at almost the same instant.

What followed was like a nightmare for Charmayne, and if she had not had the reassurance of

Kyle's continuing presence, she didn't know how she would have gotten through it.

The doctor's pronouncement that he thought the worst Raymond was suffering was a concussion but still wanted him transported to the hospital in the county seat; the police chief's questions; James Drayton's continued assertions of her father's guilt—all of it seemed too much for her to handle.

The worst had been facing her mother. Word of what had happened spread like wildfire among the people of the town and her mother heard the news before Charmayne had been able to break it to her gently.

They met at the hospital and fell into each other's arms. Kyle waited with them. Lynn and Bob arrived soon after.

When, in medical fact, it had been determined that Raymond's injury was a simple concussion and that he was expected to regain consciousness soon, the women had experienced some degree of relief. Yet still so much remained unanswered.

Her mother looked like a lost child to Charmayne. Her life had been so simple once. She had a husband, a farm, two children . . . misfortune had occurred, but it had always been financial, not personal. Now, life seemed to be crashing down upon her and she was having difficulty accepting it.

The ordeal at the hospital lasted throughout the night. Finally by morning her father came back to the world of the living, but the doctor didn't want him discussing the events of the night before and they were allowed to stay with him only a short time.

He would be released later that evening if everything went well during the day.

Kyle drove Charmayne and her mother home. It was a long, silent journey.

When they arrived at the farm, her mother went directly to bed.

Charmayne made coffee. She had existed on what the hospital called coffee all night. Now she needed the real thing and knew that Kyle did, too.

She kept herself busy getting their cups and spoons while the coffee perked. This was the first time she had been alone with Kyle since the explosion and she didn't know what to say.

Kyle sat at the kitchen table and observed her actions. He wanted to tell her not to worry, that he didn't believe Raymond was in any way responsible for what had happened, but he held his tongue. He was not going to bring it up unless she did. The night had been hard enough on her already. He saw the way her shoulders stooped with tiredness and the fine trembling of her hands.

When Kyle shifted in his chair, Charmayne was aware of it. She was aware of everything that he did, every breath that he took. She knew when he was happy, sad, distracted, worried . . . and he was definitely worried now. But he had a perfect right to be. Someone had tried to destroy his business and it looked as if her father had been a part of it.

It was funny, Charmayne thought ironically to herself. Now that something had actually happened and her father seemed to be involved, she didn't believe that he was guilty. All along she had been afraid that he was planning some form of revenge and now she knew her mistake. Her father wasn't like that. If he had a grudge, he would work it out in other ways. She had realized that at last the evening before when she had met him outside the rodeo arena.

James Drayton was lying. But then, that fact wasn't new. Everyone in town knew that he was the shame of his family. When confronted with the consequences of his actions in the past, he had always taken the easy way out. Only how was her father going to prove his innocence when he'd been found unconscious in the building? And what had he been doing in the building in the first place?

Charmayne could delay facing Kyle no longer. While the coffee still perked, she turned, her green eyes holding a clear determination.

"My father didn't do it, Kyle."

Kyle held her gaze. "I never thought that he did."

His answer surprised her. There was something more to it than simple agreement. "You suspected him?"

"My security agent did."

Charmayne's heart seemed to tighten. So she hadn't been the only one! "But you didn't believe him?"

Kyle shook his head.

"But why?" Charmayne's fingers tightened on the chair back before her. "I mean, even I . . ." Her voice trailed away as she realized what she was admitting.

His eyes narrowed. So that was what she had been worried about all along! "You suspected him?" he questioned softly.

Charmayne turned away, holding her crossed arms at the elbows. "No! Yes! Oh, Kyle, don't make me—"

Kyle scraped the chair back and gained his feet. He took the two steps that separated them. His hands gathered her slim shoulders into their possession and pulled her back against his chest. His mouth bent low to her ear.

"Hush . . . don't say any more. I understand."

Tears washed over her cheeks and she leaned her head back, turning the side of her face into the material of his shirt, needing the feel of his arms as they came out to enfold her.

"But I did!" she confessed. "I thought that he . . . Oh, Kyle. How could I? How could I think that about my own father?"

The question was a cry from deep within her. Kyle did not reply at first. He just tightened his hold. He knew that this was something she was going to have to work out for herself. He could mouth words, try to soothe her, but only she held the key to her own forgiveness.

After a time Charmayne began to wipe at the tears.

"I'm sorry," she apologized, her voice barely above a whisper.

Kyle's heart went out to the woman he held in his arms. If he hadn't come to love her before, he knew he would have now. She was everything he wanted in life. Loyal, valiant, loving . . .

"Charmayne . . ."

She turned in his arms, not wanting him to move away. The strength she drew from him was like none other she had ever received.

"Yes?" Still her voice was low.

"I want you to promise me something."

"What?"

"I want you to go to bed and go to sleep. Try to forget what's happened. I'm sure everything is going to clear itself up." If it didn't, it wasn't going to be because he hadn't worked like a fiend trying to make it so! He would accept nothing less than the truth; the truth, he knew, would acquit Raymond. "Trust me," he added. It was almost a plea.

Charmayne placed her hands over his heart. It felt so good to be close to him. She had been so afraid. It had been bad enough finding her father lying unconscious on Orion's floor, but when she had thought it was Kyle . . . Until then she had known that she loved him, but she hadn't realized just how much.

She tipped her chin and looked up at him, at the handsome face of the man she adored.

"I do," she said softly.

The sincerity of her answer was all that Kyle could ever ask. For so long he had been waiting for those words! Ever since the life of lies his uncle had forced on him, ever since his return to Kearney . . . his effort to fit back in . . . Now, to hear those highest words of acceptance from her lips was the sweetest gift he could ever receive! He let his eyes close as he savored the moment.

Through his mind passed images of a young Charmayne with her carrot-red pigtails flying as she ran along behind him, of the older version of herself as he had first seen her upon his return, of the fire that sparked at his every parry, of their first kiss, of his discovery of his love for her, of the softness and beauty of her skin and the responsiveness of her body. And now she was his totally! Kyle wondered if life had anything more wonderful to offer.

He was brought back to awareness by Charmayne's fingers resting along either side of his jaw as she pulled his face downward. She met his lips with a soft kiss.

"I love you, Kyle."

This was stated simply, as if the fact could not be disputed.

His gaze burned down at her, then he pushed himself away. If he stayed longer, he wouldn't want to leave. And there was too much he had to do that day.

Without a word he left her, but Charmayne did not feel alone. For the first time in her life she knew what it was to be complete.

Charmayne did as Kyle requested and found that she went to sleep instantly. She wasn't worried anymore. Sharing her fears, her guilt, and giving her trust worked like a sedative on her troubled mind.

She was awakened early in the afternoon by her mother, who wanted to go back to the hospital.

Margaret Brennan's green eyes were shadowed. She had not attained her daughter's peace of mind. Her sleep had been fitful. She didn't understand why her husband had been hurt . . . and in an explosion? It was hard for her to comprehend.

While Charmayne showered and dressed, Margaret went about the motions of preparing a light lunch. Several times she had to stop to wipe the tears from her eyes.

When her daughter came into the room, refreshed, she had to turn away because new moisture began to gather and threatened to embarrass her. She pretended an interest in a sprig of ivy rooting in water in a mason jar on the kitchen windowsill.

Charmayne's gaze went over her mother's plump form and compassion flooded through her. Once again it was time for her to be the stronger.

"I'll pour the coffee, Mom. Why don't you sit down?"

As if grateful for some direction, Margaret did as she was directed and stared down into her cup while it was being filled with liquid.

Charmayne took her usual seat opposite. She stirred sugar into her coffee, but her eyes never left her mother. She waited for her to speak. Finally she did.

Shaking her head, she murmured sadly, "I don't understand, Charmayne. I don't understand any of this. How did your father . . . ? Why did your father . . . ?" Her words broke off.

Charmayne's mind echoed with James Drayton's accusation. Her mother knew nothing of that and it would be better for her to remain in ignorance.

"I don't know, Mom."

"I haven't understood for a long time," Margaret went on to remark, more to herself than to her daughter.

Charmayne knew what her mother was thinking. She still thought there was another woman.

"You're wrong about that, Mom. You have been all along."

The assurance in Charmayne's voice caught Margaret's attention. She met her daughter's steady gaze and studied it for an extended moment.

"I am?"

Charmayne nodded. "Dad loves you. He would never want to hurt you."

"But something's been bothering him! I know it, Charmayne. I know him!"

"Yes. I've felt it, too. A person would have to be totally stupid not to. But I'm positive he's not seeing someone else. He as much as told me so."

Eager to believe, Margaret leaned forward, pushing her cup further before her. "What did he say?"

Charmayne shrugged. "It wasn't so much what he said, it was how he said it. I know he loves you . . . and no one else but you."

Margaret absorbed what she'd said, then proposed, "Love doesn't always enter into it."

Charmayne pushed her own coffee away and leaned forward as well. "When a man like my father gives his love, you can be sure he's not going to spoil it. Think about it, Mom. You said you know him. Think!"

The older pair of green eyes looked startled for a moment, then turned introspective.

Charmayne knew she had gotten through to her mother at last. She could almost see the working of Margaret's mind as it glided through the private sectors that belonged only to husband and wife.

Then her face reflected joy as she realized that what Charmayne had said was true. But that was soon replaced by a deep sadness as she admitted, "I doubted him, Charmayne. I can't make excuses. I'll just admit that I did. Do you think he'll ever forgive me?"

"I doubt that he even knows."

Tears glistened in the aging eyes. "Should I tell him?"

Charmayne gave a soft smile. "No, I don't think

you should. This is a perfect case of what he doesn't know not possibly being able to hurt him."

"But I was so cold to him!"

"He wasn't exactly a sweetheart himself."

"No, but—"

"Enough has happened to him already, Mom. He needs your support now. If it makes you feel any better, I had my moments of doubt, too. Only it wasn't about him seeing another woman."

"What was it?"

Charmayne sidestepped an accurate answer. "Something equally silly."

"You know you were wrong now, too?"

Charmayne nodded. "Yes."

There was silence in the room for several seconds, then Margaret decided, "We have a lot to be grateful for."

"Oh?"

"Because God spared him yesterday."

All the way to the hospital those words repeated constantly in Charmayne's brain. Things could have been so different. One wrong breath, one wrong step. Was that the way it was in every person's life? What if Kyle had given in to the pressure of disgrace in his past and not come back to Kearney? His life would have been easier. It wasn't hard to imagine that. He would be living in Dallas now, in all likelihood, and she would just be a fond memory.

Her father was awake when they entered his room. He was watching television, but there was no sound. Charmayne held back a little as her mother moved forward. Raymond transferred his blank gaze to his wife and for the first time in Charmayne's memory,

263

he let some of the emotions he was feeling come through. A haze of moisture covered his blue eyes and he made no apology. He reached out for Margaret and she hurried into his embrace. They held each other wordlessly, not needing verbal communication to speak to each other.

After a time Raymond noticed Charmayne's presence. He withdrew one arm from around his wife and extended it to his daughter.

Charmayne reacted just as her mother had. She moved to the opposite side of the bed and the three of them became clasped tightly together.

Raymond's voice was rough with unshed tears when he commented gruffly, "I guess a fellow needs something like this to happen every once in a while in his life."

Margaret sniffed and pushed away, raising a hand to straighten her mussed hair. Charmayne sat away as well.

"What are you talking about, Raymond Brennan?" her mother asked shakily.

"The shock of almost getting blown sky high. It makes a person take time to think."

When Charmayne saw that her mother was unable to ask the required question, she provided it. "What about?"

"About everything. His life, the people he loves. He begins to see that maybe what he thought was important isn't so important." He took hold of his wife's hand and held it between both of his. "I felt like I was a failure, Margaret. I felt like I had let you down. We started out our married life with the farm my parents had left me and a lot of hope. And after thirty years, what do we have to show? A much smaller place and enough debt to make a man a little crazy."

"Raymond, no—"

"Let me finish," her father said. "I thought I was feeling sorry for you, for what I couldn't give you. But, after this, I can see that I was only feeling sorry for myself."

Charmayne remained still. She knew that her parents had forgotten she was in the room.

"I can't change that, Maggie. But I can change the future. If you want to keep sharing your life with me, that is . . ."

Margaret's eyes began to glow with the power of her love and magically the years seemed to fade away. She was looking at Raymond as she had when they first spoke of their love.

"Oh, Raymond. You know I do. I love you so. . . ." She went back into her husband's arms, back into the position that had been carved for her so many years before that only she would ever occupy.

Charmayne crept quietly from the room. Her throat was tight, she had to strain to see, and there was a warm feeling throughout her body.

A short time later the doctor gave Raymond a final examination and dismissed him from the hospital, saying it was miracle his eardrums hadn't been damaged by the sound of the explosion. There were no complications from his concussion and apart from a lingering headache, he should suffer no ill effects.

Raymond would not hear of going home immediately, though. He insisted on returning to the scene of the explosion. Margaret made a mild protest, but he squeezed her shoulder and told her it was something he had to do.

Orion Enterprises this day seemed no different, at first glance, than on any other. The building still looked the same externally and there were cars in the parking area. The only difference was that this was a Sunday, which meant that under normal conditions, the parking area would be empty.

Charmayne drew her Toyota into a striped slot and cut the engine. She turned to look at her father.

"Are you sure, Dad?" This was the first time she had given any sign of questioning his decision.

"I'm sure," was the steady reply.

"Would you like me to take Mom home and then come back for you?"

Before her father could answer, her mother spoke for herself.

"No. I'm staying with you." She met her husband's gaze steadfastly. Margaret had no idea what was taking place. But she knew that she had been in the dark about a number of events over the past few weeks, and she was darned if she was going to let the situation continue. If the matter affected Raymond, it affected her. She wasn't going to let him continue carrying burdens without her help.

Raymond's eyes began to twinkle at the evidence of his wife's new sense of determination. Was he now watching the beginning evolution of his own home-grown feminist? Somehow the idea did not frighten him as it once might have. He was glad to see Margaret start to assert herself more.

"Come on, then. Let's go." He gave a cursory look around the parking area. Kyle's car was there, along with the police chief's and a few others. "It looks as if everyone we need to see is already here."

Charmayne felt her mother stiffen as she saw the refuse that was in the process of being cleared from the hall. Then when they passed into the assembly room, she herself experienced a sickening jolt. This had been the site of the blast and the damage was much greater.

Her eyes were wide with shock when they transferred to a group of men—most of them familiar, one who was not—standing to one side. Her heart jumped when she met Kyle's gray gaze.

He separated himself from the group and came over to greet them.

He held out a hand for Raymond's grasp. "Glad to see you up and around so fast."

There was an infinitesimal pause before Raymond extended his own. He said nothing. He was puzzled by Richardson's friendly manner. All the evidence pointed to his having been associated with the explosion. He had been found unconscious in a building that he'd had no business being in on a weekend evening, and he knew a good case could be made that he either was responsible for or had assisted in the resulting destruction.

Kyle held his grip. Raymond's presence at this time only confirmed his previous conviction. And combined with the evidence that had been uncovered, he was sure that Chief Stapleton would agree. Neither man had believed James Drayton's story about Raymond's part in the conspiracy. And after some checks had been made, a different motive was beginning to emerge.

The Chief had disengaged himself as well and was

now approaching their small group. He, too, spoke of his satisfaction that Raymond had not been more seriously hurt. Then he said, "There are a few things I need to ask you, though. Think you're up to answering?"

Raymond gave a short nod.

The Chief turned to Kyle. "Think we can use your office?"

"Of course," Kyle agreed immediately.

The upstairs area was unhurt except for some broken glass and dislodged small articles. Any pictures that had been hung on the walls were now tilting at odd angles.

When they started on the short journey, the Chief had indicated that Charmayne and her mother should remain downstairs. Neither woman had heeded him. Margaret walked with Raymond, her arm curved reassuringly in his. And Charmayne was accompanied by Kyle. They weren't touching, but even a blind man could see that they were a pair. The Chief gracefully admitted defeat in the face of such obvious determination.

After politely gaining permission from Kyle to use his desk, the Chief assumed the position of authority and requested that the others find seats as well. Then he took off his Stetson and laid it on the desk. His fingers remained at the fold of the crown.

"Well, Raymond. I suppose what we need to do is hear your side of what happened. And just for your information, because you weren't in any condition to know last night, we caught James Drayton as he was running from the building."

Raymond took that news calmly. "What did he have to say?"

The Chief's fingers moved over the fold, a habit he had when he was slightly ill at ease.

"Now, you know I can't answer that. You just tell me your version."

Raymond sighed. Margaret slid her hand into his.

Charmayne held her breath as tension made the muscles in her body tighten. She knew her father was innocent, but would he be able to convince anyone else?

Then she felt Kyle's hand come to rest on her thigh and a flood of feelings washed through her: reassurance, gratitude, a release from fear. He had asked for her trust and she had given it to him. She wouldn't be drawn from trusting him again.

Eventually her father replied, and his answer caused shock waves to reverberate around the room.

"I'm just as guilty for what happened here as Drayton is."

Charmayne sensed Kyle's stiffening the same moment as red-hot needles of disbelief drove into her blood. What was her father saying?

The Chief was the least affected of any of them. He looked from Margaret's white face to Kyle's and Charmayne's frozen features. Then he transferred his gaze back to Raymond.

"Would you care to explain that statement?" His words seemed loud in the deathly silence of the room.

Raymond dropped his gaze. "Because I knew what he was planning and I didn't come forward."

There was a roaring in Charmayne's ears as giddy colors danced before her eyes. She had to take several deep breaths to gain recovery.

"Did you approve?"

"Hell, no!" Raymond's head snapped up and his blue eyes bored piercingly into the police chief's.

The Chief pushed his hat away and folded his fingers together.

"Did you try to stop him?"

"What do you think I was trying to do last night!"

"He says the entire affair was your idea."

"He's a bald-faced liar!"

A slow smile lifted the Chief's full lips. "I know."

Raymond sat forward a degree. "You do?"

The Chief nodded toward Kyle. "Thanks to Mr. Richardson, here. He did a little investigation of his own and came up with a few interesting facts. Like the fact that Drayton can be traced to the purchase of the dynamite—"

"I haven't used any for years!" Raymond interrupted.

The Chief went on. "And that Drayton's been talking to a few other people besides you. Namely his cousin, John Marshall."

At mention of that name Charmayne started. What did Mayor Cliburn's opponent at the next election have to do with this discussion?

"Oh, he didn't go so far as to tell them what he was planning like he did you. But he did keep grumbling about Orion. John Marshall even mentioned it, Raymond, to your new son-in-law. He was worried about James. Felt he was getting a little off center, if you know what I mean, and thought maybe the minister could help. Anyway, adding two plus two and coming up with the correct number, we think we have the whole story. We just needed confirmation from you."

Charmayne spoke for the first time. "But why

270

. . . ?" She was still trying to figure out why James Drayton wanted to harm Kyle.

The police chief looked at her, but Kyle answered. His voice was low and contained. "Because, in his mixed-up way, Drayton thought that if he could close down Orion, the loss of the business would embarrass Mayor Cliburn's administration. Show that he was unable to protect the town's newest and most profitable business. Then his cousin would win the next election. I think he also had plans for himself. He wanted to wheel and deal a little, get his finger into some of the local political pie."

"That doesn't sound crazy, that's criminal!" Charmayne cried.

"It's both." Chief Stapleton regained her attention as well as that of the others in the room. "And he's going to have to answer for it."

Raymond cleared his throat. "I still feel responsible for what happened here."

Kyle pushed to his feet and Raymond did as well. The two men faced each other.

"Forget it," Kyle advised. "The damage isn't as bad as it looks. Orion is insured. And nothing's going to drive us out of Kearney."

Raymond gazed across at the man who equaled him in height, the man he had disliked for so long. He still couldn't say that he liked him. Too many memories of the past still clung. But he couldn't say that he completely disliked him anymore, either.

Charmayne moved to Kyle's side and took his arm. Her eyes were pleading with her father. He met her look steadily, then gave a slight shrug.

Kyle extended his hand, and this time Raymond knew that it was more than a mere handshake. Long ago the Indians of America used to smoke peace pipes when they agreed to settle their differences. The Anglo custom was to shake hands.

He met Kyle's hand with his own and both men knew a moment of satisfaction.

Later that night Charmayne was waiting for Kyle at the fork in the road. She had been unable to stay in the house. Her parents were acting like honeymooners again and she felt a very obvious third. And anyway, she couldn't stay still. She needed to do something . . . walk, run, fly! Before she and her parents had left Orion that afternoon, Kyle had asked to see her that night. And time had not passed fast enough since.

So much had been happening over the past few days, so much tension, so much worry. She had barely seen Kyle. And now that everything was settled and the future seemed to be open to them, she couldn't wait for it to get started!

When his Cadillac drew near she stepped into the street.

Kyle saw her and his heart actually leapt. He had made himself keep to the appointed time for their meeting even though every nerve within him had screamed at him to come earlier. She looked so beautiful standing there. The white sundress she was wearing set off the brilliance of her hair. He wondered fleetingly if their children would inherit that hair. He could see them now . . . and they did! But he didn't mind. Each of them was a product of their parents' need for each other, and their flame-colored hair was a symbol of love. Of course the girls would have pigtails and he would again see a version of

Charmayne running through these hills. And both the boys and the girls would have freckles. . . . His lips curved as he drew to a stop beside her.

Bringing back memories of another time, he teased, "I certainly never expected to find you waiting for me, Charmayne. I thought I'd have to drag you kicking and screaming from your door."

Charmayne's face lighted with a smile. He looked so endearing sitting there in his car with that wonderfully wicked smile on his lips and his gaze moving warmly over her face.

"Oh? And what makes you think that?"

Kyle pretended to leer. "Because I have evil intentions on your body, woman. Aren't you afraid?"

For an answer Charmayne scooted around to the passenger side of the car and practically jumped into the seat.

"Does this look like I'm afraid?"

"No." Kyle laughed, leaning forward to apply a light kiss to her lips. "It looks like you're just as anxious as I am."

Charmayne answered him with a light kiss that deepened; the smoldering fires that had been waiting for just such a moment broke into instant flame.

Charmayne and Kyle forgot everything except their need for one another. They forgot where they were, that the car's engine was running, that they were blocking a roadway. . . .

It was only the toot of a car's horn from their rear that brought them back to the everyday world.

Kyle pushed himself away and Charmayne nervously straightened her hair and bodice. Putting the car in gear, Kyle moved it farther into the fork and let the waiting car pass.

As it moved slowly by, Charmayne saw her sister's beaming smile. Lynn waved vigorously from the passenger window. Clearly she and Bob had seen everything.

When the car was safely by, Kyle folded his arms across the steering wheel and commented with seeming regret, "Well, that's done it."

Charmayne was trying to deal with the blush that had risen to her cheeks. She knew her family was aware that she was in love with Kyle, but she wasn't yet accustomed to putting on shows for their benefit.

"Done it. Done what? I don't understand."

Kyle shook his head slowly from side to side. "We're going to have to get married."

Charmayne's heart jumped. "We are?" Things were happening faster than she had thought.

"Yep. The minister and his wife saw us."

"But that's Lynn and Bob!"

"Makes it worse."

"How?"

"They'll tell your father and he'll come after me with a shotgun."

"Kyle!"

Kyle began to laugh. "Don't look so startled. I'm only kidding." He paused, the laughter disappearing. "But since the subject has been brought up . . . Will you marry me, Charmayne?"

He held his breath. Nothing in life was certain. She had already told him that she loved him, and he believed her, but that didn't mean she would agree to marriage.

Charmayne quickly regained the excitement she had felt earlier.

"Yes. When?"

Kyle's eyes danced. "Are you sure?"

"I'm positive."

His hands dropped from the steering wheel, to make instant contact with her. He loved the soft warmth of her body beneath his fingertips, the feel of her breasts pressed against his chest, the touch of her lips, and the flowery scent that seemed a part of her.

Eventually their lips parted with reluctance, their breath uneven.

"Let's make it soon," he requested huskily.

"How about next weekend?"

"Can you be ready by then? Don't you want a big wedding?"

"No."

Kyle pulled farther away to look at her more clearly.

"I thought all women dreamed of a big wedding."

"Not this one."

Kyle examined the softened features of her face and an idea occurred to him. "Is it because your parents can't afford to give you one?"

Charmayne didn't evade his question. "That's part of it," she agreed; then, when he started to speak, she continued, ". . . but not all. I don't want to waste any more time, Kyle. I love you. I want to marry you. And I want to do it as soon as possible."

"You won't regret it?"

Charmayne decided to tease him in return for all the times he had enjoyed himself at her expense.

"You mean marrying you? No, I don't think so."

Kyle punished her by trailing a kiss along the side of her neck, starting at the base of her throat and working his way up to her ear. Charmayne was trembling when he was done.

"That's not what I meant and you know it."

Charmayne threaded the tips of her fingers in his hair, holding the sides of his face with her palms.

"I know," she whispered. "And, no, I'll never regret it. I'll never regret anything about knowing you except for the way I acted when you first came back. Sometimes I don't think I deserve your love, Kyle."

Kyle grinned. "I still have the umbrella, you know."

Charmayne's eyes widened at this turn of events. She had totally forgotten about the cursed umbrella. "You do?"

Kyle nodded. "I think I may have it bronzed."

"Why?" She couldn't imagine.

"To remind us that sometimes a relationship needs a little protection."

Charmayne thought of her parents, of how not communicating fears and needs had caused such devastation in their marriage.

"We'll hang it in our living room," she decided. "And when people ask, we'll tell them that it played an important part in our relationship. But we won't tell them what."

"Why?"

She tipped her head to one side. "Do you want them to think you're married to a thief?"

Kyle chuckled.

"You weren't very happy about my coming to your rescue, were you?"

"No, but you were the only hope I had."

"Then I used it against you."

"Aren't you ashamed?"

"No. Not the least little bit. It got me what I wanted: you."

276

"No, Kyle," she contradicted. "Bribing me didn't do it. You did." Kyle remained silent, so she went on to explain, "You yourself. Nothing else. I love *you.*"

Kyle watched her another moment in silence, then turned to restart the car, a sudden intenseness appearing on his face.

"Kyle, what is it? What—?" She looked around them and saw nothing. Why was he acting this way?

His eyes caught and held her own. "One time, not too long ago, you thanked me for not making love to you in this car. I had brought a blanket along that night, but right now I don't have one. If we don't get moving pretty soon, that sister and brother-in-law of yours, not to mention your parents, might come back along this road and find us in a very compromising position in the back seat."

Charmayne's green eyes began to shine. "Oh," she said with pretended meekness. The idea that he wanted her so badly was exciting to her.

"Yes, oh."

When the car was turned and moving back down the road, Charmayne asked softly, "Where are we going, Kyle?"

He offered her a brief, burning glance. "To my house. After tonight I think we should put this back onto a more old-fashioned course. We can probably make it through a week. But not now. I need to love you, Charmayne. And I need you to love me."

Kyle's bedroom was every bit as attractive as the rest of his home, but Charmayne barely noticed. She was tinglingly aware of only one thing: Kyle. The need to delay their coming together during the ride had made their desire for one another almost unbearable.

There had been no shyness between them when they entered his home. They had come directly to the bedroom and Kyle had then begun to kiss her—intense drugging kisses that left her weak and clinging to him at the same time as a growing passion forced her to increase her response.

Within breathless seconds they were lying close together on the bed, their clothing scattered on the floor and furniture next to them, their bodies straining against each other in a mutual expression of hungry urgency. Kyle's mouth was moving over her, their legs were entangled. Charmayne ran her hands over his skin, feeling the play of his muscles as he moved, reveling in his touch, her desire to join with him completely reaching a feverish peak at the same moment he could contain himself no longer.

Charmayne cried out when he entered her. Not from pain or protest, there was none, but because of the ecstasy he was bringing to her.

Kyle halted all movement immediately, not knowing if he had hurt her. His molten gray eyes met hers and his unspoken question was soon answered. Feeling a leap of joy at her excitement, Kyle lost himself again in the sensations of sharing both love and sensual pleasure with the woman who had become so precious to him.

Their act was like a rebirth, one which would be repeated thousands of times in their life together. But each time they would discover something new . . . a reward. Kyle had once wondered if life held more for him than the gaining of Charmayne's love. Now he knew, in a deep, barely conscious part of his brain, that he would have so much more. He would be able to share in the continuation of her love. And that was the most cherished and the most exhilarating prospect his life had so far offered.

His movements increased; his arousal complete.

Charmayne heard her breath rushing in and out of her lungs, but it was as if the sound were coming from afar. She also heard the appreciative murmurs, the little guttural cries. . . . They were coming from her.

Then nothing seemed more important than their union itself and the sensations his quickened thrusts induced. Charmayne met his movement with lifting movements of her own.

Before many seconds passed, Kyle moaned, an indescribable pleasure taking hold of his body. Time seemed to have no beginning or end. There was only the here, the now.

Then he collapsed against her and the glistening perspiration of their bodies was all that separated them.

Charmayne was quivering from the heights she had just reached. She clasped her arms around his waist and held him against her. She had never felt so fulfilled—so much herself, yet so close to another person. Complete. Soaring. Satisfied.

When the chaos in their blood began to quiet, they rolled over onto their sides, their arms still holding each other tightly, their breathing still erratic.

Kyle smiled across at her and gave her nose a quick kiss.

"Are you sure you want to make a habit of this?" he asked.

"I've never been more sure of anything in my life."

His hand smoothed the curve of her hip and thigh. "Neither have I."

Charmayne burrowed her nose into the hollow of his throat, enjoying the tang of his masculine scent and the feel of his skin. They remained that way for some time.

Then Charmayne brought her face away from its resting place and looked up at Kyle. His strong chin was in the way somewhat, so she struggled up to her elbow.

"Kyle, everything may not be perfect. I mean . . . my father . . ."

Kyle pulled her against him again, a hand tangling in her bright hair. "Don't worry about him, Charmayne. I'm not. It may take time, but I think he'll eventually come around."

Charmayne sighed, deciding once again to place her trust in him.

"Yes," she said, then added, "I only hope it doesn't take too long."

Kyle said nothing as he began to stroke her hair. Tolerance was what he hoped for at first. Then from that they could take the next step.

Charmayne moved her hand along his ribs and his muscles reflexively quivered. He was very much aware of her—insatiable satyr that he was.

He smiled and touched his lips to the creamy flesh of her upper arm.

Charmayne trembled as well and his lips moved back to claim her own.

Tomorrow would have to take care of itself. Right now they had other things to do than worry about what the future might bring.

EPILOGUE

Charmayne was waiting at the front window for Kyle to come home. Normally she didn't spend her time in waiting. Her job at the mayor's office allowed her to have a half hour before Kyle stopped work for the day and she used it preparing their evening meal. Only, this day was different. She had some news she had been aching to share with Kyle for the past few hours and soon she was going to be able to tell him in person. It was not something she had wanted to confide over the impersonality of the telephone.

When she saw his long form come into view, she experienced both pride and wonder that he was her husband. Had ten months actually passed already? It seemed more like ten days. They had been so happy.

A car driving by on the highway tooted its horn to draw Kyle's attention. He glanced away from the path before him and waved back to the occupant of the car, who was waving at him. Charmayne saw the satisfied look that settled on his face as he turned to face the house again. She had learned how important it was to him that he be accepted by the town. And, to add to her happiness, ever since the explosion at Orion the townspeople of Kearney had completely taken him to their heart with offers of help and encouragement. He was one of them now.

Charmayne let the curtain liner flutter shut as she heard Kyle turn the doorknob. She moved into position to greet him, her teeth clamping down on her bottom lip to keep it still.

Kyle saw his wife and a familiar gladness entered

his heart. He would never tire of coming home to her. He held out his arms and she came into his embrace. The kiss they exchanged gave lie to the myth that after the honeymoon, passion starts to cool. Their love had been deepened by their months together as they learned to stretch and grow while at the same time learning the give and take that all marriages require.

When the kiss ended, Kyle narrowed his gaze over Charmayne's expressive features. He had come to sense her every mood.

"Okay, what's up? I know there's something."

Charmayne's eyes twinkled. She pretended to play with his tie.

"What makes you think that something is up?"

"I can tell. Come on. Give."

Charmayne looked up at him through her lashes, unable to keep one of her secrets any longer. "I talked to Daddy today."

"And?"

"He agrees."

Kyle was very still. "He does?"

Charmayne shook her head rapidly up and down. "Um-hum. He's agreed to a limited partnership, but he insists that everything be stated in writing. He doesn't want a father-in-law deal."

"He doesn't want charity."

"No."

"But I wasn't trying to give him the money! I'm serious about seeing what can be done with the farm. I know nothing about farming, he does. I know computer circuit boards, and he works with them only because he has to. I thought it would be a perfect solution. Him there, me in town."

"I know. And it is! It just took him a while to see it that way, too."

"Stubborn bastard."

"Watch it, Kyle. You're liable to ruin my grand-mother's reputation," Charmayne laughingly reminded him. "And she doesn't have a thing to do with this."

Kyle grinned. "I notice you're not trying to defend your father."

"Well, no. He's here; he can take care of himself. And if he acts like a horse's rear end, you can call him one."

"Thank you. I just did, in a manner of speaking."

She raised her arms to clasp them behind his neck, the smile still lingering on her lips. "But that's what I was just telling you. He's not acting that way any-more, at least not so much. He's finally beginning to thaw a little."

"Will miracles never cease!" Kyle exclaimed dryly.

Charmayne ignored him. "And it's a good thing that he is, too. For more than one reason."

Kyle saw the excited glow deep in her eyes and he knew there was something more.

"Why?" he asked, his throat tightening. He had a suspicion of what she was about to say.

"Because he's going to be a grandfather in about seven month's time, and I think it would be a good idea for him and the baby's father to at least be on friendly speaking terms."

Kyle let the news sink completely into his brain. What they had thought to be a fact, was one. For a moment it was more than he could comprehend. He was going to be a father. He was going to be a father! *He was going to be a father!*

Charmayne watched the play of emotion move over Kyle's face. She loved him so. And this child was merely an extension of her love. She waited for his reaction.

Just like in the movies, Kyle whooped and started to twirl her around the room. Then suddenly he stopped, a fearful expression coming into his eyes.

"God, I'm sorry, Charmayne. Did I hurt you?"

"Kyle, don't be ridiculous. You can't hurt me, not like that. You're acting as if you've stepped out of the eighteen hundreds."

Kyle frowned. "Maybe they had a point. Should you keep working?"

"Kyle!" Charmayne's temper began to bristle. "Stop being silly. Of course I'm going to continue working. There's no reason—"

"I will not have my wife delivering our baby in the mayor's office!"

Charmayne's temper instantly cooled. She could just imagine the consequence that little event would have on Mayor Cliburn's nerves. He had been jolted enough by all the events that had happened months ago when his opponent in the upcoming election had quietly withdrawn his name from the ticket. Her having a baby in his office would send him into a nervous breakdown—ex-Marine or not!

"No," she teased, "I thought I'd have it in a tree. . . . Come on, Kyle. Stop sounding so stuffy. I know you're not."

Kyle relented somewhat, realizing what a complete fool he was making of himself. "Well, it's not

284

every day a man finds out he's going to be a father" was the excuse he made for himself.

"And it's not every day a woman finds out she's pregnant, either."

Immediately Kyle felt a rush of regret. God, what an idiot! She had just given him some of the most important news of his life and he was acting like the ass he had moments before called her father. Was it some fatal flaw in all men that caused them to be so insensitive at times?

With a melting look, he cradled her gently to him.

"No, I'm sure it's not." He paused. "Are you happy?"

"Extremely."

"Do you think it's a boy or a girl?"

Charmayne giggled, and to his amazement she sounded a lot like Groucho Marx when she said, "Well, I certainly hope so!"

His grin widened. Every time he thought he knew all there was to know about her, she came up with something else. His life was going to be one of constant discovery.

"I do, too, my love," he agreed, "I do, too."

She lifted her smiling face away from his chest and looked up at him. Kyle gazed down at her . . . at the brilliant red hair and the freckles that he now knew did cover every inch of her body, and her beautiful smile . . . and he knew what a lucky man he was.

She had given him her dreams.

LOOK FOR NEXT MONTH'S
CANDLELIGHT ECSTASY SUPREMES:

CANDLELIGHT Ecstasy Supreme

$2.50 each

At your local bookstore or use this handy coupon for ordering:

DELL BOOKS
P.O. BOX 1000. PINE BROOK, N.J. 07058-1000   B161A

Please send me the books I have checked above. I am enclosing $_____ (please add 75c per copy to cover postage and handling). Send check or money order—no cash or C.O.D.'s. Please allow up to 8 weeks for shipment.

Name _____

Address _____

City_____ State/Zip _____

☐ 13 **BODY AND SOUL**, Anna Hudson 10759-8-11

☐ 14 **CROSSFIRE**, Eileen Bryan 11599-X-39

☐ 15 **WHERE THERE'S SMOKE...**, Nell Kincaid 19417-2-16

☐ 16 **PAYMENT IN FULL**, Jackie Black 16828-7-15

☐ 17 **RED MIDNIGHT**, Heather Graham 17431-7-12

☐ 18 **A HEART DIVIDED**, Ginger Chambers 13509-5-18

☐ 19 **SHADOW GAMES**, Elise Randolph 17764-2-19

☐ 20 **JUST HIS TOUCH**, Emily Elliott 14411-6-39

$2.50 each

 At your local bookstore or use this handy coupon for ordering:

Dell DELL BOOKS
P.O. BOX 1000. PINE BROOK. N.J. 07058-1000   B161B

Please send me the books I have checked above. I am enclosing $ _____ (please add 75c per copy to cover postage and handling). Send check or money order—no cash or C.O.D.'s. Please allow up to 8 weeks for shipment.

Name _____

Address _____

City _____   State Zip _____